#SELFIE

The Hashtag Series #4

by Cambria Hebert

Published by: Cambria Hebert Books, LLC

http://www.cambriahebert.com

Interior design and typesetting by Sharon Kay of Amber Leaf Publishing
Cover design by MAE I DESIGN
Edited by Cassie McCown & There for You Editing
Copyright 2015 by Cambria Hebert

ISBN: 978-1-938857-72-0

#SELFIE

CHAPTER ONE

BRAEDEN

Ass was everywhere.

Round ass, perky ass, ass you wanted to grab, and ass you wanted to smack.

I guess you could say I was an ass man.

And there was definitely no better place to partake in the view than on a beach where the ladies liked to strut their stuff in tiny bikinis.

There were some ladies that probably needed more coverage than a teeny bikini, but I still looked. Ass was ass. I wasn't about to discriminate.

Besides, confidence was sexy, too.

• • •

Even with all the eye candy on display, my eyes kept wandering back to one particular booty. Every time it happened, my teeth clenched and I mentally told myself I was a fucking moron and I'd better get my head on right before I did something I would regret.

To help distract myself from the ass that just wouldn't quit and my wandering eyes that didn't want to listen to my brain, I drank beer.

It's not like I had to be anywhere other than right where I was.

The sand. The surf. The sun and my family. Nothing else I needed.

Except maybe the ass I kept eyeing to grow warts and a tail so I'd quit looking.

Yeah, I said I didn't discriminate, but even a guy like me had standards.

"You okay, man?" Romeo asked from my left. We were chilling in some beach chairs in the sand.

I glanced his way. "Do I not look okay to you?"

He smirked. "You're looking a little buzzed."

"All hail Corona!" I said and held up my bottle.

Romeo laughed. Down by the water, Rimmel shrieked, and we both watched as she ran from the surf as it crashed against the shore.

"How's she doing after everything?" I asked, still watching her. Missy and Ivy were in the water with Trent, who was trying to teach them how to surf.

I gave the guy credit. He had way more patience than me. Rim wasn't surfing or swimming. In fact, she hadn't even gotten her toes wet. Not that I could blame her for the aversion she had to water.

"She's hanging in," Romeo answered and took a sip of his beer. "This week's been good for her. No drama."

The reason we were all even here enjoying this fine Florida beach for spring break was because Romeo wanted to give Rimmel something besides all the drama they'd been plagued with since they got together.

I mean, seriously. The two could fill an entire season of some old lady's favorite soap opera with all the shit they'd been through.

"Hey, man. If I haven't said it, thanks for inviting me. And for paying for our sweet-ass house on the sand." I jerked my thumb over my shoulder toward the beach house Romeo rented for the week.

He shrugged. "We're family." He pulled his eyes away from Rim and glanced at me. I could feel his stare even through his shades. "Which is why I know something is up. There a reason you're already buzzed and it's just past lunchtime?"

"Should I start calling you Mom?" I asked but averted my gaze.

"You know I could give two shits if you want to drink. Hell, I got a beer in my hand. It's spring break. But I know you. What's up?"

I muttered a curse under my breath. "It's nothing."

"I could call Rimmel over here to badger it out of you," he threatened.

I groaned. She would too. Good God, she'd be like a damn dog with a bone. I had a weak spot for my little sis. She'd drag it out of me.

I couldn't let that happen.

Shit would hit the fan.

"Fuck no." I groaned. "Look, I got some stuff on my mind is all. Nothing I care to say out loud. I'll handle it."

Romeo was silent a moment. "I can respect that," he said. "You know I got your back, right? Just say the word."

"Yeah, I know." And I did. Romeo wasn't just my best friend. It was like he said. We were family.

Rimmel came walking up the sand, and I could almost hear Rome's pulse spike in reaction. I didn't even need to look to know he was taking in the way she looked in her bathing suit—which was not a bikini, thank God. Sisters and bikinis did not mix.

Setting his beer in the sand, Romeo held out his arm. Rimmel climbed into his lap and threw her feet over the side. Sand from her toes fell all over my arm.

"You need more sunscreen," she told me.

I grunted. "I'm working on my tan."

"If you get any tanner, people will mistake you for an Indian," she joked.

"Find any good shells?" Romeo asked, drawing her attention away from my tan.

"No, the tide's coming in. I need to get up early tomorrow. The best ones are found in the morning. *If* someone would let me out of bed."

Romeo grinned. "I'll let you up early tomorrow, *if* you go to bed early tonight. You do need your rest."

"We both know you ain't letting that girl get any rest," I quipped.

Rimmel laughed and nudged me with her sandy feet. "How about it, B? Want to hunt for shells with me in the morning?"

"I love ya, but hells no. I ain't getting up that early. I'm working on a hangover." I held up my beer.

"Beer's gross." She pulled a face.

"Better than Smurf Balls," I countered.

Romeo held out his fist and we pounded it out.

"I'll go seashell hunting with you tomorrow, baby," Romeo said.

Behind my sunglasses, I rolled my eyes. Rome was totally whipped. I'd never seen him like this before with anyone. Rimmel totally changed him, and if I were honest, she sort of changed me, too. Not that I was whipped, but I wasn't totally appalled by the fact Rome was, and that was something. If anything, sometimes I felt a pang of jealousy for the easy way the pair seemed to connect. I'd never had that kind of relationship with a woman before.

Not that I wanted one.

Trent came jogging up and snatched his towel off a nearby chair. After he'd rubbed it over his wet hair, it stuck out everywhere. Reaching into the cooler, he grabbed a beer.

"How's surfing going?" Rimmel asked.

"Those women would have a better chance at getting eaten by a shark than actually standing up on that board in this century," he muttered, but then he grinned. "It's pretty damn entertaining."

"How's it going with Missy?" Rimmel asked slyly.

The fact that Romeo invited Trent to take off some of the pressure of Missy and me ending up in the same room alone all the time was sort of a relief. I liked Missy a lot, but there was no future there. There never would be.

"She's a cool girl." Trent shrugged.

I knew what that meant. There probably wasn't a future with him and Missy either.

Rim didn't seem to understand what I did, because she said, "Do you like her?"

Romeo and I laughed. Trent joined in.

"What?" she said innocently.

Romeo rubbed her back. "You can't just ask a guy if he likes a woman."

"Well, why not?" she demanded.

"Because guys don't sit around and talk about their feelings like a bunch of girls," I told her.

Rimmel rolled her eyes. "Whatever."

Grinning, Trent took a pull on his beer. He gazed down at the waves where Missy and Ivy were still playing around with the surfboard.

"What's Ivy's deal?" he asked.

I shifted my gaze to him.

"Ivy?" Rimmel asked. I heard the interest in her tone.

"Yeah. She seeing anyone?" Trent replied.

I drank some beer; it was getting warm and tasted like piss.

"No, she's not. She hasn't been dating very much," Rim answered, but from the sound of her voice, I knew there was more to it.

I grunted. "She probably can't find a guy wanting to deal with all that maintenance."

Rimmel kicked me gently.

"Ah, one of those chicks, huh?" Trent murmured.

"I don't know," Romeo jumped in. "She's been pretty chill lately. Different than she used to be."

Trent glanced back down to the water. I followed his gaze.

The girls were towing the surfboard out of the water and laughing at whatever they were talking about. Both Missy and Ivy were wearing bikinis, and both of them were sporting nice golden tans from all the time we'd been spending out here.

I averted my eyes and stood. "The beer needs more ice. I'm gonna go grab some." I picked up the cooler. "You guys want anything?"

"Water," Rim said.

I nodded. "Water for my sis."

● ● ●

The girls approached and dropped the board in the sand. "That thing weighs about a hundred pounds!" Ivy remarked and grabbed a towel to start toweling off her body.

I couldn't help but notice the way the water drops glistened on her sun-kissed skin and the way her red bikini hugged all the right curves.

I turned away and started for the house.

I definitely needed another beer.

CHAPTER TWO

Spring Break is almost over.
How much of it will you
remember?
#AlcoholInducedAmnesia

... Alpha BuzzFeed

IVY

Spring break at the beach sure beat spending it at home with my brothers, my parents, and the rest of my family who all dropped in constantly and liked to ask a million questions about everything.

I loved my big family, but sometimes it was nice to avoid all the questions.

Especially when I spent half of my sophomore year at Alpha U making choices I wished I hadn't. The last thing I felt like doing was answering questions I had no intention of answering honestly.

• • •

But that didn't matter.

Those things were over.

My eyes were open, a big part in thanks to Rimmel.

She helped me realize it was okay to be exactly who I was. I didn't have to try so hard to be the person I thought everyone wanted me to be. She also taught me when the right guy came along, he would like me for me.

And if he didn't… he wasn't worth it anyway.

Seemed like this was a lesson I should have learned in high school, not as a sophomore in college, but maybe I was a late bloomer.

Okay, I wasn't a late bloomer. I just got a taste of freedom since coming to Alpha U, and now that I wasn't constantly surrounded by family who watched my every move, I had more room to try things out.

And I tried lots of things.

Most of which I regretted.

But no more.

I wasn't going to be the girl who partied and drank too much. I wasn't going to sleep with random guys, thinking it might lead me to Mr. Right. And I certainly wasn't going to get so drunk that some psycho could take advantage of me to hurt people I cared about.

I closed my eyes against the thought.

It made me feel dirty even now, months later.

It seemed it didn't matter how much I tried to distance myself from it or tried to forget. There was no forgetting I'd slept with Zach.

Actually, I *didn't* remember much about the actual sex. I just remembered coming back to my dorm with him, some foreplay, and waking up naked when Rimmel came home the next day.

God, I'd been mortified when I fully woke up and realized what happened. I even tried to tell myself we hadn't actually slept together, that maybe he left before it got that far. But I couldn't deny it very long.

I felt the evidence between my legs the second I got up.

I shuddered and tried to cut off my thoughts.

But they were persistent.

I don't know what was worse: the fact I slept with Zach or the fact we hadn't used a condom.

God.

* * *

Could I respect myself any less?

And then to find out he'd used me to hurt Rimmel, one of my best friends?

There wasn't enough soap in Wal-Mart to make me feel clean again.

So I vowed to lay off the alcohol. I would still drink—I was still in college after all—but never enough to let myself get to that point again. Never enough to not know what I was doing.

If only I could forget. If only I could wipe away the fact I let him touch me.

The sound of the sliding glass doors behind me broke into my thoughts, and I glanced over my shoulder. My body tensed when I saw who it was, and I rolled my eyes.

"What do you want?"

"Just coming to make sure you aren't burning my dinner," Braeden quipped as he came closer.

I was standing in front of the grill, the scent of charcoal and hamburgers filling the breezy air around us.

"I know how to use a grill," I snapped.

"But you don't know how I like my meat," he goaded, stopping just behind me. I felt his breath as he leaned in, right beside my ear. "Pink in the middle."

My tongue slid over my teeth. "You smell like a brewery." I spun and shoved him away. "It's gross."

He stumbled back a step but didn't go any further. He wasn't wearing a shirt. He was all tan muscle and low-riding board shorts.

It was totally annoying.

I turned back to the grill and lifted the lid to check the burgers.

I felt him behind me again, peering over my shoulder. "They look done."

"They need a few more minutes," I argued.

He made a rude noise and reached around me to grab the spatula out of my hand. I moved it away before he could.

"Look," he growled, and reached even farther around me, so much that I could feel the solid wall of his wide chest against my back. Gently, he wrapped his hand around the handle of the utensil, just above where

• • •

mine was. I told myself the sizzle I felt was because my skin was so close to the open flame.

I started to jerk back, but he tightened his grip and stepped closer.

"You need a lesson," he murmured.

I was totally surrounded by him.

God, had he always been this big? He towered over me, around me. The way he held his arm, it was almost like it was wrapped around me as well. I was practically encircled by him. I couldn't go back because he was there. I couldn't run forward because the hot grill was there. All I could do was stand there.

And feel him.

He moved the edge of the spatula and sliced into the center of one of the burgers. "See? Perfection."

"I can't see anything," I grumped. To be honest, I wasn't even looking at what he was showing me. I couldn't concentrate.

I should have just agreed.

His other arm came around me so I was completely enveloped in him. If I leaned my head back, it would rest in that hollow place between his neck and shoulder. I imagined what it would feel like, how safe that would feel.

"Can you see now?" he was saying.

I jerked and looked down. Thank God he couldn't see my face; surely my cheeks would be red. Using both hands, he showed me the inside of the burger.

He was right. It was done to perfection.

"Fine," I bit out. "They're done."

Laughing, he pulled away. "Of course they are. I'm always right."

"Whatever," I muttered and sidestepped so I wasn't so close to him.

"If you're so worried about your meat, then you finish cooking them." I thrust out the platter I'd brought out to put the burgers on.

His amused smirk made me want to hit him in the head with it.

He took it from my hands. "Fine. I will."

"Fine," I bit out and then stomped away toward the house.

Inside, Rimmel was standing in the kitchen with a huge container of strawberries in front of her. "Please tell me those are for daiquiris."

"You get the alcohol; I'll get the blender," she said.

I wasn't going to get so drunk I'd forget anything. But I was going to drink just enough to maybe forget the feeling of Braeden against me.

CHAPTER THREE

BRAEDEN

I wasn't sure what time it was when I stepped out of the house and onto the deck. It was late, well past midnight, and everyone else had gone to bed hours ago.

I couldn't sleep. I felt restless and a little bit caged up.

The moon was heavy in the velvet sky, the bright rays glistening off the ocean waves and making the water look like it was dancing with glitter. The sounds of the surf crashing against the shore were loud, so loud they could drown out a man's thoughts.

I draped my forearms over the railing and gazed out across the beach. It never stopped moving, even while everyone else slept, and for some reason, the constant it represented soothed whatever was going on inside me.

There were more stars in the sky here than I'd seen anywhere else. They filled the night with dots of light, breaking up the otherwise inky darkness.

Tomorrow, we'd all pack up and get on a plane. Sadly, the beach and stars would be replaced with cool spring air and semester finals. Romeo would be leaving for training camp soon, and most everyone else would be leaving for the summer, back to wherever they came from.

Then there would just be me.

And probably Rim.

Next fall when classes started, Rome would be off with the NFL, and college life would go on, but everything was going to be different.

I felt it changing already.

* * *

Wind blew off the water, pulling at my shorts and brushing against my skin. It also brought with it a sound other than the calmness of night.

My body went rigid and I pushed off the railing, looking down at the sand.

I saw nothing.

But someone was there.

A scream bounced around with the whipping wind. It sounded close, but was it a trick of the wind?

Another shrill scream pierced the night.

Without another thought, I tore across the deck and raced down the set of private stairs that led to the beach. The sand was a lot cooler without the sun's rays to heat it, and my bare feet sank in even as I darted off in the direction from which the scream had come.

Down here, I saw the shape of a woman darting through the dark across the sand. I knew the second she saw me because she angled her body toward mine and quickened her pace.

"What—" My question was cut off when she leapt at me.

The crazy bitch literally threw herself on me, practically climbing up my body and winding her legs around my waist.

"Whoa," I said, even as my arms locked around her. "What's wrong?"

"Braeden, thank God you're here!"

My head snapped up at the familiar voice. I caught a flash of blond hair billowing out around her before she ducked her head into the crook of my neck.

"Ivy," I growled. What the hell was she trying to pull? God, this chick was a piece of work. I grabbed her around the waist to pull her off me, but she made a sound and tightened her arms and legs.

It was then I felt the slight tremble in her arms.

Okay, maybe this wasn't an act. Maybe something had happened.

"Hey?" I murmured. Without thinking, I rubbed her back gently. "What's going on?"

Her voice was muffled against my skin. All I heard was, "—attacked me."

My entire body went rigid. Someone fucking attacked her? Oh, hells no. Ivy and I might not like each other much, but she was Rimmel's best friend. And beyond that, we'd all been hanging out for months now.

Ivy wasn't all bad. She sure as hell didn't deserve to be attacked.

"Who?" I demanded, scanning the beach for some guy who was about to get his ass beat.

"It hurts," she whined.

My glare snapped back to her and she stared up at me with wide eyes. Something in me shifted. "What hurts?" I asked softly.

"My toe." I swear her lower lip jutted out in a pout.

Wait. What?

I shook my head. "Did you just say your toe hurts?"

"Haven't you been listening?" she demanded. "Some angry crab attacked me!"

I blinked.

A crab attacked her? This girl was off the fucking chain.

"You mean to tell me you're clinging to me for dear life because a crab pinched your toe?"

"I think it's bleeding," she replied seriously. "It was a really big, angry crab."

I laughed and the wind carried the sound down the beach. I hoped the crab heard. "It probably took one look at you and attacked."

"It's not funny!" she snapped.

It sure as hell was funny. I palmed her waist, enjoying—a little too much—the way it dipped in on each side, like it was built just for my hands, and tried to pry her off me again.

Shrieking, she grappled to hang on.

"Now what?" I sighed.

"I'm not putting my feet down there again."

"You mean down there on the ground where people walk?" I asked dryly.

"It's dark. There might be more crabs."

"Well, we *are* on the beach," I reasoned.

She reached up and pulled my hair.

"Ow!" I yelled.

"Stop making fun of me!" she demanded. "It hurt and I refuse to walk."

"And you think I'm going to carry you?" I scoffed.

This chick had a serious wakeup call coming.

"Please?" Her fingers, which were still in my hair, reached out and smoothed where she just pulled. Chills scattered down my bare arms. The wind out here was getting cold.

"Fine," I muttered. It would be easier to cart her curvy ass back up to the house than to stand here and argue with her about walking. Besides, the second I put her down, she'd probably start screaming again.

Ain't nobody got time for that.

She sighed like the fact she didn't have to walk was a great relief and leaned forward to wrap her arms around my neck. Her chin rested on my shoulder, and she wiggled her ass a little closer, tightening her legs around me.

I didn't like Ivy.

But I was a guy.

She was pressed all along my bare chest and her legs were wrapped around my waist.

• • •

Obviously, all thought went down south, and a lot of blood started rushing that way, too.

"What the hell are you even doing out here this late?" I asked gruffly as I started to walk.

"It's our last night. I wanted to spend as much time on the beach as I could."

"How'd that work out for ya?"

"Ha-ha."

I was just about to tell her she needed to go on a diet when she turned her head so her cheek was pillowed on my shoulder and a sigh rushed out of her mouth. I felt her breath dance along my skin.

She really wasn't that heavy.

When I reached the stairs to the house, I hesitated, figuring she could walk up the damn steps herself.

But I didn't put her down.

I kept walking, still supporting her weight and my own.

At the top, I walked a couple feet across the deck to the sliders that led into the house. Inside was completely dark and still. But everything else around us seemed to be charged with energy.

"You gonna need me to carry you to bed?" I asked, the words coming out a lot huskier and a lot less sarcastic than I intended.

She pulled back, some of her body losing contact with mine. Her hands were on my shoulders and mine were still wrapped around her back.

"I think I can manage." Her voice didn't sound quite as mocking as it usually did, either.

My gaze dropped to her mouth. She had full, heart-shaped lips. Usually, I didn't notice just how kissable they were because they were usually hurling insults my way.

The tension in the air seemed to spike. The wind blew around us, grabbing a thick strand of her hair and blowing it across her cheek. As she reached up and pulled it back, our gazes collided.

"Braeden?" she whispered.

I was on her before my name even fully left her lips. It echoed through a hollow place inside me I hadn't realized was there.

We were like two sides of Velcro that fused together to create an unbreakable bond. I was the rough side and she was the soft. Normally, I wouldn't say there was one soft thing about Ivy Forrester, but tonight was different.

Tonight, it was all I could feel. There wasn't a single, solitary rough thing about the girl in my arms.

All the insults, snide looks, and barely contained dislike we slung at each other over and over again for months piled up. It created a stack of tinder, a mound of kindling that up until this moment had stayed cold and dry.

But no more.

The second she pulled back and her blue eyes landed on mine, the second she wrapped her legs around my waist and sighed against my neck, we were a forest fire waiting to happen.

All the pent-up angst between us turned from hate to desire and combusted in one great explosion.

The force of emotion that erupted pushed us even closer together, and now here I was ravaging her mouth like a wolf who hadn't been fed in months and was being offered a thick cut of juicy, rare meat.

• • •

I pulled her tightly against me, close enough I could feel her ribcage dig into my chest. I kissed her so fiercely our teeth banged together, but instead of pulling back, I licked my tongue over the spot and kept kissing, kept going back for more.

Her hands slid up the back of my neck and into my hair. It was short, but she still found a way to tangle her fingers in, to grip my scalp and return my kiss with an intensity that matched my own.

I'd never had anyone kiss me back with the same kind of roaring passion as this.

Not ever.

It was so heady, my brain lost focus and pure instinct ruled. Two great steps brought us up against the house. Pinned between the wall and me, Ivy raked her hands across the back of my shoulders, her nails leaving a tingling trail.

I growled, once again feeling more wolf than man, and sank my teeth into her lower lip and pulled. Her flesh filled the inside of my mouth, and I sucked at it, wanting even more.

• • •

A small mewling sound slipped from her mouth, and she wiggled her hips in a circular motion, rocking the center of her thighs against me.

Holy fuck, I was so hard it hurt. My hips surged forward, but she was up too high, so my cock didn't collide with the part of her it wanted.

I ripped my mouth away and dragged in a ragged breath.

Ivy collapsed back against the side of the house, her chest heaving and her nipples so hard they poked through her clothes. I reached between us and rolled one between my fingers. When she gasped and bit down on her lower lip, I damn near came in my pants.

Keeping one hand on her breast, I grabbed her hair with the other and pulled her close again, taking her mouth and owning it.

Our tongues danced together, and I swear I explored as deep into her mouth as I could go.

It just wasn't enough.

Bringing her with me, I moved into the house. Because we'd been here a week, I knew the pattern of the furniture well enough that I was able to maneuver around it even as I continued to assault her mouth with my own.

The way her legs tightened as I walked made me feel like I was on fire. Burning up from the inside out.

We reached my room, and I all but kicked the door before rushing inside. Behind my head, she grabbed the door and pushed it closed.

Ivy was so tightly wrapped around me that when I let go and crawled over the bed, she stayed right there with me. When I settled, her legs loosened and I pressed my body along hers, and we sank into the mattress together. Two bodies as one, making a single indent in the center of the bed.

Her hands skittered across my back muscles, squeezing and rubbing as she went until they slid into the waistband of my basketball shorts and over the bare skin of my ass.

I ripped my mouth away from hers and shoved my face into the pillow just above her shoulder. All my limbs were quivering with need and my heart beat so fast I genuinely thought it might be in danger of bursting.

* * *

Ivy's teeth sank into my shoulder, and her hands palmed my ass and pulled it in. My hips responded instantly, thrusting into her center. My erection was hard and unforgiving and practically demanded entrance.

She moaned, the sound causing her teeth to release my skin, and her chin tipped up, exposing the pale, creaminess of her neck.

I left my rod right there where it was—teasing her core— even rocked a little so she would shudder as I sucked my way down her neck to her collarbone.

"Oh my God." Her words sounded more like a prayer than anything. Her voice was almost unrecognizable to my ears. Her hands pulled free of my shorts and dug into the flesh on my back.

I took her lips again. She tasted like strawberries, and it reminded me of the daiquiris that were flowing freely at dinner and then later when we were all playing cards.

I ripped my mouth off hers and did a pushup so my body was raised up off hers, parallel to the bed. "Are you drunk right now?" I demanded.

• • •

I could've asked nicer, but just pushing out the words was difficult. The only thing I wanted to push right now was my cock inside her body.

"What?" she gasped, her eyes totally unfocused.

I let out a string of curses and shoved myself off the bed. I didn't even bother trying to hide the huge-ass tent in my pants. She'd already felt it anyway.

She pushed up onto her elbows and looked at me, a little awareness coming back into her expression.

But then her eyes dropped, down to the place I wasn't bothering to hide, and her teeth sank into her lower lip.

I groaned. "Don't fucking do that."

"You're wet," she murmured.

I glanced down. It was dark in here, but with the light from the moon coming through the window, I could see a dark spot on the front of my shorts.

I glanced back up at her thighs that were still spread.

She was wearing a dress thing, which meant when I was between her legs all that had been between us were her panties. Panties that were clearly soaked with her need.

Need so strong it soaked me too.

I moved fast, surprising us both, and clamped a hand around her ankle. Slowly, I towed her down the bed, toward me.

"Look. At. Me," I ground out and held her chin so I could look into her eyes. "Are you drunk?"

Her eyes cleared a bit, enough that I could tell the only fog in her eyes was from what was going down between us.

"I had some drinks," she said. "Hours ago."

"So you're not," I surmised.

She shook her head slow. "They didn't work."

"Excuse me?" I said, impatient as my fingers left her ankle and started climbing up her calf.

"Turns out tequila isn't enough to drown out the way you felt against me."

My eyes snapped up.

Earlier at the grill. She'd been affected by me just as I had been by her.

"I've seen you looking," she confided. "You like the way I look."

I groaned. "God help me, I fucking do."

Her eyes took in my bare chest, and I admit I puffed it out a little to give her more to see.

"I'm not drunk. Not even close. I know exactly what I'm doing right now, Braeden."

Well, if that wasn't a fucking hand-carved invitation, then I don't know what was.

I dropped to my knees right there in front of the bed and dragged her down until her legs dangled off the side, her dripping center right near my face.

She pushed up onto her elbows and fisted a hand in the hair above my forehead. "Hey, what about you?"

"I've had some beer," I murmured and slipped a finger inside the edge of her panties. Holy shit, she was shaved bare and soaking wet. "But don't you worry, sweetheart. I'm still more than able to perform."

She collapsed against the mattress and arched her back into the air. My finger dipped inside her, finding her hot and tight.

"I'm not stopping."

· · ·

"No one asked you to," she shot back.

I pulled my finger back and reached beneath her dress for the waistband. My fingers met string. She was wearing that damned bikini that drove me nuts all goddamned week.

I pushed to my feet and took her hands. I knew she was surprised when I yanked her to stand. Hell, I preferred her on her back, too.

But I had to do this.

I ripped the cotton dress over her head and threw it onto the floor.

My upper lip curled when I took in all that skin covered by nothing but triangles of fabric and strings.

Her bikini was red.

It was barely there.

And the way her body looked in it…

More than once this week, I had to stop myself from pounding some random guy for staring.

It didn't matter who stared at her.

Ivy wasn't mine.

I didn't want her.

But tonight… tonight I did.

* * *

Tonight she was mine.

I dipped my finger beneath the feeble string and followed it all the way around to the back of her neck where it tied. The goose bumps that rose across her skin weren't lost on me.

"I don't ever want to see this bikini on you again," I rasped and pulled the end of the tie. I tugged slowly as I caught her eyes with mine. "I don't want anyone else looking at you in it. Ever. Again."

I released the strings and the top fell down, revealing a pair of perky, round breasts.

I was an ass man—we all know this—but that didn't mean I couldn't appreciate a fine pair of tits when I saw them.

I palmed them both. I filled my hands with her warm, supple flesh and kneaded gently. I wanted to be rough and fast. Need hammered in me almost like adrenaline. Almost like this was do or die.

But I couldn't treat her body like that. Not now that I was staring at it, almost completely bare and unprotected.

* * *

I rubbed my thumbs over her erect nipples, and she purred, her forehead coming forward to rest on my shoulder.

I liked that.

It was almost like she couldn't stand. It was almost like she needed me to hold her up.

I left her breasts and skimmed my fingers down her waist, following the hourglass shape of her body until I met the ties on either side of her hips. Her body trembled from being so close to mine, and it made me feel powerful.

I pulled both sides at the same time and let go. The fabric fell and tangled at my feet. Quickly, I pulled off the top, which was low around her waist, and it joined the rest of her clothes on the floor.

I couldn't wait another second. I shoved my hand between her legs and cupped her sex. She groaned and lifted her head.

I captured her lips once more as I delved a finger into her opening. One of her hands wrapped around my bicep and held on while her other did a little moving of her own down into the waistband of my shorts.

Without any hesitation, her fingers wrapped around my throbbing rod and started pumping me slowly, to the same rhythm I moved my finger inside her.

Her hand was like a hot shower in the center of a snowstorm, like medicine to an ailing man. It was exactly everything.

I slid another finger inside her, spearing her with two. She whimpered and her knees buckled. Both of us fell back onto the bed. We started kissing again, and I lost myself in her, in the way she felt.

Eventually, she grew impatient. Her hands started pulling at my shorts, and I couldn't stop my throaty chuckle from filling the room. I left her lying in the center of the bed to pull off my shorts and dig around in the duffle lying by the door.

I felt her molten stare when I pulled out a condom, and then I reached in for another.

One wasn't going to be enough.

* * *

I tossed the extra onto the pillow near her head and then used my teeth to rip open the foil packet in my hand. I could wrap myself in my sleep if I had to. I could wrap myself even without the light of the moon. It was second nature, so it didn't take long.

When I climbed between her legs, her hand shot out and palmed my balls. Gently, she cupped them, felt their weight, and then dragged her fingers down the inside of my thigh.

I grabbed her hand and nipped at her fingertip. She laughed, but it was a short-lived sound, dying in her throat when I reached for her other hand.

After threading our fingers together, I pinned her arms above her head. She looked up at me with eyes full of anticipation.

I thrust into her—one deep plunge straight into the heart of her body.

My body registered it all at once. Slick. Hot. Tight.

But while my body was overwhelmed with sensation, my brain totally blanked out.

● ● ●

A sudden stillness came over the room. It was like we didn't even breathe. I looked beneath me. She looked up.

I knew the shock written on her face was mirrored back at her.

Something passed between us, something even my brain didn't comprehend. My chest tightened and a burning sensation erupted right below my ribs.

Ivy untangled her hands from mine, reached around my ass, and pulled me in farther. When I tried to move, she made a sound and clutched at me some more. I remained buried so deep inside a faint voice warned me I might hurt her.

But then she started rocking.

Small, fluid movements against me. We were so tightly pressed together, my pelvis rubbed against hers.

Tension coiled low in my stomach as she rocked, her movements becoming faster, her thrusts becoming harder.

How the hell was I on top but she was in control?

I tightened my hands into the sheets, prepared to take over.

"Right there," she whispered.

I felt her body begin to shake, but then her eyes went wide. A shocked, almost frightened look replaced the pure bliss from just seconds ago.

I pulled back immediately, not leaving her body completely, but almost.

"Did I hurt you?" My voice was hoarse.

"No," she was quick to say, but she wouldn't look me in the eye.

I grabbed her chin and forced her eyes up. "Tell me."

"It felt good," she rushed out. "Better than ever before."

She squeezed her eyes shut, embarrassment written on her face.

And then I understood.

CHAPTER FOUR

> #TrueFact
>
> Decaf coffee is like having sex
> without an orgasm.
>
> ... Alpha BuzzFeed

IVY

I didn't know it could be like this.

I wasn't a virgin. I'd had more than a couple partners in bed.

Sex wasn't something new to me.

Yet this feeling was.

The way my body seemed to open up just for him. It was almost as if there were some secret combination inside me no one knew. Not even me.

But Braeden knew.

. . .

The sensations that took over my body were foreign and quite frankly wicked. I felt like I'd just discovered an itch I didn't know I had. It was too good. It was too enticing. It was too overwhelming.

It was scary.

"You've never had an orgasm." He dropped the words into the moment, blowing up my world.

As much as I wanted to be embarrassed, as much as his discovery should have totally blown whatever the hell had come over us, it didn't.

"I…" Words failed me.

A slow, seductive smile spread across his face. Even in the dark, I could see it reach his eyes. That smile held a lot of things. Passion, surprise… greed.

"I want it," he announced.

Like just the declaration would make it his.

Who was he to think he could just demand I give him something like that? The jerk. I was about to tell him what I thought of his demanding ways when he slid his well-muscled arms between my back and the mattress, pulling my body flush up against his. His hips surged forward and his cock went deep again.

My eyes rolled back in my head.

Braeden started moving. He was so large and hard he filled me completely. I could feel every inch of him, and it was delicious.

His movements mirrored the way I moved earlier, and something inside me throbbed so desperately it was almost painful. Confused, I started to pull away.

His palm grasped the back of my head and he pressed me deeper into the mattress.

"Ivy."

It wasn't the first time he'd said my name.

But it might as well have been.

My eyes locked on his, and I felt him between my thighs; his patience and will was unmatched.

"Give it to me."

And then it happened. My nails dug into his back, my toes curled into the sheets, and pleasure rolled over me like a giant wave in the sea. It literally flowed through my entire body as I started to moan.

Braeden covered my mouth with his as I groaned and whimpered.

I was totally helpless to the way he milked my body. I'd never in my entire life felt anything more powerful.

When my body, totally spent, fell back in languid stupor, he rose above me, holding himself up on his arms, and drew back, only to surge into me again.

My mouth opened, but no sound came out.

Braeden totally took over and pumped his hips until his entire body went rigid and I felt his hot release inside me. When he collapsed on me, his skin was slick with sweat and his body jerked with little aftershocks.

So did mine.

Braeden had just become my own personal earthquake. Everything inside me felt rattled and shifted. The composition of my insides would never be the same again.

I didn't mind the weight of him over me; in fact, I was grateful for it. Without it, I would surely float away. At least this way I stayed grounded.

Eventually, the electricity in the air evaporated, leaving behind two naked people piled on a bed. The sound of the ocean waves outside the window seemed to intrude, and the reality of what just happened settled in.

I just had sex with Braeden.

Braeden.

The guy I hated. The guy who slept with girls and then vanished, leaving them brokenhearted. I saw firsthand what he was capable of. After all, he did it to one of my best friends.

Missy was never going to forgive me for this.

All the muscles in my body tightened. My stomach clenched. The euphoria of my very first orgasm was being intruded upon by the fact the person who gave it to me was irrevocably off-limits to me.

I was a terrible person.

Braeden pushed away and walked into the adjoining bathroom. He didn't say a word. I wondered if he was having the same mental breakdown.

I almost laughed.

Yeah, right. Braeden didn't care about stuff like this. How many times had I heard him say it? He just had fun. He didn't have feelings.

I rolled onto my side and closed my eyes.

* * *

How in the hell did he pull off no feelings after what just happened between us? Had everything I just experienced been totally one-sided?

Did it even matter?

He came out of the bathroom, leaving the light on but pulling the door around so the room was mostly still dark. The mattress dipped beneath his weight, and I felt him move close behind me.

Now that my body wasn't taken over by some evil alien—evil alien = Braeden's touch—my brain was fully comprehending the implications of what just happened.

When Braeden grasped my shoulder and tugged, I rolled onto my back but avoided his stare. The muffled chuckle over me made me want to punch him.

And maybe poke out his eyes with my fingers.

But then he did something totally unexpected.

His large, warm palm landed on my thigh, and he tugged so my legs fell open. Before I could kick him, I felt a soft, cool cloth between my legs.

Oh, it felt nice.

I glanced at him, surprised.

He wasn't looking at me, but he smirked. "Didn't expect that, did ya?"

It was the absolute last thing in the history of earth I expected.

"I know you don't really need cleaned up," he began, "since, you know, we used a condom." How was he so totally comfortable talking about this with me? "But that was pretty intense. You're kinda small."

I gasped at the shock underlying his tone.

"And this surprises you?" I demanded.

He shrugged as he gently held the cool cloth between my legs. "Yeah. I guess it does."

"I'm not a slut," I deadpanned.

His white teeth flashed against the dark. "Never said you were."

"Not in so many words," I muttered.

"I just thought this might help," he said, wisely avoiding the issue. "I hope I didn't hurt you."

I didn't want to be affected by his consideration.

Yet I was.

"You didn't hurt me," I whispered.

• • •

We lapsed into silence. Intimacy clouded the room; it was far thicker now than when he'd actually been inside me. There was something very intimate about him touching me, about him caring for the most secret spot on my body, without the suggestion of sex.

Oh my God, what had I done?

A few minutes later, he withdrew his hand—leaving the cloth in place—and cleared his throat. "I still don't like you."

Some of my freakout actually calmed.

"I still don't like you either," I agreed.

Chuckling, he flipped the comforter up over me. He reached for his cell lying nearby before he lay back down beside me. I should've been running out of this room.

I wasn't ready to do that yet.

He checked the time and grunted. "Couple hours 'til the sun comes up."

Was he saying that because he wasn't ready for me to leave yet either?

Of course not. This was Braeden.

"Relax. I have no intention of sleeping over. I'll be out of here in a couple minutes."

"Like it never even happened," he murmured.

Something pierced my chest. "Believe me. I'm not telling anyone."

The screen on his phone lit up again and shined in my eyes when he held it up in the air above us.

"What are you doing?" I asked.

"Taking a selfie." The image of us lying in a rumpled bed—me with swollen lips and messy hair and him with a look of smug satisfaction across his face—reflected back at us.

The image was exactly like the fleeting moment we shared before.

Intimate.

I turned my head and looked at him. He was looking up at the screen, smiling for the camera. I took just an instant to stare. His strong, square jaw, his full lips and high cheekbones. He was incredibly good looking and at the same time, incredibly maddening.

"I thought you said this never happened," I remarked, still watching him.

I heard the click of the camera. I knew he'd taken his selfie.

He tossed the phone aside and turned so our faces were mere inches apart and his dark, unreadable eyes stared into mine. "Maybe some things shouldn't be forgotten."

My stomach did a flip. Beneath the comforter, my hands flexed

"I still don't like you," I told him again.

A ghost of a smile appeared on his face. "I still don't like you either."

"This can never happen again," I said, serious.

"I'm not interested in a repeat."

I felt a pang of something I didn't want to acknowledge.

I rolled out of the bed and tried to take the comforter with me, for coverage. The jackass was lying on it and wouldn't move.

I dropped it. "You're such an asshole."

"Yep."

I hurried to pull on my swimsuit cover up. It was made out of combed cotton and so comfortable.

Suddenly the idea of being naked with him nauseated me.

After I gathered up the pieces of my bikini and crept to the door, I stopped and turned. "I'm not this person… not anymore. I'd appreciate it if you didn't tell anyone this happened." Damn the emotion in my voice. I'd already given him too much. Showing him anything more was suicide.

A wave of guilt washed over me. Guilt for so many different reasons.

"What happens in spring break stays in spring break," he quipped. I relaxed, realizing he probably hadn't even been paying attention to the sound of my words. Hell, I'd been lucky he even heard them.

I slipped out of the room, into the dark hallway.

Braeden's words echoed behind me.

Funny, they didn't make me feel any better. If anything, now I felt worse.

CHAPTER FIVE

BRAEDEN

I honestly had no intention of ever touching Ivy.

From the moment we met, she irritated me.
Sometimes just looking at her made me want to run my
fist through a wall.

And that kind of emotion was dangerous.
Especially for a guy like me.

I only tolerated her because of Rimmel. Even with
all of Ivy's faults, she was loyal to my little sis, and that
alone kept me in check.

I'm not really sure what came over me.

Fuck.

That's a lie.

I know exactly what came over me. I couldn't ignore the way she wrapped herself around me. The way she fit in my arms like she belonged. I had every intention of tossing her on her shapely ass the second we hit the deck.

But there was no one.

No one between us in that moment. No Romeo, Rimmel, or Missy. No sarcastic jokes hanging in the air. The irritation I always felt seemed distant, and undeniable desire was front and center.

There wasn't even the sun, the bright light of day to shine some sort of barrier between us. The dark saw it all. The dark knew the truth.

The breeze off the ocean whispered and taunted. It stripped us both bare.

Lies only work if the person you tell them to believes them. When Ivy looked up at me, I saw the truth. I saw neither one of us believed the lies we were telling.

So I kissed her.

I slammed her up against the house and stroked my tongue deep inside her.

I didn't stop.

I couldn't.

We went at each other like we always had: full throttle. Except this time, it wasn't with hate. It was with fucking desire.

I stared at the door for a long time after she slipped out.

This was good.

This needed to happen.

Now that it was out of our systems, we could go back to barely veiled contempt, and no one would ever have to know.

I rolled to the side and tucked an arm beneath the pillow and my head. My gaze landed on the extra, unopened condom I'd thrown beside us on the mattress.

In the heat of the moment, I thought once with Ivy wasn't going to be enough.

I was wrong. Once was more than enough.

It had to be.

. . .

It was all we were going to get.

● ● ●

CHAPTER SIX

> Friends are like boobs.
> Some are big. Some are small.
> Some are real and some are fake.
> #WhatKindOfFriendAreYou?
> ... Alpha BuzzFeed

IVY

My body still hummed.

Like literally, everything beneath my skin still pulsed from what happened last night.

Okay, fine, it had been only hours ago. But I preferred to think of it as last night. It seemed further away, less present in my mind. God knew it was still all too present for my body.

Even though my brain was horrified by what I'd done, my body was so satisfied it made me feel guilty.

Damn Braeden.

Damn him for making me so divided inside.

I just prayed he kept his word and didn't tell anyone. Especially Missy.

Missy and Braeden weren't together; they never really were. Yes, they had a "friends with benefits" relationship, but that had been last fall, before winter break. So technically, me hooking up with him shouldn't be a big deal.

But it totally was.

Missy might not say it, but I knew she was still hung up on B. I knew she'd wanted more from him… had hoped the casual relationship they had would turn into more.

It took her a while to come around once Braeden stopped calling. She pulled back from our group, pulled back from dating. And for that, I hated Braeden. I hated guys like him. So cocky and charming. They only ever thought about themselves, never about the girls they slept with and left.

But the past few weeks, Missy had been coming around; she was more like herself, and being around Braeden didn't seem to bother her as much. We all managed to spend an awesome week here at the beach with barely a single tinge of awkwardness.

Until I broke the girl code and slept with the guy Missy wanted.

She'd been asleep when I snuck past her room on the way to mine last night. Her room was dark and silent, and I let out a huge breath of relief no one seemed to hear the romp Braeden and I just had.

Even though I went to bed super late, I was still the first one up. I was too keyed up after what happened, my body and mind unable to sleep. I tried, but all that happened was me reliving every second I'd spent with Braeden as I lay there in the dark.

So I got up. I showered and blew out my hair. It was the first time since we got here I actually styled it straight. There'd been no point with all the time we spent in the ocean. But today we were all leaving. Getting on a plane and flying back to Maryland, back to Alpha U.

After I distracted myself by styling my long, blond hair and did a minimal makeup routine, I got dressed. Since we were flying, I put on a long maxi dress with a bold black and white chevron print. The top of the dress was all black, making it look like I was wearing a black tank top with a skirt even though it was all one piece. I figured it would be comfortable for the plane yet still offer some warmth on my legs when we landed. I was also going to add a black cardigan. Maryland wasn't going to be as warm as Florida.

I didn't bother with jewelry; I wasn't in the mood. The only thing I was wearing was the bracelet made of seashells from a beach shop nearby. All three of us got one to remember the week we spent here together.

Looking at it just then made my stomach hurt.

No one else was in the kitchen, so I put on a pot of coffee and waited impatiently for it to brew enough for a cup. Once I had a mug full of caffeine and sugar, I carried it out onto the back deck. I stood at the railing beneath the early morning sun and stared out at the glistening waves.

As I sipped at the coffee, I saw Romeo and Rimmel down the beach. Rimmel had a bucket in her hand and was searching in the sand for shells. I smiled.

• • •

She finally dragged Romeo out of bed to go seashell hunting.

I watched the pair with a bit of envy as a wave crashed close by and rushed toward Rimmel. She'd been so intent on the shells she didn't notice the water until it was close, and even from this distance, I saw her body react when she saw.

But Romeo was there. He wrapped his arms around her and lifted her just before the water touched her. It rushed around his feet and ankles, but he didn't seem to notice. He was too busy kissing her.

Sometimes I wondered if I would ever know what that kind of love felt like.

The sliders behind me opened and my body tensed, afraid it was Braeden. I wasn't ready to see him yet. I didn't know what it would be like between us.

"There you are," Missy said and sidled up beside me at the railing.

"Hey." I gave her a smile and sipped at my coffee. "Can you believe the week is already over?" I asked, gazing back down the beach toward Rimmel and Romeo.

• • •

"It went by fast," Missy agreed, following my gaze. "Those two really are perfect together."

"Yeah," I agreed and turned back to her. She was wearing a pair of navy loose, lightweight pants with a high waist and a fitted red T-shirt tucked into the waist. Her dark hair was pulled up in a messy bun on the top of her head and she had a pair of large white sunglasses on her makeup-free face.

Missy was gorgeous. She was tall and thin, moved with grace, had olive-toned, perfect skin and wide gray eyes. In all honesty, she could be a model. That's how beautiful she was.

And since I was standing here being honest, I could admit sometimes she made me feel like a frump. Out of the three of us, I was probably the most plain. Rimmel had the whole adorably rumpled thing going on, and when she let me style her, the rumpled look turned into unique beauty. Rimmel might not realize it, but all her "imperfections" made her very eye-catching. Hell, she'd caught Romeo's eye.

I'd hate her, but it was impossible. She was so incredibly genuine. I'd much rather have her as a best friend than an enemy.

Missy made most girls look plain. She was just naturally glamorous. Most eyes went to her when she walked in a room.

And then there was me.

I was somewhere in the middle of the unintentional beauty and the natural beauty. More average. I guess it's why I tried so hard with my appearance. Well, that and I just really loved clothes.

I was average height, not short or tall. I wasn't fine boned or long and lean. I filled out my clothes, honestly more than I'd like. I wasn't heavy, but I was curvy. My hourglass shape sometimes frustrated me because trying to dress it wasn't always easy. Some days I wished I had the kind of body everything looked good on, like Missy, and sometimes I wished I didn't care how I looked, like Rimmel, but I didn't and I did.

My blond hair was highlighted to be brighter because if I didn't, it would look like I soaked my head in dirty dishwater on a daily basis. Ew. My blue eyes didn't seem that exotic or spectacular when I scrutinized them in the mirror, and my skin was on the pale side—it lacked the golden glow Missy always seemed to have.

Basically, I was high maintenance. Most people probably thought I dressed cute, styled my hair and always had makeup on because I was self-absorbed. They probably thought I spent too much time looking in the mirror and assumed I thought I was better than everyone else.

You know what they say about assuming.

(ASS-U-ME = makes an ass out of u and me)

The truth was I did that stuff for me. To make me feel good about myself. There was nothing worse than walking around with this voice constantly whispering inside your head that you aren't good enough. That people would cast their eyes your way, only to immediately dismiss you as someone who didn't deserve a second glance.

So yeah, I styled my hair every day and I put on makeup. I wore cute jeans and heels to make me a little taller. I wore tops that accentuated the curves I had

* * *

instead of hiding them. Everyone always thinks blondes have it easy, that they're the most beautiful.

It's not true.

Being blond and blue-eyed gets me more distasteful looks than being exotic-looking ever could. I'm stereotyped before I even open my mouth. My mom used to tell me girls were just jealous. Maybe she was right. However, it's hard to believe someone could be jealous of the way I look when I wouldn't be.

I'd rather have gorgeous dark, shining hair I never had to color. I'd rather have olive-toned skin that didn't need the help of bronzer. And I sure as hell would rather have less body.

But I didn't.

Dying my hair dark would totally wash out my skin and it wouldn't go with my light-colored eyes. And these curves of mine? They weren't going anywhere. I tried for years—all through high school—to diet and exercise them away, but eventually, a girl gets tired of trying.

Eventually, a girl wants a slice of pizza.

So I work with what I have. And I try to be the best version of myself, even though on most days, my best version still feels kind of lame.

Still, I'd never show the way I actually felt on the outside. I'd rather people think I was shallow and full of myself than insecure and vulnerable.

I'd rather sling out a witty comeback than let anyone get the better of me. Over the years, I'd built up a strong defense for the softness inside me, so much so it was part of me now. Sometimes even I forgot about the weakness I kept hidden deep, so when I felt it— when it reminded me it was there—it frightened me.

For some reason, that weakness was reminding me now.

"Ivy?" Missy's voice cut into my inner thoughts. She tentatively touched my shoulder. "Are you okay?"

I gave her a bright smile and nodded. "Of course."

"You seemed a million miles away," she replied, still eyeing me cautiously.

"You caught me." I shrugged. "I was staring at the piece of man candy down there running on the sand."

Missy turned to stare at the guy who was conveniently running down the beach with no shirt. His back muscles were cut and glistening with sweat under the early morning sun.

"He's definitely enough to distract anyone." Missy elbowed me in the side gently.

The truth was I hadn't noticed him at all. I probably wouldn't have if I didn't need an excuse for my lapse into La-La Land a few moments ago.

I wagged my eyebrows, and she laughed. "So," I began, taking another sip of coffee, "I need the details."

"The details for what?"

I rolled my eyes. "Girl. You and Trent. So what's up with that?"

Missy sighed and glanced out toward the ocean. "Girl," she mirrored my tone, "you've been here all week. You know what's up with that."

I made a snoring sound. "Look, we all know certain people were hoping you and him would hit it off this week."

Missy glanced my way. "I really don't like it when people try to get involved in my love life."

"That's what friends are for. So come on," I fished. "Do you like him?"

Smiling, Missy shook her head. "You should run a dating website."

I made a rude sound. "Gross. The last thing I want is a bunch of disgruntled women trying to blame me because they ended up dating a dog."

We both laughed. Wind blew up from down on the beach and pulled my hair in all different directions. "I'm going to take your evasion to my question as a no, you don't like Trent."

Missy leaned her forearm on the railing of the deck and angled her body toward me. A few strands of hair had come loose from her bun and waved wildly around her face. "Trent is a really great guy. And he's definitely easy on the eyes."

"But?"

"But he's not Braeden."

I choked on the coffee I was drinking. It spewed back out between my lips and splashed back into the half-empty mug as my body was racked with coughing.

Oh my God.

Did she just say what I thought she said?

My mind was spinning as I tried to calm my racing heart and swallow down the rest of my coughs. After a few minutes, I seemed to be able to rein in it. Sitting the cup aside on the railing, I sucked in a deep breath.

Missy was watching me closely, and I shook my head. "Sorry. Wrong hole." I dabbed at my lips with the back of my hand, making sure there wasn't coffee all over me and trying not to smear my makeup in the process.

"You good?" she asked, concerned.

"Yeah." My voice was hoarse, and I cleared my throat and said it again, this time more confident. Then I threw out my hands as if to stop everything around us. "I'm sorry, but did you just say you're still into Braeden?"

I didn't have to disguise the disgust in my voice.

'Course, I wasn't sure who I was more disgusted with. Her or me.

Missy shrugged, suddenly shy. But she couldn't be shy with me. Not after that bold statement.

• • •

"I thought you were finally over him, Miss," I pressed.

"Why, because I stopped wallowing in the fact he wasn't calling anymore?"

"Well, yeah. And we've all been hanging out. You even agreed to weekend pancakes with us all. This week…"

"This week?" she prompted.

"You and Trent…" I echoed again.

Flashes of last night wouldn't stop assaulting me. His mouth. His abs—good Lord his abs. The way he felt between my thighs. I turned abruptly away from Missy and toward the ocean. I forgot about my coffee and I bumped the mug.

It fell over the side of the deck. I grappled for it, but it was too late. Missy and I watched as it fell down into the sand dune among lost seashells and tall beach grasses.

"Oops," I said.

"Was what I said really that surprising?" she asked, amusement clear in her tone.

I groaned. "I need to go get that."

"You can't. People aren't supposed to climb on the dunes." She pointed to a sign posted near the public access next to our house. It promised hefty fines if anyone was caught climbing.

"I'm not climbing," I countered, flipping my hair over my shoulders. "I'm retrieving."

"Just leave it down there."

I probably should have. I mean, really, it was a stupid mug. There were a dozen others just like it inside. But if I stayed here, I'd have to finish this conversation. I'd have to listen to Missy tell me she was still interested in B. In the guy I had hot sex with just hours ago.

"No one will even know I went down there," I said and rushed toward the side of the deck that led down to the parking beneath the house.

"Ivy!" Missy hissed.

"I'll be right back!" I called and rushed down the stairs. Once I was standing on the concrete parking pad beneath the house, I leaned up against one of the stilts the house was on and dragged in a ragged breath.

• • •

Get it together, Ivy! I told myself. If I reacted like this every time she said his name, everyone would know what happened without me saying a word.

So what if she still had a thing for him? He already made it clear—the big jerk—that he wasn't interested in her that way. It's not like her feelings were going to change anything. Other than make me feel worse about what I did.

However, that was my cross to bear, and I could do that quietly.

Feeling much stronger and less caught off guard, I pushed away from the thick wood pole and went to the side of the house underneath the stairs. I hesitated a moment because it was cooler and shadier under here. The deck kept the sun off the sand and the grasses were grown up well past my knees.

What if there were creatures living down here?

I told myself to get over it and pushed forward. My feet sank into the sand as I climbed beneath the deck and walked along the house until I came to the edge of where the deck above ended.

"Hurry up!" Missy called from above me.

I looked up to see her staring down at me. She pointed toward the mug, and I followed her direction to where it lay nearby.

The weeds brushed against my skirt and pulled at it. Shuddering, I gathered the fabric up in one hand and bunched it up around my knees as I made my way over the mug.

"There's a lot of crap down here," I yelled up. A Frisbee, a beach ball without its air, scattered shells, a couple straws, and empty plastic cups littered the sand. It was cold beneath my toes and so was the grass that brushed against my calves.

The sounds of the beach were a little muted down here, and it sort of felt like I was in a whole other world.

Sounds from up above caught my attention, and I looked up, squinting against the bright sky. Missy turned away from me and was looking toward the house. Footfalls against the deck vibrated the wood, and I started praying.

Please be Trent. Please be Trent.

"What the fuck are you doing?" boomed a voice overhead.

My teeth snapped together. It wasn't Trent.

"Washing my car," I spat.

Missy told him about my mug, and he laughed.

"How much of that coffee did you actually drink before you dropped it? Apparently not enough." Braeden was clearly amused by his unwitty banter.

Missy's light giggle floated above, and I narrowed my eyes. Oh no she didn't just laugh.

"Jerk face!" I yelled and then totally turned my back on the both of them. The mug had fallen near a patch of tall grasses, so I had to reach my hand into them to get it.

Before I did, I parted the foliage and peered in, making sure there wasn't something else in there. I heard talking above me, but I ignored it. I ignored him.

My hand closed around the ceramic and I lifted it. Well, part of it. The other half was still lying in the sand. Figures. Stupid thing was broken. Since I was already down here, I was going to pick it up. Even though, by the looks of everything lying around, no one else ever bothered to clean up after themselves.

Once I collected the pieces of the mug, I straightened up, one hand full of the glass and the other holding my skirt up so I didn't trip.

"Be careful," Missy called down.

"Wouldn't want you to trip and break a nail." Braeden chortled.

I tossed my hair back and glared up. The smartass remark died on my tongue as the breath in my lungs stuttered.

He was leaning over the railing, watching me with a red hat turned backward on his head. From where I was standing, he really wasn't much more than a dark shape looming overhead, but he still affected me. He still caused awareness to crash through my limbs.

I jerked my face away and started walking toward the underside of the deck. My foot stepped on a large shell and my ankle turned a little. Stumbling, I threw my opposite foot out to catch my balance.

"Ow!" I howled as sharp pain sliced through on the bottom of my foot. I fell backward, the pieces of the broken cup falling into the sand beside me.

CHAPTER SEVEN

BRAEDEN

I didn't think. I just reacted.

I leapt over the railing with ease. The distance down and the uneven sand I would be landing on didn't even cross my mind.

It didn't matter.

I landed like a cat, no trouble at all, and the second my feet hit the sand, I moved forward. Ivy was almost beneath the deck, but not quite. Her back was to me and she was sitting up, hunched forward over part of herself.

She was muttering some pretty damn colorful curse words beneath her breath, and my face split into a smile. "Another angry crab attack you?"

She stiffened and looked over her shoulder. Long blond hair cascaded down her back and partially over her shoulder, creating a waterfall around her.

God, she was beautiful.

Wait. No. No, she wasn't.

I cleared my throat.

"Braeden?" She glanced up, surprised. "Did you jump down here?"

"Well, you screamed like you might be dying," I quipped.

"Hardly." She tried to roll her eyes, but it turned into a grimace. "I need a Band-Aid," she said pathetically.

I bit back a smile and crouched down beside her. "Let me see."

She leaned back a little so her body wasn't blocking my view. The movement brought her closer against me, and the scent of cinnamon wrapped around me. My stomach muscles tightened and I jerked slightly. There was no way she could have noticed, but her head tilted back and her eyes found mine.

We stared at each other for the span of a few heartbeats, neither of us moving or saying a word until someone called down from above, wanting to know if we were okay.

I blinked, bringing myself back from the edge—the edge I always seemed perched on around her—and motioned for her to show me what was wrong.

She lifted her foot into her lap, and I looked down.

I heard myself mutter something, but I was back to not thinking again.

She had the cap of a beer bottle sticking out of the bottom of her foot. Blood oozed out around it and dripped into the sand.

I cradled her foot in my hand and gently stroked my thumb along her heel. A shudder moved through her, and I glanced up.

"Hurts, huh?" I murmured.

She blinked. "Uh…" She blinked again. "Yeah."

Using one hand, I reached around to the base of my neck and pulled my T-shirt up over my head. I didn't say anything when I reached for her again, and without any warning, I yanked the cap free.

Her breath hissed between her teeth and she smacked my arm.

"Hey!" I snapped.

"That hurt!" she yelled, but it came out more like a whimper.

I tossed the cap over my shoulder and glanced back down. Fresh blood welled. "It's over now," I said gently and used my shirt to wrap around her foot.

Once the shirt was in place, I pressed her foot between my hands, applying a little pressure.

Really, I just wasn't ready to let go.

"Braeden?" Her voice caressed me. Being down here mostly concealed by the deck in the cool sand and low lighting brought back last night. It reminded me of the undeniable electricity between us.

I thought for sure it would be gone.

It was still there.

One of her toes was red and looked scraped, too. I touched a fingertip to it. "You hit your toe, too."

"That was from last night."

I smiled. "Ah, yes. The angry crab."

Our eyes met again. I reached between us, my fingers itching to tuck her hair behind her ear, but I stopped just before I made contact.

What the hell was I doing?

I pulled back and released her foot. "Come on. Let's get your clumsy ass up the steps so you can clean that up before we gotta leave."

"I'm not clumsy," she snapped and pushed to her feet. I started to help her, but she pulled away.

"Thank God for that," I retorted. "Rimmel is all the clumsy I can handle."

She made a face and turned away to take a step. But she didn't make it very far with one foot down for the count.

"C'mon," I drawled and wound an arm around her waist. She relented some of her weight to me, and we started toward the concrete pad under the house.

"The mug," she said, whirling to go back.

"Leave it." I tightened my arm.

"But—"

"But nothing," I snapped. "That fucking thing is the reason your foot's all sliced up."

The vehemence in my voice shocked us both.

Before I could say anything, someone turned the corner and headed straight for us. It was Trent. His eyes went right to Ivy and stayed there. When he saw my shirt around her foot he frowned.

"What happened?"

"I got in a fight with a bottle cap, and it won," Ivy replied.

Trent chuckled. "Beer is one tough opponent."

"I'll keep that in mind." Ivy's voice was dry.

We made it to the concrete, and I all but lifted her onto the flat surface.

"Getting up the stairs like that isn't gonna be too fun," Trent observed.

I thought about the way I carried her up a set of similar stairs just last night. Carrying her up today would just be the right thing to do. We'd be here all day if I had to help her drag herself up.

Before I could pick her up, Trent did. He swept her right out of my grip and up against his chest. I felt my eyes narrow.

Ivy squealed.

"I'll help you clean that up," he offered.

"You mean you aren't going to tell me how clumsy I am?" Ivy asked, and irritation punched me. Was she trying to annoy the shit out of me right now?

"Clumsy?" Trent smiled down at her as we made our way to the stairs. "Nah. That cap had it in for ya."

"I know!" Ivy agreed.

Of course she would. Missy was coming down the stairs as we were going up. Her eyes bounced to all of us, and then I thought I saw a look I didn't recognize pass behind her eyes when she glanced at Ivy and Trent.

It was almost calculating.

I remembered when Trent casually asked Rome and me about Ivy's status.

Did Missy think Ivy and Trent made a good couple?

I felt my upper lip curl at the thought, like I'd just eaten something sour. Ivy and Trent?

Hells no.

A hand slid over my arm and I glanced up. Missy was standing close, gazing up at me with worry in her gray eyes. "Is she okay?"

"Yeah, she just cut her foot."

"You just leapt right off the deck."

I glanced down at her hand, where it still rested against me. Then I looked back up. "Well, yeah. Rim woulda kicked my ass if I just let her lay down there."

Missy's lips curved up. "How did she manage to get your heart?"

"Who?" I demanded, a little bit of alarm pulsing through me. How did she know about last night?

Missy gave me a look. "Rimmel," she spoke slowly.

Right. Rimmel.

Trent disappeared around the side of the house with Ivy in his arms, leaving Missy and me here alone. I shrugged. "She's good for Rome. She's family."

Missy tilted her head to the side and regarded me. Even through her shades, I could feel her stare. "You got any more room left in there?" She pulled her hand back from my arm and poked me in the chest, just above the heart.

What the fuck was she asking me? I swear, chicks might as well speak Spanish. I decided charm would be the best answer here. Charm with a side of truth. I gave her a lopsided smile. "Haven't ya heard? I'm like the Grinch. My heart is two sizes too small."

She laughed and pulled back. "I better go see if Ivy's okay."

We walked together around the side of the house toward the sliders. Inside, I could see Ivy sitting on the kitchen counter and Trent standing in front of her with a first aid kit beside him. Missy went ahead, but I hung back for a second.

The familiar heat of anger swirled inside me, practically appearing out of nowhere. My fingers curled into my palms, and I took a deep breath. There was no reason to be getting so worked up. I just needed to chill.

The boards of the deck vibrated underfoot, and I glanced around at Romeo and Rimmel, who were coming toward me. Rim had a bucket of shells in her hand and flushed cheeks I knew weren't from the morning sun. Romeo was right behind her with a pair of shades wrapped around his eyes.

"What's going on, B?" Romeo's tone was casual, but I knew he sensed more. We'd been friends since first grade; we read each other well. He knew me. He knew my inner workings. He knew things most everyone else didn't.

"Ivy cut her foot," I replied.

Rimmel gasped. "Is she okay?"

"I'm sure she's being a drama queen," I muttered.

She smacked me in the stomach and then handed me her bucket of shells. "I'll go see if she needs help."

I was pretty sure she was already getting help, but I didn't stop her from rushing in the house.

Romeo was watching me when I set the bucket down by my feet. "You straight?"

I pulled the hat off my head and ran a hand through my hair. "Yeah."

"What's got you so worked up?"

"Fuck," I muttered. "It just hits me sometimes. Ya know?"

"Yeah." Stepping closer, he palmed my shoulder with his hand and turned me toward the ocean. "Just look at the waves. Be one with nature and shit."

I laughed. "Dude. You are so lame."

"You totally feel peaceful right now," Rome cracked.

I guffawed.

Romeo grinned and slapped me on the back. "You're welcome."

I snickered. Even though I laughed, I did owe him thanks. I did feel better. More in control. Romeo always knew how to pull me back. I glanced over at him, feeling grateful.

He must have seen the sincerity in my gaze because he shook his head. "I just spent a long time picking up seashells on the beach. If I have any more girl moments today, I'm gonna grow tits."

"On that note…" I scooped up the bucket and held it out. "Here's your shells. I'm gonna grab some coffee."

• • •

"Whoa," Romeo said after I turned toward the sliders.

"What?"

"Trent and Ivy." He gestured inside with his chin. "Guess Trent really is interested."

"Poor guy," I muttered and walked in.

Ivy was still sitting on the counter with Trent right in front of her. Missy and Rimmel were on either side of him, and everyone's attention was focused down.

"Does it need stitches?" Rimmel worried.

"Nah," Trent answered as he tore open a large Band-Aid.

I ignored them all as I went for the coffee maker on the other side of the kitchen. As I was walking past, Rimmel grabbed my arm. "What do you think, B? Think it needs stitches?"

The muscle in my jaw jumped when she pulled me into the situation I was trying to avoid, but when little sisters asked for your opinion, you gave it.

"Let me see," I said, and Trent angled off to the side so I could move forward to look.

My shirt was lying on the counter beside Ivy, and I could see the stains of blood. Trent was holding her ankle, supporting her foot, and I focused on the cut, not the way his fingers wrapped around her.

It was good slice, and if it had gone any deeper, she probably would need stitches. However, it seemed like Trent had cleaned it out well and the bleeding was pretty much stopped. It looked like it hurt, though, all red and raw-looking.

I glanced up at Ivy. Her cheeks seemed a little pale, but when her eyes found mine, her gaze was steady. "How's the foot, Blondie?"

"Nothing a Band-Aid won't fix."

I felt the side of my mouth kick up in a half smile. "Sounds good to me," I agreed and moved away, retreating to the coffee.

I poured a cup, and when I turned back, Trent was smoothing the Band-Aid on her foot. I tossed some of the brew down my throat. It burned.

"Thanks," Ivy told him. The softness in her voice had me throwing back another gulp of the black stuff. I

• • •

felt Romeo's eye, but I avoided it and stepped out of the kitchen.

"I'm jumping in the shower before we gotta leave," I called, not really talking to anyone specific.

"Wait," Ivy yelled.

I turned back.

She lifted my shirt up and held it out. "I sort of ruined your shirt."

I shrugged. "Toss it. It's just a shirt."

Not waiting for her to reply, I disappeared down the hall, away from everyone.

It was just a shirt.

Just one night.

Just one more thing for me to forget.

CHAPTER EIGHT

Actions speak louder than words?
#Truth
But some words are just too beautiful
to ignore.

... *Alpha BuzzFeed*

IVY

Damn, baby.

Two words.

Two words that were spoken millions of times during an average day of everyone's average lives.

But he said them.

And when he said them, it was anything but average.

He spoke them so well they replayed in my brain over and over again, like some annoying song you hear on the radio and can't get out of your head. Except this song wasn't annoying.

Every time those words replayed, I recalled the way he looked when he said them, and a piece of me literally melted. If it didn't stop soon, I was going to be nothing but a puddle.

No one had ever called me baby before. I mean, sure, I got the occasional, "Hey, baby," pickup line that was sort of like hearing nails on a chalkboard.

Oh, but this was so different.

It was the way I sometimes heard Romeo talk to Rimmel when he thought no one else could hear. The way it seemed to rumble out of him with so much emotion, yet without seemingly any thought. He spoke like it was an endearment, like I meant something to him. Something other than the girl he insulted so often it could be considered a hobby.

Even so, this was Braeden. The king of "having fun," the king of avoiding what he so *un*-charmingly referred to as the feels. He might have said it, but I knew I shouldn't read too much into it. He acted like he hadn't even heard himself speak. That was the worst part, that those two whispered words could mean so much to me and him not even realize he'd spoken.

And so I heard them on repeat over and over again, wanting it to stop, but also never wanting to forget.

I was totally screwed up.

I mean, seriously.

"How's it feel?" Trent asked. His voice was so close I wondered how I'd forgotten he was standing there.

I glanced up and smiled. "A lot better. Thanks for helping me get it cleaned up."

"Next time you want to get in a fight with a bottle cap… maybe just don't."

I laughed. "Yeah, maybe."

His smile was lopsided, and the tooth to the left of his two front teeth was slightly crooked, giving him an ornery, rakish look. This week was the most time I'd ever spent with him, the most I'd ever really seen him. I mean, sure, I knew him. He hung out in Romeo's crowd and was always with the Wolves. We went to the same parties, and I saw him around campus, but I

● ● ●

hadn't really ever bothered to get to know him. I'm glad I did, though, because Trent was a great guy.

He liked to laugh and seemed to have one of those easygoing, Namaste personalities. You know, the even-keel kind of vibe that never really went off balance.

He was the complete opposite of Braeden, who always seemed to be walking on a fine line between aggression and intensity.

I watched him as he gathered up the empty bandage wrappers and leaned away to toss them in the nearby trashcan before he screwed the cap back on the antibacterial cream. Trent was good-looking, like the kind of good-looking you did a double take to see.

I was beginning to think to be friends with Romeo, you had to be smoking hot.

He was a big guy, of course, being a college football player. Trent had a wide chest and shoulders that tapered down into a narrow waist and hips. His skin was golden from the week we spent here at the beach, and the warm color only drew more attention to how defined his body was. His hands were large, too, and his skin was warm like he'd been sitting in the sun.

* * *

At least that's what I'd thought when his entire palm wrapped around my heel and ankle as he fixed up my foot.

His hair wasn't blond like Romeo's, and it wasn't dark like Braeden's. It was somewhere in the middle—a sandy-brown shade that complemented his hazel eyes. He had wide cheekbones, a strong brow, and a straight, almost-perfect nose. He had that clean-cut look so many college guys had, even though the top of his hair was too long and flopped down over his forehead.

I don't know how long I stared at him, but it was long enough he seemed to notice. A slow, knowing smile tugged at his mouth and his golden-greenish gaze caught mine. "Think you're gonna be able to walk on that?"

I swallowed and tore my eyes away to glance down at my foot. My dress had ridden halfway up my thighs while everyone was assessing my foot and trying to clean it up. The ankle of the cut foot was thrown over the top of my knee—so unladylike for a girl in a dress. I dropped my foot so it could hang off the counter and tugged the dress until it fell down, covering all my legs from sight.

"Oh yeah, I'll be fine," I mumbled.

Trent didn't say anything, but he did muffle a laugh as he slid his arm around my waist. I stiffened at the unexpected touch. Did I mention he wasn't wearing a shirt? The skin of his arm and chest was just as warm as his hand had been earlier.

"Have you already been out in the sun?" I wondered out loud.

"I went for a run on the sand this morning," he replied. His voice was low because I was so close he didn't have to talk loud.

With one arm, he lifted me off the counter and lowered me carefully to the floor. I put most of my weight on the uninjured foot and balanced with the toes of my other. I wasn't quite ready to find out how it was going to feel to walk with a chunk of skin missing from the bottom of my foot.

"Thanks," I murmured when I was firmly on the floor.

• • •

He didn't pull back right away; he waited to make sure I was steady before stepping back and palming some stuff lying nearby. "You should take some of these big bandages. Keep them handy in case we need to change the Band-Aid on the plane."

"We?" I glanced down at the small stack of wrapped bandages in his hand.

"Yeah," he replied casually. "If you need help getting it changed, just let me know."

I took what he was offering and looked up. "Okay." My voice was weak. I wanted to kick myself.

I became acutely aware of everyone else in the room. Trent and I seemed to have a captive audience. I jolted back from him and took in everyone with a sweeping glance. "I'm just going to make sure the bathroom is cleaned up and everything of mine is packed before we do a final run-through of the rest of the house."

"I'm going to do that in our room, too," Rimmel agreed and pulled away from Romeo.

Romeo looked at me. "Just put your stuff by the door. I'll load it into the car for you."

• • •

"Thanks."

Trent leaned forward and reached behind me, his arm brushing against my bare shoulder. "I'll toss this for you." He stepped toward the trashcan.

As he did, I caught a flash of blue material in his hand.

"No," I gasped.

Surprised, he turned. "It's ruined."

I glanced down at the shirt in his hand. Braeden's shirt. The one he wrapped around my foot to help stop the bleeding.

"It seems silly to throw away a perfectly good shirt." What a lame thing to say.

Trent shrugged. "B said to toss it."

I should have just let him throw it away.

But I couldn't. It felt like I was losing something. Something I wasn't ready to let go of.

"Since when do I listen to anything that moron says?" I quipped and made a face. Trent smiled. I reached for the shirt, and he let me have it. "It's his Wolf Pack shirt. I feel bad I got blood all over it. I'll try to get it out, and if it doesn't, then I'll toss it."

I tucked the shirt beneath my arm and left the room, feeling like I needed to run but unable because of my stupid foot.

That was the last time I attempted to clean up after myself—especially when it was posted I shouldn't.

I was moving so slow that Rimmel slowed her pace on her way and glanced at me with worry in her eyes. "Maybe we should have had that checked out."

I waved away her worry. "I'm fine. Besides, we don't have time to sit at the doctor's office. We have a plane to catch."

She didn't seem convinced. I smiled reassuringly. "If it looks bad when we get back to campus, I'll go to the clinic, okay?"

That seemed to make her feel better, and she nodded. "Okay."

Her concern suddenly choked me up. The well-meaning, honest way she looked at me like she truly cared.

It made me feel small.

Guilty.

• • •

Tears pressed against the backs of my eyes and I pulled in a shaky breath.

"Ivy?" Rimmel took a step forward.

I laughed it off and fought for control. "Don't mind me. I think I have the spring break blues. All this sun and sand has been so awesome that going back to classes and cool weather is making me depressed."

"Can't say I'm all that excited about going back, either," Rimmel admitted. Just by the drop in her voice, I knew this was something she had yet to tell anyone.

All thoughts of myself fled—it was a relief—and I focused on her. The past two semesters had been rough on her. More than rough. She'd been pushed so many times to her breaking point, yet she stood here still. It left me wondering what it was that kept her from snapping.

"If you ever want to talk, I'm here for you," I told her earnestly. "You know that, right?"

Rimmel smiled. "Yeah, I do. Thanks, Ivy."

I nodded. Once again, guilt assaulted me. Here I was feeling sorry for myself about choices I made… about actions I took. Basically, damage I did to my own life. Yet there were people like Rimmel who were dealing with fallout from things she had no part in creating.

Romeo came around the corner and we both looked up. His blue gaze latched onto Rimmel, and it was like he saw exactly what was going on inside her. Like he saw past her skin, beneath the smile. It was like he knew.

"I'm afraid I have bad news," he intoned.

Rimmel stiffened immediately and so did I.

"What now?" I groaned. "Please tell me they didn't let him out of the loony bin early for extra-psychotic behavior."

God, that was just what everyone didn't need.

Romeo shook his head. "I'm afraid it's worse."

"What is it?" Rimmel asked, worried. "Is it your arm?"

"Murphy is getting fat."

It took a minute for the stupid sentence to sink through the horrendous thoughts Rimmel and I were both having.

* * *

Several silent beats later, we looked at each other and Rimmel snorted. I laughed.

"You call that an emergency?" I snickered.

Rimmel smacked him in the middle.

"Feline obesity is a very serious issue." How the hell did he keep a straight face when he said this crap?

"I take it your mother has taken a liking to my cat and is feeding him a million treats a day?" Rimmel asked.

Romeo draped an arm across her shoulders. "Yes, I didn't think it was possible anyone could feed our cat more than you, but Mom's managed it."

Rimmel giggled. "I can't wait to see him."

"Let's go pack." Romeo steered her down the hall, and I turned toward my bedroom door.

Before I went in, I looked back at the pair as they walked away. Romeo glanced over his shoulder at me and winked.

I flashed him a grin even as something in my stomach sank.

I was so glad she had someone as good as Romeo. Someone who would take care of her even when she could take care of herself. Even the strongest people needed someone to lean on sometimes. Even people with the best of intentions sometimes made mistakes.

Seemed like the past few months of my life was filled with them.

I felt lonely just then. I was standing in the center of a beautiful beach house filled with my very best friends, but I was utterly alone.

Who would make stupid jokes about feline obesity when I felt down? Would anyone ever be able to see beneath my skin, at what swirled beneath? Would I ever be anything more to someone than just a one-night stand?

I was afraid the answer to everything I just asked myself was a very loud, very resounding no.

CHAPTER NINE

BRAEDEN

I was feeling pissy.

Rome could tell, I knew, but thankfully, he didn't try to distract me or talk me out of it. It wouldn't have worked anyway. Sometimes a guy just felt pissed.

Okay. Sometimes I just felt pissed.

I hefted the last of the girls' shit down the stairs and out into the driveway. Why women needed so much stuff I had no idea. I mean, hell, they walked around in tiny-ass bikinis all week, not like they needed the fifty pounds of crap they brought with them.

Except for Rim, of course. She had one bag, one full-coverage swimsuit, and one thankful big brother.

"That everything?" Romeo asked when Trent and I handed over the last of the haul.

"I hope the hell so," I replied.

Trent snickered. "Dude, I don't even want to know what's in those bags."

Rimmel came down the steps with a list in her hand and stopped beside me. I glanced down to see the checklist the rental company left of all the things that needed to be taken care of before we left. "Everything is done," she stated.

I noted the neat checkmarks beside each item and smiled. "Only you would find homework on spring break."

She elbowed me in the gut, and I made a sound like it hurt. It didn't, but I didn't want to make her feel bad. It wasn't her fault she was harmless as a fly.

"Sweet. Let's go, then. The airport is waiting," Romeo said.

Trent glanced at the red convertible. "You sure we're all gonna fit in there?"

"Like sardines in a can," I muttered.

"We'll make it work," Romeo said.

"Easy for you to say. You're driving," I cracked.

He gave me the finger.

"I'll sit in the back because I'm smaller. One of you guys can take the front," Rimmel offered.

Technically, we had one person too many for the car. However, instead of calling a cab or renting anything else, we were just going to put the extra person in the back. It was illegal, but who the hell cared?

Missy and Ivy came out the door and started down the steps. Ivy was moving slow and Missy kept her pace, holding her arm like she was an old lady with a broken hip.

"Move your ass, Blondie!" I yelled. "We're gonna miss our flight."

"Braeden!" Rimmel scolded me. "She's hurt."

I grunted. "It takes a lot more than a bottle cap to take that one down."

• • •

From the stairs, Ivy told me to go suck an egg. I looked back at Rimmel and lifted an eyebrow. "She's so delicate."

Rimmel glared at me, and I knew I was about to get a lecture. God help me. If any other woman tried to lecture me, I'd tell 'em to piss off. But Rim was different. She'd somehow gotten her way in my heart and made a place there. I was really good at keeping women out of there, but this was different. This wasn't a romantic type of love; it was family. She was family.

In my pocket, my cell rang. "Sorry, sis, I gotta take this," I said, trying to sound so sad I would miss her instructions (okay, I didn't sound sad at all) and pulled it out.

It was my mom.

"Mom," I answered and turned away from the group.

"Hi, Braeden, honey," she said. "I'm just calling to make sure everything is still on schedule with your flight home."

I was twenty-one years old and my mom still called to check up on me. She'd probably still do it when I turned fifty. "We're heading to the airport now, Mom. Everything's good."

"Okay, well, you boys have a safe flight. And Rimmel, too."

"Will do."

I expected her to say her usual good-bye and end the call. But she hesitated.

"Mom?" I intoned. "Is something wrong?"

"Oh, no," she laughed, but it was strained. "I just miss you is all."

"I'll stop by once I get settled back on campus." Or maybe I'd just swing by on the way from the airport. I didn't like to think of her sitting around worrying about me. Or being lonely.

She'd wanted me to live at home when I went to college, and I did freshman year, but I wanted to live in the dorm. I wanted a little more freedom, some space that was just mine. So I moved on campus. Sometimes I felt bad about it.

"I'll look forward to it," Mom said, breaking into my thoughts.

"Cool. I gotta go or we'll be late. I'll call you when we land." I turned back to everyone. Trent was helping Ivy into the car, his hand on the small of her back.

I shoved the phone back into my pocket and went to the car. Trent was getting ready to squeeze himself in the backseat with the girls.

"You want the front, dude?" I asked.

"Nah, you can take it," he replied.

I slid into the front and spun the hat on my head so it wasn't backward anymore and then pulled it low on my forehead. The inside of this car felt like a pair of jeans with too much ass in them.

I ignored the chattering of everyone in the back as Romeo pulled away from the house and onto the main road. The vacay had been a fun time. And last night…

Well, I wasn't going to think about that anymore.

Ten minutes down the road, a bare foot came up between the seats and rested on the center console between Rome and me. I glanced over and caught a flash of red polished toes and the edge of a Band-Aid.

"Your feet stink," I snapped.

"Who sprinkled the bitch in your coffee this morning?" Ivy retorted.

I sat up, leaned around the seat, and stared at her from beneath my hat. She was in the middle with Missy, poor Rim squished up against the door, and Trent was on the other side of Ivy. Her hair was falling around her shoulders and her arms were crossed over her chest.

I felt our eyes connect; even with my hat partially blocking my gaze, my eyes still found a way to fix on hers. A shock of awareness jolted me, like a shot of tequila that lit a fire all the way from my throat to my stomach and then fanned out to coat my limbs.

Ivy's teeth sank into her lower lip, and I had an acute memory of sucking it into my mouth and licking over it with my tongue.

There was no way she could know what I was thinking. I gave not one indication. Still, her body tensed and she pulled back her foot, withdrawing as far away from me as she could.

"Is it hurting?" Trent asked.

She ripped her eyes away from me, breaking the half-drunk feeling washing over me. "A little."

"Propping it up probably would help."

Was he a doctor now?

"I wouldn't want anyone to pass out from my stench," she cracked.

Hell if it didn't make me laugh.

"If you stink, then I've got a third nipple," Trent said.

Her gasp was amused and exaggerated. "Where?"

His rumbling laugh filled the space behind me, and I rolled my eyes.

"You saw me without a shirt just this morning. Did you see any extra parts?"

"I think I'm gonna need a barf bag," I announced. Romeo laughed.

"I think everything was where it should be," Ivy stated like she hadn't heard me speak at all.

"Give me your foot," Trent said, laughter still in his tone.

I didn't bother looking—I kept my body trained toward the front—but I heard a little bit of movement. I imagined Ivy crossing her leg over her thigh and Trent pulling her injured foot into his lap.

"That okay?" he asked.

"Yeah, it's good. Thanks."

"Looks like it started bleeding again." I imagined him cupping her foot in his hand and staring down at the Band-Aid he placed there earlier.

"Well, I did hurry down the steps. People were rushing me." Her tone was directed at me. So was her snarky attitude.

I opened my mouth to tell her to shut it, but Trent spoke before I could.

"I can change it for you."

"I might as well wait 'til after I am through walking around the airport." I noticed the bitchy tone in her voice had been reserved exclusively for me.

I grunted and turned up the radio. Hopefully it would drown out the sound of her ear-splitting voice. I'd rather listen to nails on a chalkboard than hear her syrupy, slightly southern-accented voice talk to Trent like he was some kind of hero.

He put a bandage on her foot for chrissakes; it's not like he saved her from amputation.

I spent the rest of the drive to the airport with the brim of my hat pulled low over my eyes and ignoring the small confines of this car. Once we got to the airport, Romeo stopped in the unloading zone to let everyone out before he pulled around to return the rental. After I helped him unload the bags, I started to climb back in the passenger seat, figuring I'd just stick with him and give myself a break from all the women.

Before I could shut the door, Romeo caught it and leaned in. "Rim wants to grab a coffee before we head to the gate."

I rolled my head across the seat and looked at him. "You want me to stay with her?"

"It's a big place, lots of people. Trent seems to be pretty caught up in helping Ivy walk. Plus, he's hauling more than half the luggage."

I glanced past Rome to Rimmel standing on the sidewalk and sighed. "I got her."

"Thanks, man."

"No thanks needed. She's family."

● ● ●

We pounded it out, and he jogged around to the driver's side. Over the hood, he called out to Rimmel, "I'll meet you at the gate. Stick with B."

I slung my bag over my shoulder and stepped up beside her as she rolled her eyes. Taking her bag out of her hand, I added it to mine.

"Babysitting again?" she asked.

I shrugged. "I could use a coffee."

I get why it irritated her that Rome and I pretty much shared the responsibility of looking out for her, because it would probably piss me off, too. But it wasn't going to change.

"Come on," she muttered, and the five of us walked into the bustling airport. It was a bright place, full of glass and light, with white shiny floors that stretched out as far as I could see. People hurried across it, dragging bags with wheels behind them.

"You want me to take some of that, man?" I asked Trent. He was carrying his bag, Ivy's fifty pounds of crap, and half of Missy's.

"I got it," he grunted.

Ivy was standing next to him, favoring her uninjured foot over the other. Missy was glancing down at the paper in her hand and then up at the signs. "This way," she said and motioned us all toward the machines that would give us our boarding passes.

There were so many dispensers that there wasn't a long line. Rimmel and I stepped up to one, and I ushered her in front of me so she could go first. As she was typing in her info, I glanced next to us where Missy was using the computer. Behind her was Ivy, and Trent was close by.

Her black-and-white dress fell almost to the floor and skimmed her body, outlining the curves I'd gotten to know a lot better just last night.

The way her light-blond hair contrasted against the tan on her long, slender arm was something my eyes found very fascinating, and I stood there like a schmuck and stared.

I knew she felt my gaze. She glanced at me out of the corner of her eye but then quickly looked away.

"Ivy, you mind giving me a hand?" Trent asked, pulling my attention.

The skirt swung around her ankles when she turned and glanced up at him. "Seriously, Trent, you look like a pack mule. I can carry some of that."

"My momma taught me better than that," he drawled and then flashed his teeth at her. "'Course, my momma probably wouldn't approve of what I'm about to ask you to do."

My shoulders tensed as I eavesdropped on their little one-on-one.

"I'm intrigued," Ivy replied, interest in her tone and a slight smirk on her face.

Could she be any more obvious? I mean, shit, we were in an airport for shit's sake. This wasn't the time or place to pick up her next hookup.

"I need my ID." Trent's shit-eating grin stretched out across his face, and he motioned toward his conveniently full hands.

"Oh, where is it? I'll get it for you."

"It's in my pocket." He swiveled his hips so his pocket came forward. "Mind grabbing it?"

Oh, he was smooth. The fucker. That's the kind of shit I would pull.

Ivy giggled. My back teeth snapped together.

She stepped forward and slid her hand down into the front pocket of Trent's jeans. Did she really have to stand that close to him? Did he really have to look down at her like he was hungry and she was a damned donut? Her entire hand disappeared. How the hell deep were those pockets?

"Braeden?" Rimmel's voice cut into my thoughts and her hand brushed my arm.

I ripped my eyes from Ivy's search mission and looked at Rim. "Hmm?"

"It's your turn." She motioned to the machine like it was obvious.

"Cool." I dropped our bags at my feet and turned my back on everyone as I typed in everything.

I could hear Ivy laughing, Missy talking, and the low rumble of Trent's laugh.

I ripped my pass out a little rougher than I meant and grabbed up our bags. "We're gonna grab some coffee. You guys cool?" I directed the words to everyone but looked at Missy. I wasn't about to watch Ivy feeling up Trent anymore.

Missy frowned a little, and I realized my voice had been harsh. I took a deep breath and gave her my best charming smile. "You need some joe, Miss?"

Her frown disappeared and she smiled. Missy was hot, like magazine hot. And she wasn't that bad in bed either.

Made me wish I liked her as more than just a friend.

"I'm good, but thanks for asking."

I draped my arm across Rimmel's shoulder and started walking. "Cool. We'll see you guys at the gate."

Rimmel didn't say anything as I led her away and to the closest coffee shop. Of course there was a line. After a few minutes of standing there in silence, I felt my little sis staring.

"What?" I asked.

"What's wrong with you?"

I glanced at her and smirked. "Nothing. I'm perfect."

"And I'm Victoria Secret's next swimsuit model."

I groaned. "No brother wants that image in his head, Rim."

"You're acting strange. What's up?"

"Strange how?" I hedged. Why was it she always knew when something was going on? I blamed all the damn books she read all the time. Girl was too smart for her own good.

Rome was never gonna get away with nothing for the rest of his life.

"Braeden," she warned.

I smiled. I liked when she tried to act all tough and intimidating. The line moved up and we went with it.

"You want one of those girly drinks?" I asked, looking at the menu. The guy in front of us snickered and glanced over his shoulder at us.

"Sure." Her voice was syrupy sweet. "Just get me the one you always drink."

I glowered at her and the man's muffled laughter floated back to us.

She seemed rather proud of herself at that comment, so proud it took her mind off my interrogation, and I wasn't about to remind her. Yet the second I ordered—regular lattes with sugar for me and Rome and some vanilla macchiato thing for her, with a drizzle of chocolate and caramel—and we moved over to wait for our order, she put her hands on her hips and glared.

"Well?"

"It's nothing. My mom just sounded a little off when she called."

She dropped her arms and her face softened. "Oh, is she okay?"

I tugged on a stray piece of hair that had come out of the huge mess piled on her head. "Yeah, she's cool. I just think she's lonely. I've been gone a while."

"I don't think I really thanked you for coming to Florida when Romeo called. For being there for me like you were."

"BBFL," I said.

She smiled. "You're the best big brother anyone could have."

The barista called out my name, and Rimmel went over, grabbed the coffee, and handed it to me. When the other two were set down, she grabbed them up and we headed toward the gate.

She sipped her coffee, and after a few minutes of us dodging rushing people, she said, "Want me to come with you to see her? Romeo, too? We can all visit her, maybe make her feel less lonely."

If Romeo was gonna settle down with a woman and commit to being a one-woman guy, then he'd made a damn good choice. Rimmel was probably the most selfless person I knew.

"I'm sure she'd like that," I replied. "But I think I'll just stop by first, make sure everything is cool."

"Maybe we can have dinner with her this week?" she asked hopefully.

"Sure, that sounds good."

Rim had only met my mom a handful of times, but Mom knew how much my little sis meant to me. And Rimmel seemed to just slip right into my life, like she'd always been there. It was like because she cared about me, then she cared about everything I cared about, too.

The seats around our gate were full; it appeared the flight back to Maryland was going to be totally packed. However, even in all the people, my eyes found Ivy.

She was sitting with Missy and Trent over by the window.

I was glad to be going back to Alpha U, back to my normal schedule and dorm where she wouldn't be around all the time.

"Hey," Rimmel said, stepping in front of me as we drew closer. I stopped walking and focused on her. "You know you can talk to me anytime, right? Little sisters make really good listeners."

I half smiled. "Yeah, thanks."

She seemed a little unsure about her openness, a little shy about letting me know she cared. "I mean, I know you have Romeo, and he'd be the one you would go to—"

"Rim." I cut her off and dropped the bags beside us. "I know. I love you, too." I hooked an arm around her and pulled her in. It wasn't a full-on hug because she was holding two coffees and I was holding one, but it got the job done.

I felt her shock at my words. That I actually said I loved her out loud like that.

I cleared my throat. "You know, as a sister."

Her giggle was muffled against my shirt. "I love you, too."

I didn't think those words would mean so much to me. Hell, I hadn't really thought I'd be telling her I loved her in the middle of the airport.

But her willingness to say she cared touched me. It dug underneath the pissy mood I was in and the annoyed feelings I had toward Ivy.

For a long time, my family consisted of just my mom and me. Romeo and his parents were main constants in my life, too. But this was the first time I'd let in a girl. No, it wasn't romantically, but it still meant a lot. In fact, the shock Rimmel just displayed I felt, too. Maybe that's why I was so protective over her. Because letting in people was just as rare for me as it was for her, and because I wanted to protect it.

"I leave you two alone for five minutes," Romeo drawled as he came up behind us.

Rimmel pulled away and went to him. I wasn't a relationship guy, but the devotion I saw in her eyes when she looked at him sometimes made me feel like I should be.

"Got you a coffee." Rimmel held out the cup to him.

Romeo took it and leaned down to kiss her on the head. "Thanks, baby."

"Car returned?" she asked.

"Yep."

"I'm gonna miss that convertible," she sighed.

"Hey now, don't be saying that around the Hellcat."

"Well, at least I could drive the convertible," she cracked.

Rome grimaced. "The Hellcat is probably gonna miss that convertible."

"Hey!" Rim admonished and poked him in the ribs.

Laughing, Romeo pulled her close.

I turned away from their disgusting, lovey displays of affection. Rome was so whipped. How the hell he got so twisted up inside for some girl—no offense to my little sis—was a damned mystery.

I wasn't ever going to get twisted up like that. Being whipped was the last thing I ever planned to be.

Without meaning to, I looked at Ivy. She was laughing along with Missy at something Trent was saying.

Letting women in, letting that kind of emotion in was dangerous. I knew all too well the kind of damage a relationship with too much of anything could cause.

I was better off alone.

CHAPTER TEN

#LateNightMusings
Friends are like boobs. Some are
small. Some are big. Some are
real and some are fake.
#WhatKindOfBoobRYou

#BuzzBoss

IVY

I needed a shower.

For more than one reason.

Sitting on a plane full of crowded people wasn't fun. Sitting next to Missy, my best friend that I betrayed, was worse. Still feeling Braeden on my skin?

Torture.

All I could think about while I hobbled through the parking lot of the airport with Missy and Trent in tow was a shower. I didn't care it wouldn't be a private bathroom like I'd been using for the past week. I didn't care I was going back to the dorm, back to classes, and back to regular life.

I just wanted these feelings to go away.

This war inside me needed to stop. What Braeden and I did had been so wrong, but *oh my word*, it felt so good.

I couldn't stop thinking about it. About the way the orgasm, my first one, was like a riptide inside my whole body. It circled and circled, gaining momentum, and then everything in me collapsed and was pulled into the swirling center of unmatched pleasure. My whole body splintered apart. I didn't know it could be that way.

Why?

Why did I have to experience something so powerful with him?

And then I had to sit next to Missy—the girl who wanted him—on the plane home. Trent sat in the same row, and that thankfully curtailed any girl talk, but I knew I wouldn't be able to avoid it forever.

Maybe after a shower, after some space and time to think, I would be better prepared. Prepared to shove what happened into the deepest recesses of my mind. I would be able to talk to Missy about him and the way she felt without feeling like a horrible person.

The drive back to campus wasn't terribly long. We didn't really talk much. I think everyone was just glad to be off the plane. The first place I went was to the frat house where Trent was president. It was the first time I'd been back since the night before the big championship game Alpha played in.

The night I slept with Zach.

When I parked the car at the curb, a sick feeling wormed its way into my gut. A cold sweat beaded my forehead, and I felt sick and sort of panicked.

My fingers tightened around the steering wheel as I tried to contain the panic clawing my throat.

What the hell was wrong with me?

Get it together!

Unable to sit in the enclosed space of the car another second, the door burst open, and I catapulted out onto the pavement. My foot protested when I landed, but I didn't care. Pulling in deep breaths, I tried to curtail the way I was feeling.

Flashes of that night assaulted me. Of people laughing, dancing, and the crush of bodies filling the house. A familiar laugh flirted through the memory. It was Zach's.

I shuddered.

"Ivy?" Trent said, reaching out to touch my arm.

I jerked away, taken aback by his sudden appearance.

"Whoa," he said and pulled back. "You okay? You're not looking so good."

I leaned against the car door and mustered a smile. "Sorry. I think all the travel is catching up to me. I'm feeling a little carsick."

It was a lie, but it was better than saying looking at the house he lived in made me feel like I was going to have a panic attack.

"Can I get you some water? You wanna sit down?" The concern in his voice was genuine and surprisingly brought me back to the present.

That one time with Zach had been a horrible, horrible mistake. It was never going to happen again. I never had to see him again. It was history.

I looked at Trent. His attention was wholly focused on me, and it made me feel good to be the center of someone's sights even if it was for only a few moments.

"You're a sweet guy."

He placed a hand over his chest like I shot him. "That's the kiss of death," he moaned.

"What?" I laughed.

"No guy wants to hear how sweet they are."

"Then what do they want to hear?" I asked, totally amused.

"That they're badass." He shrugged like it was obvious and I should know this.

I laughed again and held out my fist for a fist bump. Guys liked those. "You're totally badass, Trent."

He flashed me a wide smile and reached for my fist, but he didn't return the bump. Instead, he grabbed my hand and tugged me hard. I wasn't prepared for that, so I tumbled forward into his chest.

"We don't fist bump. We hug," Trent said as he pulled me into the circle of his arms. Automatically, I returned the embrace, laying my cheek against his shoulder.

I felt his hand in the ends of my hair before he pulled back.

"I had fun this week."

"Yeah." I smiled. "Me too."

Why did I suddenly feel like the air was charged with more than just a friendly good-bye?

"I'll see ya around, right?" he asked.

"Of course!"

Trent leaned in the door of the car and said bye to Missy. When he pulled back out, he pushed a hand through his sandy-colored hair and winked at me. "See ya around, Ivy."

I waved and climbed back in the car. I didn't look at the house again. I was afraid it would ruin the peace I'd manage to get back since we pulled up.

As I drove away from the curb, I felt Missy's eyes. I looked over at her. She was grinning like she'd just found a giant diamond.

"What?" I asked.

She smiled wider.

I sighed.

"He's totally into you."

"Who?" I wondered, though I knew exactly where she was going with this. I was so not up for a conversation about my love life—or lack thereof—right now.

"You know who!" She smacked me in the arm. "Trent totally has a thing for you."

"Umm, I think Romeo was trying to set him up with you."

"The only thing between me and Trent is friendship. But you two…" Her voice turned calculating. "You two make a good match."

"What?" I said a little too high. "No."

Missy nodded. "Uh-huh. You had to see the way he was looking at you. And the way he was this morning at the beach house. He totally took care of your foot."

Her voice was turning dreamy. I rolled my eyes. "Missy—"

She cut me off. "And the way he watched out for you at the airport and helped you with your bags."

"He carried your bags, too," I pointed out.

"Not all of them."

I groaned. This was ridiculous. I was tired of thinking about guys. Of talking about guys. For the first time in years, the idea of having a boyfriend was totally unappealing.

"I don't want to talk about Trent."

"Since when do you not want to talk about guys?" Missy pressed.

Since I slept with Zach like a giant ho, then fell into bed with the guy you had your eye on. I wanted to say it out loud, but I didn't dare.

Taking my silence as some kind of mutiny, she sighed. "Fine, we'll talk about Trent later."

Oh, goody gumdrops.

"Besides, I want to talk about Braeden."

"Braeden?" I asked nervously. "He's my least favorite topic."

Missy fell quiet for a moment. I felt her scrutiny. I worked hard to keep my face devoid of any kind of emotion.

"Is something going on with you and Braeden?"

"What?" I gasped and slid her a surprised look. *Shit. Shit. Shit!*

"What makes you think that?"

"Things just seemed more tense than usual between you two today. Did you get into another fight? You know, worse than usual?"

I relaxed a little. "Well, I'm not usually trapped in a car or an airplane with his royal pain in the ass," I cracked.

Missy laughed. "I guess not."

"Frankly, I'm glad to get away from him for a while." That was said with complete honesty.

"You shouldn't hate him, you know," Missy said quietly when I pulled into the parking lot of our dorm building.

"I don't hate him," I hedged. "Just strongly dislike."

"I know it's because of me. Because of how things ended with him and me."

I didn't want to talk about this right now.

"He was upfront about us. He never said we were anything more than what we were. It was just fun."

"But it wasn't," I said vehemently. "Not to you."

"At first it was. But then I got to know him. He's so… intense, you know?"

Oh, did I. "I guess?"

"And he's fun. Even though we were kind of just friends with benefits, he still made me feel special."

I whipped the car into the first open spot I saw, cut the engine, and ripped the keys from the ignition. Saying nothing, I got out and popped the trunk.

My foot hurt as I dug our bags out of the back and handed them to Missy. When the trunk was closed, I couldn't ignore Missy's comments anymore.

"I know you liked him," I began. "A lot. But I just don't think he's the guy for you, Miss. You deserve so much better than a guy who just wants benefits with none of the commitment."

I was a hypocrite. I know.

"Maybe. But I want him."

I felt like she punched me in the gut.

"I want a million dollars," I cracked.

"Maybe you should play the lottery." Missy smiled as we dragged our stuff toward the dorm.

I laughed.

• • •

"I saw him watching me, you know."

My steps faltered. "What?"

Missy nodded. "This week on the beach, at the house. Sometimes I would catch him staring. Admiring the view." She smirked.

I thought he'd been looking at me.

I even said it last night… He didn't say I was wrong.

'Course he wouldn't! He was about to get laid! He'd let you believe whatever you wanted.

Suddenly, I was incredibly unsure. And incredibly embarrassed. Would I never learn?

Missy went on like I wasn't totally dying of embarrassment. "Maybe the time we spent apart made him miss me. Maybe seeing me play around with Trent in the ocean made him jealous."

I swallowed. Is that why she seemed more interested in Trent than she actually was? Maybe what I thought of as her flirting in the ocean was actually just her putting on an act for Braeden.

* * *

She mistook my silence for something else. "Oh!" she gasped. "I don't like Trent. Not like that. I promise."

"Yeah, I think I got that," I remarked dryly.

She held open the door to the building, and I went ahead inside.

"I just didn't want you to think I was trying to put the moves on him. Especially with you two starting something."

"We aren't starting something."

"Yes, you are," she sang. "And I fully support it. Just because I might have used Trent a little in Florida to make Braeden jealous means nothing. I know you like him. I would never ever put the moves on a guy you were into."

My heart sank. "You're a good friend, Missy."

"Hos over bros," she called out and turned down the hallway toward her room. It was on the first floor, and Rimmel and I were on the second. "Call me later!"

I escaped into the stairwell and collapsed against the closest wall.

It was official.

#SELFIE

I was going to best friend hell.

CHAPTER ELEVEN

Make-ups, Break-ups and Hook-ups
#ReportsOfSpringBreakDramaComingIn
#BuzzBossTellsAll
... Alpha BuzzFeed

BRAEDEN

We landed in a small airport in Maryland. It was more expensive to fly into this airport because we had to take a hopper flight from Baltimore, but the smaller crowds and short wait times for luggage return made the cost worth it.

My truck was parked in the long-term lot, since, originally, I was gonna ride here with Trent, but then Rome called and asked me to come early. It's a good thing I did. If things had gone even an inch worse, someone would have needed to be there to sweep Rimmel up off the floor.

Hearing the gunshots in the hotel room we knew Romeo was in had been one of the scariest moments of my life. And I'd had some shit-tastic ones. But Romeo was my brother—since the playground that day in first grade. Tommy Bromley was a bully and the biggest kid in class. He decided one afternoon he was gonna own me.

I wasn't big like I was now.

I was skinny, hadn't grown into my feet, and I was scared of my own shadow.

Still, when he pushed me down and told me to give him my lunch money, I forgot what a scaredy cat I was. I got angry—real angry. Sometimes I think that was the day my temper was born.

And then Romeo walked into my life at exactly the right moment. He'd always been the water to my fire. The extinguisher to my flame.

I pushed myself up off the rough mulch and shoved Tommy back. I saw the shock register on his face. He never in a million years thought little Braeden would fight back.

However, I was tired of being scared. Tired of being pushed around.

Still, my display of defiance didn't deter him. It got me punched in the nose. There I was, not even seven years old, and I was standing there on the playground with a bleeding nose and a bully trying to take my lunch money.

I wanted to cry.

Yet even at that young age, I knew I couldn't.

Never let them see you cry. It was something my mother told me more times than I could count. But there was so much emotion bottled up inside me, so much hurt and fear, it had to go somewhere.

It channeled into rage.

With a battle cry I'd heard on morning cartoons, I lunged forward, sinking low and running. I rushed Tommy and plowed my slight form into his middle. I had the advantage of surprise on my side. I had the advantage of being really pissed off.

We went down in a heap, me on top of Tommy and a circle of kids closing in to watch the unfolding scene. They were all hollering and cheering, but I barely registered the sound.

I drew back my small fists and delivered a rain of hits. Tommy started screaming, telling me to stop, but I hit him again.

Tommy had size on his side, so he was able to roll and force me off. Then I was the one pinned to the ground. I saw the flash in his eyes. I knew what was coming. He drew back his meaty fist, and I prepared for a black eye to go with my bloody nose.

But it never came.

Romeo—back then still known as Roman—caught Tommy's arm and pulled him off me.

"Hey!" Tommy yelled.

"You deserved it!" Romeo yelled back.

Just then a teacher broke through the crowd with a stern expression on her face. I was still lying on the ground bleeding, and Tommy was glaring at Romeo.

"Tommy Bromley, what have I told you about starting fights at school?" she yelled.

"It was him! He attacked me!" Tommy pointed at me.

I stared up at the teacher with wide eyes. I was going to get into so much trouble for fighting at school.

"He's a liar," Romeo stated, calm as could be. "Tommy's been bullying everyone and taking our lunch money. When Braeden said no, Tommy gave him a bloody nose."

The teacher glanced down at my nose and her eyes widened. "Is this true, Braeden?"

I glanced at Romeo.

And that's when I knew.

I knew we'd be best friends forever.

I nodded at the teacher, and Tommy was taken to the office. He got in trouble, moved to another class, and a year later, moved to another town.

Romeo and I became inseparable.

And eventually, he became my brother.

So when I saw his body sprawled out on the hotel floor, unmoving, after hearing those shots, my world as I knew it threatened to crumble around me. And

Rimmel… when she saw, the way she cried over his still body ripped out what was left of my heart.

I was forced in that moment to push away my own mind-numbing pain and focus on her, because if Romeo had died then, I was all Rimmel had left.

Thank fuck he hadn't. Thank fuck for the bulletproof vest that saved his life.

I'm just glad all three of us walked away with our lives.

Romeo didn't have his car in the lot. His dad drove them to the airport so he wouldn't have to leave the Cat here. Ivy drove her and Missy here, and Trent got a ride from one of the guys at his frat house.

Since I wasn't going straight to campus, Romeo and Rimmel rode with me, and Trent caught a ride with the girls. He didn't seem to put off by that.

I needed to have a talk with that guy. He could do better.

After I dropped off Romeo and Rimmel at his place, I drove to my mom's. Like Romeo's parents, she still lived in the same house I grew up in. Except our house wasn't as big or in a ritzy neighborhood.

My house was in a regular, middle-class neighborhood, not even ten minutes from Rome's. It was a one-story brick, ranch-style house with a finished basement where I spent a lot of time as a kid playing video games.

It was on the corner of the street so it had a pretty decent-sized yard where Romeo and I used to play football when we were kids. In the front yard was a mature tree that was starting to show signs of life now that spring was coming along. It was maybe sixty-five degrees here, and the sun was shining bright, but it was a long way from the balmy breezes I'd just spent a week enjoying on the beach.

I pulled my truck into the newly sealed driveway and hopped out. Instead of going up the walk to the front door, I just keyed in the entry code on the side of the single garage and the door began to open. Mom's Honda was parked inside, and it looked like it needed a wash. The blue paint was grayish from all the winter weather that was finally leaving us alone.

I made a mental note to take it down to the car wash and clean it out for her.

My mom hadn't had the easiest life, but she always did right by me, and she always put me first. It seemed like washing the car for her, cutting the grass, and doing stuff around the house was the least I could do.

When I pushed through the door leading in the house, the rich smell of pot roast wafted toward me, and my stomach grumbled. Damn, I loved pot roast. Mashed potatoes, gravy, and some bread…

"Mom!" I called out.

"In here!" she answered.

After I kicked off my shoes, I stepped through the laundry room and into the kitchen. She was standing at the counter, stirring a pot on the stove. Steam rose from the inside and made a cloud over her head.

"Please tell me those are potatoes," I groaned.

She laughed and turned. "Your favorite! I thought you might be hungry after the flight."

"That's why you're my favorite lady ever." I hugged her, lifting her so her feet dangled off the floor.

"Braeden James, put me down!" she demanded and slapped me on the shoulder.

"Ugh, Mom. Why do you have to call me that?" I set her down and snagged a roll off the basket on the counter beside her.

"Because it irritates you."

I shoved the entire piece of bread in my mouth, and she gave me a look. When I was small, it would have been intimidating, but now I thought it was amusing.

"Did ya miss me?" I asked around chewing.

"Manners!" she reminded, and I grinned. By the look on her face, I knew I had bread stuck in my teeth. She sighed and then turned away, but not before I saw her smile. "You know I did."

"What've you been up to?" I went to the fridge and pulled out a bottle of water. There was surprisingly a lot of food in there. She usually didn't have too much because she lived here by herself. Usually, it was just girl stuff like yogurt and bagels. She kept most the good stuff in the pantry and freezer for when I came over to raid the cabinets.

"You must have really thought I'd be hungry when I got here," I said as I uncapped the bottle.

She smiled. "Oh, just the usual, working and book club."

I grunted. I would never understand why anyone would voluntarily read anything and then go sit around and talk about it.

"Now that the weather is warming up, I'll start planning the garden for this year."

Mom was an avid gardener. Every year, she planted a garden in the backyard and tended it religiously. She said she liked being outside because she felt less cooped up.

"Just let me know when you're ready. I'll pick up everything you need with the truck."

"So tell me about Florida. How is everything with Rimmel?" I'd given Mom a basic rundown of some of the stuff going on with Rim and Romeo. She didn't know everything, but enough for her to understand why I had to take off early and miss some classes before spring break actually started.

I sat at the table in the kitchen—we didn't have a fancy dining room—and told her a little about Rim's dad and some of the stuff that happened. Mostly, I talked about spring break and the time we spent at the beach.

While we talked, she mashed the potatoes, then pulled a salad out of the fridge and set it on the counter. I watched her as she worked, and I ate some more rolls. It was nice to be here, to be at home. Spring break had been a blast, but I needed a break from everyone and everything for just a little while.

Even as I relaxed, I noticed something. Something seemed different about Mom. She seemed a little stiff. Like she was waiting for me to figure out something she didn't want me to know. Like a ticking bomb that didn't have a countdown meter and was just set to spontaneously explode.

I didn't press, not when she announced dinner was ready and I piled my plate high with food. I didn't ask when we were sitting at the table together, eating just like we'd done a thousand times before.

I was curious.

But I was also hungry.

And when a man was hungry, he ate. He didn't ask questions that might interfere with his appetite or the good-ass food on his plate.

After I inhaled my second heaping serving, I dropped my fork and sat back, feeling pretty damn satisfied. "That was some good eats, Mom."

Over the rim of her mug, she stared at me with an amused expression. Her eyes were blue, but not the same kind of blue as Ivy's. Moms were a little grayer, a little more subdued, sort of like a sky promising a storm.

Considering all the storms Mom had weathered, I wondered if maybe her eyes used to be brighter but changed to reflect her life.

Her hair wasn't nearly as dark as mine; while mine was nearly black, hers was true brown. More of a chestnut shade, without a hint of gray. Hell, she probably dyed it like most women. Who knew what her natural color actually was? But her eyebrows were brown too, and they drew attention to the lightness of her eyes.

"Did they have food in Florida?" she mused.

"Nothing like you make," I complimented.

"Quite the charmer, my son." Mom set her decaf (what was the point of decaf?) on the table and reached into the cabinet. She was dressed in a pair of jeans and a plain black T-shirt. She wasn't a big woman, but I wouldn't really call her petite either. More average, I guess. Her hair was pulled up into a ponytail, and she wasn't wearing any makeup. She rarely wore it outside of work. But really, she didn't need to. She was an attractive woman. For a mom, anyway.

When she turned back, she was carrying a plate of brownies. I groaned when she set them in front of me. They were my favorite, fudgy and gooey with chocolate sprinkles on top.

I didn't tell people how much I liked sprinkles.

Sprinkles were for kids, and I was a man.

But Mom knew, and she always had some around.

"Ohmigod," I muttered as I shoved about three quarters of my first brownie in my mouth. "This is the best brownie I've ever had."

"You say that every time I make brownies," she reminded me as she picked up her coffee again.

"I really mean it this time." I shoved the rest in my face and reached for more. The brownies melted in my mouth, and the sprinkles added that little bit of extra something.

I liked me a little extra somethin'-somethin'.

I ate half the plate. I probably could have eaten them all, but I wanted to save some for later. They were too good to eat all at once.

After I helped Mom clean up and pack up some stuff for me to take back to campus, it was beginning to get dark. Classes started up again in the morning, and it was back to the grind.

"Braeden," Mom began, and my attention snapped to her. I knew that tone. I knew whatever I sensed before was about to come out. "I need to talk to you about something."

"What happened?" I scrutinized her face, but I couldn't tell what it was. She just looked worried. And vaguely scared…

"Are you sick?" I demanded. Worry filled my chest and squeezed. What if she was? What if she'd been for a long time and hadn't wanted to tell me?

"No!" she replied adamantly. "I'm fine." She came forward and laid a hand on my forearm. "I'm healthy as a horse."

I blew out a breath. That was good. "Okay, so what has that look on your face?"

She pulled back and paced toward the table. The way she wrung her hands in front of her was familiar.

Then it clicked.

At my sides, my hands balled into fists.

"It's him, isn't it?"

She stopped in her pacing, leaving her back to me. She really didn't have to answer, but she did anyway.

"He called while you were gone last week."

The urge to ram my fist through something was so potent it knocked me back down a couple notches.

"What the hell did he want?" I ground out.

She turned and met my eyes. "He wanted to talk to you."

I laughed. It was a cold, bitter sound. "I hope you told him to hold his breath while he waits."

"He asked to see you."

I reacted physically, jack-knifing away from the counter where I was leaning and thrusting my body forward. "He can go to hell."

Mom sighed. "I pretty much told him the same thing."

I grunted. Whatever she said wasn't enough. Mom just didn't have the mean streak in her she needed to deal with him.

"How the hell did he even get this number?" I'd had it changed. More than once.

"Apparently, he's been trying to get ahold of you for a while."

"Fuck him!" I roared. Mom flinched, and I felt bad.

"Watch your language," she said, sounding every bit the mother she was.

"Yes, ma'am," I muttered.

She came forward and laid a hand on my cheek. "I don't want to upset you. I even debated on telling you about the call. But you're grown now." Her eyes turned wistful. "And I'm so very proud of you. Therefore, I felt it wasn't my right to keep this to myself. You have a

* * *

right to make your own choice about whether you want to get in touch."

"You really think there's a choice?" I asked. Damn the way this still made me feel.

Stepping back, Mom pulled a piece of folded paper out of her back pocket and laid it gently on the counter beside me. I didn't even look at it.

"It's been a very long time, Braeden. I just want you to know I will love you no matter what. If you want to return his call, I'll love you just the same."

It had been a long time.

But it still wasn't long enough.

I left the paper lying there, ignored. "Thanks for telling me. I love you, too, Mom."

She wiped at her eyes and stepped away. "You better be getting back to the dorm. You need some sleep before classes start up again tomorrow."

I grunted. "Yeah, and now I gotta get up early and train like a beast because of your damn good cooking."

Her laugh was light, but it was genuine and made me feel a little less heavy.

"You gonna be okay here? I can stay the night." I'd move back in if she needed me.

"I'm fine. Honestly. And it's not your job to worry about me. I'm the mom. Not you."

I made a face. "I'm too handsome to be a woman."

She laughed. "Well, there is that."

She moved around the kitchen, putting the brownies and a few other snacks and stuff into a bag, and then held it out for me.

"Rimmel wants to have dinner sometime soon. You up for that?"

"Of course!" She beamed. "I like her. She's a sweet girl."

"She likes you, too."

"So tell me," Mom probed. "When are you gonna bring a girl like that home to meet me?"

"Now why would I want to go and do that?" I drawled. "Then I'd have to share all your cooking."

After we hugged and said good night, I went out and climbed in the truck. I tossed the bag beside me on the seat and blew out a breath. *What the fuck had he called for? Why now? What could he possibly want?*

I started up the truck and gunned the engine, listening to the sweet sound of the V8. My truck wasn't pretty like the Hellcat, but it was full of testosterone. And even though I'd never tell Romeo, I knew damn well my beast could roll right over the Cat and still have a hundred thousand miles in him.

I gunned the gas one last time for good measure and prepared to back up. When I turned to look out the back window, I noticed the bag of food had fallen over and the containers were spilling out across the seat.

I picked them up and restacked them in the bag.

That's when I saw it.

Instead of throwing it away like she should have, Mom tossed the folded piece of paper inside. I stared at it for a few minutes and then snatched it up.

When it was unfolded, I stared down at my mother's handwriting.

Your father called. He wants you to call him back.

Beneath the words was a phone number I didn't recognize.

I crumpled it up and threw it on the floorboards of the truck.

Fuck that. Calling him was the last thing on earth I'd ever do.

• • •

CHAPTER TWELVE

> #NoticeToTheFaculty
>
> Students today spend more time on homework than ever in recorded history.
> #GiveUsABreak #HomeworkSucks
>
> ... Alpha BuzzFeed

IVY

Ah the tangled webs we weave.

I have no idea who said it. I have no idea where I heard it. But it was the only thing in my head as I dragged my ass out of bed.

Hey, I might be a zombie, but I could still rhyme. (Head + bed… Never mind.)

The first week back from spring break had been long and arduous. I swear the professors knew we were all still partially hung-over and depressed the time off was over, so they wanted to further our torment by assigning even more work than normal.

School really wasn't my thing.

Socializing, checking out what everyone was wearing that day, and walking around campus… I liked all that. But I could do without the coursework.

It didn't help that I had no idea what I was majoring in. Here I was almost a junior in college and still had no direction. My parents liked to remind me how much they were paying for me to "find myself" every chance they got.

I liked to remind them they told me I had to go to college.

Even so, declaring a major was something I was going to have to do. I just wasn't ready to commit to any one thing. Any one job. There were so many things out there that seemed interesting. I did know what I didn't want to do.

I didn't want to sit behind a desk.

I didn't want to wear boring pantsuits and stuffy blouses.

I didn't want to be at the mercy of a boss who liked to tell me what to do.

And I sure as hell didn't want one of those nine-to-five, forty-hour week life sentences.

My criteria ruled out a lot.

But it didn't really point me in any direction.

I groaned as I tossed one of the many pillows onto the heap of blankets half spilling onto the floor. It was too early to think about this. I'd do it later.

After coffee.

After I saw Braeden.

I groaned again. Thoughts of him weren't allowed. Hell, if I thought I could get out of our usual pancake breakfast without a million and one questions from Rimmel and Missy, I wouldn't go. Why did I even agree to weekend pancakes? Sundays were supposed to be for sleeping in!

Okay, it was already after ten.

I guess it wasn't that early.

Rimmel spent the night with Romeo last night, so I had the room to myself this morning. After I made a trip to the bathroom, took a quick shower, and brushed my teeth, I came back and walked around in my panties and bra.

Hey, it wasn't every day a girl had her dorm room all to herself.

As I was rummaging through my drawers for something to wear, I saw something I shoved in there and "forgot" about. I didn't really. I pretended I forgot about it when really, I looked at it every single time I got dressed.

Pathetic. That's what I was.

I should get rid of it. But I knew I wouldn't. Not yet anyway. It made me feel… Well, I don't know how it made me feel.

I slammed the drawer closed and yanked open another. I was so not in the mood to get cute this morning. This week had been tough, and I was exhausted.

Aside from the heavy classwork and the pressure I was suddenly feeling to pick a major—and a direction for my life—my brain never shut off. Like ever. I thought about Braeden. I thought about Missy. I even thought about Trent.

I definitely avoided them all. It was quite the task trying to avoid people you had deliberately made part of your life.

It was exhausting.

And so were the dreams.

But I wasn't going to think about any of that.

I was going to get dressed, smile, and eat pancakes.

When it was done I could hide out in the room the rest of the day and watch makeup tutorials online.

I loved doing makeup. I loved watching other people do makeup. There was something peaceful and mind-clearing about starting with a blank canvas—a fresh face—and enhancing its natural beauty.

I glanced at the clock. I was late. So I did something I never did.

I threw on a pair of sweatpants. Yes, they were the cute kind. Fitted but a little slouchy. They were hot pink with wide pockets slashing across the hips. The bottoms sported wide bands and hugged my ankles.

On top, I threw on a white tank and a black T-shirt. It was cotton, but it draped and felt like silk. I tucked just the front of it in so the waist tie was exposed and didn't look lumpy beneath the hem of the shirt.

The only makeup I bothered with was some cherry-flavored lip-gloss and some mascara. My hair was in a messy bun high on my head, with a few strands falling out around my neck and face. I left it that way and added a pair of gold aviator sunglasses like a headband.

On my way out the door, I grabbed my oversized Michael Kors bag and shoved my bare feet into a pair of slip-on Sketchers. The diner we always met at wasn't far from campus and it only took a few minutes to get there. The sun was bright and the sky was blue as I walked through the full lot and through the glass door.

At least the weather was warming up. Spring was good; it was happy.

Rimmel waved from a table across the room when I stepped inside. I was the last one here, and there was an extra person sitting at the table. Trent.

I smiled and waved as I made my way through the crowd and noted the look in Missy's eyes. She totally invited Trent. And I bet the reason the only empty seat at the table was beside him was her doing, too.

On the other side of Trent was Missy. On her other side was Braeden. I avoided looking at him. To his right was Rimmel and then Romeo. I took the seat between Romeo and Trent.

"Sorry I'm late," I said and picked up the menu. "I overslept."

"You look good," Trent told me, offering a smile.

I smiled back at him. "Thanks. I was in such a hurry, I barely looked in the mirror."

"Well, that's obvious," Braeden cracked.

There was a loud thud beneath the table. "Ow!" he groaned. "Rome, you better get your girl. She kicked me!"

Rimmel snickered and so did I.

The waitress came, and all of us ordered. When my coffee arrived, I took a sip and moaned in appreciation.

"Good stuff," Trent remarked, leaning close to speak only to me.

"You have no idea," I agreed. "Is it just me or are the professors trying to punish us for spring break?"

Trent laughed and leaned back in his seat. As he moved, he flung out both his arms so one rested on the back of my chair and the other on Missy's. "Oh, they are in total annihilation mode."

"I'm definitely not going to miss the work load next semester," Romeo said.

"I'm gonna miss you," Rimmel said.

He kissed her on the temple and yanked her chair so it was right up against his. "I'll still be around." He promised.

It was kind of hard to believe next semester Romeo wouldn't be here. He'd be a pro football player. I'd gotten used to having him around. When he first got involved with Rimmel, I wasn't sure how we'd get along, but as time went on, I could honestly say he was my friend. I liked Romeo, I liked him a lot, and I really respected him.

I hoped he could say the same about me. Even though deep down I wondered if I deserved his respect.

We chattered on about classes, the latest Buzz notifications, and, of course, football until our food arrived. When my pancakes were finally in front of me, my stomach growled like it hadn't seen food in a week.

"Someone's hungry," Trent teased and shoved an entire slice of bacon in his mouth.

"I'm not the only one," I shot back.

He grinned and bacon stuck out of his teeth.

I laughed and shook my head. I felt something cold from across the table so I glanced up. Braeden was watching me. Watching us.

Our eyes connected, and for a split second, I was jolted with electricity no one else seemed to feel. I looked away quickly. This was the first I'd seen Braeden since we came back from spring break. I was hoping whatever seemed to unleash itself between us at the beach would be gone.

But it wasn't.

If anything, it seemed harder *not* to look in his direction.

"So what's up with you, Ivy?" Missy asked as she took a drink of her OJ.

"What do you mean?"

"I've barely seen you this week."

"I haven't seen you at all," Trent added.

"Like I said, classes this week have been insane. I have so much work. I've been busy trying to get a jumpstart on it all. With finals at the end of the semester, I want to get a lot of the work out of the way early."

Rimmel was nodding. "Me too. I've been in the library a lot."

"You look tired," Missy pressed.

"I'm not wearing makeup," I countered.

Braeden dropped his fork, and everyone looked at him. "Let's just cut to the chase. You look like shit, you haven't been butting into everyone's lives, and Missy wants to know why."

"I've just been busy," I said hard. I told myself his assessment of the way I looked didn't hurt my feelings (even though it totally did). "And enjoying a week free of you."

Rimmel changed the subject, and the guys started talking football again. I picked at my food; I wasn't as hungry as I thought after all.

A few minutes later, Trent leaned close, putting his lips almost against my ear. "You definitely do not look like shit."

My lips curled into a smile. I glanced at him. "You don't have to say that."

"I know."

It was silly, but his kindness made me feel better. "Thank you."

I felt Braeden watching us, but I didn't take the bait. The second I looked at him, I'd be vulnerable. He would say something asswipe-ish, and I'd get my feelings hurt. Again.

Usually, I was stronger, but not this morning. This morning I was just tired and, yeah, maybe a little depressed.

Missy started talking to him, taking his attention, and I breathed a silent sigh of relief.

"So there's a frat party at the house this Friday," Trent said. He was directing his words at me but speaking loud enough for everyone else to hear. "You guys game?"

"Sounds like fun," Missy replied.

"I don't know," I hedged. The thought of going back to that house made my stomach turn. I set down my fork and quit pretending to eat. "Maybe."

"You know I would, man, but some of your guys there still hold a grudge about everything that went down with Zach."

A sour taste in my mouth erupted at the mention of his name.

Trent nodded. "I'd keep them contained, but I totally understand."

"Maybe we can all go out Saturday night instead?" Missy suggested and looked at Braeden.

"What d'ya have in mind, Miss?" he asked.

"Screamerz?"

"I had fun last time we went," Rimmel remarked.

Romeo got this smug look on his face, and I wondered why. When Rim glanced up at him, she blushed, and I knew they were sharing some kind of private moment they must have had at the club.

They were so in sync. They didn't even have to speak to hold a conversation. I longed for that.

"What do you think?" Trent asked me, a twinkle in his eye.

I smiled. "Sure, it sounds fun."

"After another week of classes, we're gonna need a round of Smurf Balls," Missy said.

Braeden and Romeo groaned. The memory of the guys tossing back the blue drinks was still hilarious.

The rest of the breakfast was blissfully uneventful, but I was still glad when it was time to go. Out in the parking lot, I climbed into my car and expelled a long breath. I waved at Romeo as he drove past and then did the same with Trent and Missy.

I was about to pull out of my spot when a big red truck pulled up and stopped in front of me, blocking my car's path.

I glared at him through the windshield, and he smirked. Seconds later, he jumped down and came over to the driver's side.

I rolled down the window. "Move your hunk of junk!"

"Woman, don't you know better than to insult a man's truck?"

"Don't you know better than to tell a woman she looks like shit?" Ah! I wished I could snatch those words back the second they left my mouth. I basically just admitted what he said hurt me. Admissions like that gave a guy like him too much power.

He stopped and rocked back on his heels. "That pricked your infallible armor, did it?"

"What do you want, Braeden?"

"There's something you need to know." The serious tone in his voice perked me up.

"What is it?"

He stepped forward and rested his hands on the windowsill of my door. When he leaned in, his eyes reminded me of the coffee I drank before I added in some cream. The dark depths of his stare swept over my face, sort of like he was taking inventory, making sure it was all still there.

"I thought you should know," he began. His hair seemed a little longer than usual, a little more unruly. My fingers itched to delve into the wayward strands, to feel the silky texture against my palm.

"That I still don't like you."

It took a moment for his words to penetrate the spell he'd cast on me. But once they did, I wanted to smack him.

I settled for whacking his hand with an empty CD case from the seat next to me.

"Ow!" he howled, jerking back.

"I still don't like you either!" I snapped and rolled up the window.

Braeden didn't seem the least bit put off. If anything, he seemed proud he annoyed me. I watched him walk back to his truck and hoist himself inside.

I didn't notice the way his Levi's molded around his tight rear end as he walked.

Before he drove away, he looked back one last time.

I ignored him.

CHAPTER THIRTEEN

> #24 is heading to the NFL. That means there will be an opening for a new campus alpha. #WhosItGonnaBe #CastYourVote
>
> ... Alpha BuzzFeed

BRAEDEN

Fucking sweatpants.

They were tricky little bastards. Meant for comfort, meant for laziness, meant for making a guy's eye move right on by.

But that isn't what they did.

I'd never seen Ivy so dressed down before. Usually, she was on point with her style and outfits. I'm surprised she even owned a pair of sweatpants.

When the minutes ticked by and she didn't arrive at breakfast, I started to wonder if she was coming. I hadn't seen her at all since we got back from spring break. Not that I'd been looking for her. But if she was avoiding me, I wanted to know. I needed to be prepared to explain to Rimmel why her BFF wasn't hanging around so much anymore.

Just when I began concocting crazy but slightly believable lies for my sis, Ivy breezed through the door, late, and I swear at least three guys' heads swiveled to check out the way she strutted through the pancake house with those bright-pink sweats molded to her fine ass.

Day-um.

No one was overlooking the girl who didn't try this morning. In fact, more people were looking than I cared to admit.

She was sexy as hell with her hair all a mess, sunglasses perched on her head, barely-there makeup, and an outfit that said she was sexy without even trying to be.

I didn't notice she looked a little tired until Missy pointed it out. It made me curious about what was going on with her.

Since when did I care about her life?

She acted like she normally did, meaning barely glancing in my direction. It wasn't anything new, but my inner reaction to it was.

I didn't like it.

In fact, it kinda pissed me off.

Watching Trent whisper in her ear half the damn morning wasn't my idea of mealtime ambience either. I was just glad it was over.

Because last week had been full of everyone getting back into the swing of things—AKA Rimmel lived in the library—dinner with my mom got put off. Not that I was heartbroken or anything. Honestly, I wasn't anxious to go home. I knew Mom would ask me about the message from my father. She'd want to know if I called him.

I'm pretty sure hell was still ablaze with sinners and brimstone, so yeah, no. I didn't call. I wasn't going to.

Why she even seemed inclined to imply I should shocked the hell out of me.

I didn't want to talk about it. I didn't want to think about it. I wanted to forget.

I'd been trying to do a lot of that lately.

I couldn't hide from my mom forever, and I did ask her to dinner, so when Rimmel texted to set something up, I couldn't say no. When I called Mom to see if she was still up for it, I felt guilty for staying away so long. She offered to make us all a home-cooked meal and said how much she was looking forward to it.

And so here I was, pulling into the driveway of the house I'd grown up in. After I killed the engine, I sat there staring at the rancher for several long, silent moments. Frankly, I was surprised my mother still lived here. A lot had happened in her life at this place. Some good, but more of it bad. Hell, if I were honest with myself, I would admit the real reason I needed my own "space" over at the dorm was to get away from the memories here.

The bright-green, spotless Hellcat pulled up behind me. In my rearview, I watched Rimmel bounce around in the passenger seat and Rome say something to her that made her laugh. A smile pulled at the corner of my mouth. I honestly couldn't have loved her more if God had made her my biological sister. The innocence and openness of her heart despite the shitty hand life dealt her shocked me.

How she hadn't become jaded seemed a miracle to me. It was something I wanted to protect. I hoped Rimmel never lost that innocence about her. I realized her openness was something Rome and I somehow had been given, because she wasn't like that with everyone. It had taken Romeo a while to get in.

Seemed like it took less for me. Maybe that's because on some level, my little sis and I recognized each other. I understood her walls better than most.

Even still, Rimmel and I were different, because once someone got behind that wall she kept up, it was all rainbows and unicorns. Happy times and gummy bears. I wasn't Willy Wonka. I didn't have happy times and gummy bears inside me.

I had a wall and then another one.

She appeared at my window, craning her neck to see inside the lifted truck. I laughed and popped open the door. "Hey, tutor girl."

"What are you doing sitting in the driveway?" She was holding a large bouquet of sunflowers, almost as big as her head.

Her dark hair was down around her shoulders, looking pretty tame, her clothes matched a little too well and didn't swallow her whole, and I knew right away she hadn't dressed herself.

This was Ivy's handiwork.

"You trying to make me look bad by showing up here with flowers?" I asked.

She snorted. "As if you could look bad."

"Well, Rim, some people need flowers and some are just naturally amazing." I sighed like it was a chore.

Behind her dark-framed glasses, hazel eyes rolled. "And some people have big egos."

I grinned. "Rome."

"What's up, B?" We pounded our fists in way of greeting.

Rimmel muttered something about us acting like cavemen.

"You boys gonna eat in the driveway?" Mom's voice carried through the mild spring air.

She was standing in the front door with a kitchen towel in her hand. I plucked the flowers out of Rim's hands and dashed across the driveway. She let out a yell behind me and Romeo chuckled.

"For you." I presented the flowers to my mother. She took them and patted me on the cheek.

"They're beautiful. Thank you, Rimmel." Mom looked around me to her guests.

"I'm insulted," I cracked and moved into the house. "I've brought you flowers."

Usually they needed to be planted in her garden, but she liked that shit. It counted… right?

"Thank you so much for having us, Caroline," Rimmel said politely.

Little sisters were suck-ups.

"Thanks for coming, honey," Mom crooned.

I made a gagging sound.

"Mom!" Romeo greeted her a lot less politely but way more familiar than Rim. "What's cooking?" He swept her up in a bear hug, and she swatted him with the towel.

"Lasagna."

* * *

"Hope you made a whole pan just for me," Romeo replied. "'Cause I'm starving."

"Me too," I added.

"How did I know you would say that?" I felt Mom looking at me, studying me. I knew she probably wanted to ask about him.

But she didn't. She wouldn't. Not in front of my friends.

"Wash up. It's almost ready," she instructed.

Rome and I took off for the bathroom like it was a race. We'd been doing it since we were seven and it would probably never change. Except of course now we were both too big to fit through the bathroom door at the same time.

Mom and Rimmel were talking animatedly out in the kitchen and their voices carried down the hall.

"How's the arm, Rome?" I asked, glancing at the arm he'd broken several weeks ago. It used to be in a sling, but now he just wore a brace. And when it was under his jacket, it appeared there was nothing wrong at all.

He grunted. "Healing up. Now that we're back, I'd like to get some extra training in on the field. You game?"

"Hells yeah," I said as I scrubbed my hands. I could use an outlet for some of the pent-up crap inside me. Some days I felt like a caged animal. I missed football season; I missed the team and the practices that kicked my ass.

I was a damn good player, but I'd never been quite as serious about it as Romeo. I'd done it more for the rush, for the outlet being on the field provided.

The lasagna was banging and so were the salad and garlic toast she made to go with it. The dinner conversation was light, and I spent half of it teasing Rimmel about everything I could think of. Mom grilled Rome about his arm and physical therapy, which was something she was interested in as a nurse. I'd learned a long time ago that nurses never really left their jobs at the hospital. Being a nurse was an around-the-clock gig, and for Mom, caring about people was, too.

• • •

Romeo and I were plowing through our second slice of cheesecake and Rimmel was helping Mom with the cleanup when the phone rang.

She still had one of those ancient phones that hung on the wall. A landline. It practically belonged in a museum. I'd asked her a hundred times why she didn't just cut it off and use her cellphone exclusively. She said it was for safety and she wanted it in case she ever forgot to charge her cell.

I wasn't gonna argue with anything that made her feel safe. Hell, I'd put a landline in every room of this house if I thought that's what she wanted.

"I'm surprised that thing doesn't spit out a cloud of dust every time it rings," Romeo drawled.

I cackled. "Good one."

"You boys." Mom chuckled and padded across the kitchen to pick up the receiver.

She was barefoot tonight and dressed in some black pants Ivy would call leggings with some kind of long, silky shirt in a pale yellow. Her dark hair hung in a single braid down her back, and it reminded me of that chick from *Hunger Games*.

"Please tell me you aren't going to eat another piece," Rimmel said, motioning toward the half-gone cheesecake on the table between Romeo and me.

I was thinking about it.

Romeo caught her around the waist and pulled her into his lap. She settled there like there was no place else she'd rather be, and something in my chest felt hollow. They had an easy way about them, not because their relationship had been easy—hell, they could fill up an hour of *Jerry Springer*—but their feelings were. It's like they never doubted they belonged together.

A coldness seeped into the room, stillness. It pushed away all my thoughts of cheesecake and sappy love. I felt the tentacles of something I didn't like creep across the floor like a stalker in a bad horror movie.

"Just a second," Mom said.

My fork clattered against the plate.

I knew.

I knew what the wooden tone, the lack of inflection in her voice, meant.

It was him.

He was fucking calling here again.

● ● ●

I spun in the seat and glared across the room. Mom pulled the receiver from her ear and held it at her side. We looked at each other. "It's for you."

I shoved out of the chair so hard it clattered onto the floor. I wanted so badly to rip the phone from her hand. From the wall. But I forced myself to take it calmly. Acting like a caveman would only make things worse.

I'd go to the gym afterward and hit the bag if I needed to.

"Braeden." Mom's voice begged for some kind of understanding.

I laughed. It wasn't a nice sound.

"Don't ever call here again," I snarled into the phone. Then I slammed it back on the base on the wall.

Even with the loud clattering of the phone being hung up, silence descended upon the room. It was like we were in a movie and someone hit pause.

Breath heaved in my lungs and fingertips curled into my palm.

Hate.

It was a strong emotion. Probably the strongest I'd ever known.

And right beneath it lay fear.

Both of those feelings originated from the same place. Both of them were inspired by the same man.

My father.

The silence was shattered when Romeo cleared his throat. He stood up, taking Rimmel with him, and placed her on her feet.

"I ate way too damn much. I'm gonna need to hit the gym and work it off."

It wasn't lost on me the way he stepped in front of Rimmel like he felt the need to protect her.

Which pissed me off. I swung around to face him.

Did he really think I'd hurt my damn sister?

He held his ground, like I knew he would. I stared into his face, just looking for a fight. He'd give me one if that's what I wanted. It wouldn't be the first time.

But I couldn't deny there was no hint of warning in his eyes. He wasn't shielding Rimmel from *me*, just the situation.

Some of me deflated. She didn't need this. BBFLs kept drama away, not brought it in.

"Yeah," I said after a few breaths, "I could go for a workout."

Romeo fished the keys to his Hellcat out of his pocket and handed them to Rim. "Don't rip the transmission out on the way back to campus, baby."

"Romeo?" I heard the question in her voice, the wariness.

"It's okay. We'll be at the gym. I'll come by your room in a couple hours."

I knew I should say something. Something to make her less freaked out. But I was afraid to open my mouth. I was afraid I would start yelling and never stop.

Romeo appeared beside me. "Let's go."

I left without a backward glance at anyone, not even Mom.

It was an asshole thing to do. But I never said I wasn't an asshole.

Out in the yard, I heard her say something. I heard Romeo reply. He was probably promising her he'd make sure I was okay. It wasn't the first time he'd made that promise.

I thought a long time ago he'd never have to make it again.

And just like that, I was transported back to the past. Back to the memories I wished I didn't have.

● ● ●

CHAPTER FOURTEEN

IVY

Two weeks.

Two weeks since Braeden and I combusted into a pile of limbs in his bed.

Every. Single. Day.

That's how often I thought about that night. It's like I was some old, musty house being haunted by ghosts of the past. It didn't matter how many showers I took. I still felt his touch. It didn't matter how many insults he'd flung at me over the past few months. Hell, even since that night, they didn't matter.

• • •

I didn't love him.

But I didn't hate him either.

Not anymore. There was no way I could hate someone—the only one—who gave me the most pleasure I'd ever known in bed.

I'd seen him twice since our weekly pancake breakfast. The first time, I ducked into a building so he wouldn't see me. The second time, I didn't notice him until it was too late. When we locked eyes across campus, my belly flip-flopped and my palms grew sweaty.

He smirked like he knew the kind of effect he had on me.

I flicked my hair over my shoulder and narrowed my eyes. If he wanted a fight, I'd give him one.

But some dark-haired beauty slipped up to his side and said something. He looked away, and I used it as my chance to escape.

Missy, Rimmel, and I had lunch a few times this week. A couple times, I made up an excuse and didn't go. I couldn't believe how this one mistake, how one night, could seriously be affecting the rest of my life.

Oh, wait.

I guess I did know.

It happened with Zach, too.

Hell, that's partly why I was in this situation.

The morning I woke up and realized what happened made me take a long, hard look in the mirror. I wasn't the kind of girl who got so drunk she'd sleep with anyone. I wasn't the kind of girl who partied too much and stayed out all night.

Yet that's who I was acting like.

And frankly, I scared myself. I was on a dangerous path. A path I was afraid if I wandered too far down, I'd get lost and never find my way back.

It seemed so cliché to think, but growing up was hard. Here I was almost a junior in college, two years living on my own and making my own choices, and I was doing a shitty job. I had no major declared and my grades were decent, but not as good as I knew they could be. I partied every weekend, slept with a few guys (including Zach… What the hell was I thinking?) and made out with more than I cared to admit.

And to top it all off, I slept with Braeden. The guy I hated. The guy my best friend wanted.

What's worse? My body craved him. I needed more.

So it wasn't really just one thing affecting everything. It was a culmination of choices, mistakes that led me here—sitting in my dorm, feeling depressed, insecure, and wishing I hadn't agreed to go to Screamerz tonight with everyone.

If I tried to get out of it, Missy would call me on it. I'd rather go and be miserable than try to explain anything to her.

Since it was Saturday and I didn't have classes today, I went to the campus gym and worked out. Then I grabbed some food from the food court, carried it back to the room, and vegged out in front of my laptop with my favorite movie of all time, *Clueless*.

After that, I did some homework and read ahead a couple chapters in one of my classes so I wouldn't be so slammed next week.

Rimmel was volunteering at the shelter today, so I had the room to myself. Missy texted a couple times to make sure we were all still going out and to ask me about outfit choices.

I felt like wearing sweatpants. Hell, I felt like wearing no pants. I smiled to myself and wondered what everyone would say if I walked in wearing what I was dressed in now.

The expression on certain people's faces might be worth it. But the one on others wouldn't be. Not to mention I'd be embarrassed as hell.

Even if I didn't feel like dressing to the nines for our night out, I would. Braeden was going to be there. Missy was, and probably half the campus would be, too. I'd never let anyone see me down. I knew I needed to make some changes in my life, starting now. And I would. But I would still look good for it.

I glanced at the clock. Rimmel was going to be home to get ready soon, so I dragged myself off my bed and changed into a pair of pajamas with bottoms, tucking what I'd been wearing in the back of my dresser drawer before sliding it closed.

Afterward, I pulled up a makeup tutorial I watched earlier in the week and watched it again so I could copy the look for tonight. It was super cute and perfect for a fun night out. It was fairly neutral, but the eyes were slightly smoky and the outer corners were accented with white-and-black polka dots. They were so small you'd have to be sitting close to notice them, but the effect was stunning, and I really wanted to try my hand at it.

Since I was doing something a little more involved with my makeup, I decided to keep my hair simple and wear it straight and sleek. As I watched the tutorial, I divided the blond strands into sections and started flat-ironing it.

I was halfway done when I heard Rimmel at the door. I paused in styling and spun in my chair. Rimmel stepped in holding her oversized bag in front of her.

"Hey, girl," I called.

"Hey!" She stopped beside her bed and kicked off her sneakers. Her hair was a disaster, and I knew it was gonna take me a while to fix it. Maybe I'd do some kind of braid. Braids were pretty and fast.

"You been hanging out here all day?" she asked, casual.

"I went to the gym," I said and spun back around toward the laptop.

"Didn't hang out with Missy?"

"Nah, I wanted to get some homework done before we all went out tonight." Before she could ask me anything else—this girl was like a dog with a bone when she suspected something, and I was starting to think Rimmel definitely suspected something—I asked, "How was the shelter?"

"Busy." Rimmel sighed. "A lot of animals have come in lately. So many of them need homes."

Her words made me sad. Like a genuine gnawing sadness to think about all those animals sitting in a cage with no one to love them. To my surprise, tears filled the backs of my eyes and threatened to spill over.

I kept my back to Rimmel so she wouldn't see and worked on another section of hair. "I'm sorry to hear that."

I realized I sort of felt like a stray. Not really sure where I belonged. I wasn't homeless—I would always have a place with my parents and brothers—but it

* * *

wasn't exactly my home either. I guess I felt more displaced than homeless. Lost, wanting to be found.

"Well, I hope you don't mind…" Rimmel's voice trailed away. "But I sort of brought home a stowaway."

I put down the flat iron and spun around.

Rimmel looked sheepish, but that wasn't what caught my eye. Her bag was moving. Or rather, something inside it was.

"Isn't it only a stowaway if you didn't know it was there?" I asked warily.

Rimmel giggled. She totally knew that thing— whatever it was—took a ride with her all the way back here. She set the bag on her bed and reached in. When she turned back, I saw what was in her arms.

"O-M-Geeee!" I squealed. "That is the cutest thing I've ever seen!"

Rimmel laughed. "I know! I couldn't just leave her there. Poor little girl."

I abandoned my hair, laptop, and chair. I didn't rush over because I was afraid I'd scare her, but I was totally wanting to smoosh her little face.

Rimmel was holding a Chihuahua puppy, and she couldn't be more than two pounds.

"Hi," I crooned to her. Now let it be known, I might not be dedicating my career and part of my life to animals, but I did have a soft spot for them. I'd grown up with big, slobbery dogs and cats my brother's had to climb trees to get down.

And yes, they were the reasons the poor cats were in the trees. (Note to cats everywhere: hiding in trees will not keep little boys away. It will only make them into monkeys.)

I'd never had such a tiny little thing, though. "Can I hold her?" I whispered, like my full voice would be too much.

"Of course!" Rimmel smiled and held out her hands. The puppy was so little she fit in both Rimmel's hands.

I picked her up and cuddled her against my chest. "Aww," I crooned at her. "Aren't you just the cutest thing ever?"

Her little body was trembling a bit, and she climbed up my chest a little farther. Her ears were bigger than her head and had long wisps of hair flying off them in all different directions. She was the color of wheat, with brown eyes and a pink nose. She was fluffy and tiny and wiggly.

Basically, this puppy was everything a little heart stealer should be.

Against my arm, I felt her little tail wiggle, and I laughed. She looked up at me and licked my chin.

My heart turned over. The sadness I'd been plagued with for weeks suddenly seemed a little lighter. My mood a little brighter.

I carried the puppy over to my bed and sat down. When I spread my legs and put the little girl down on the comforter, she sniffed around and tripped over a wrinkle in the fabric.

Laughing, I played with the hair on her ears. She had puppy breath and a little fat belly.

"What's her name?" I asked Rim.

"Doesn't have one yet," Rimmel replied, coming over to pet her. "She just came to the shelter today."

"How could anyone drop such a precious little thing off at a shelter?" I asked.

The puppy grabbed hold of the hem of my T-shirt and started tugging. Rimmel and I both laughed at her valiant yet very tiny efforts.

"Someone found her on the side of the road. They didn't know where else to bring her but then remembered the shelter from all the publicity the fundraiser generated."

I blinked back tears. Gah, I was an emotional disaster. Maybe I was PMSing. Lord, I hoped so. I couldn't be this screwed up. Yet the thought of this tiny little baby roaming the street alone and hungry totally wrecked me.

"Thank God you took her in!" I proclaimed as the pup gave up on my shirt and curled up right against my leg.

"Well, the shelter really is full, but we would never turn away an animal that needed help."

"How old is she?" I asked, stroking her light-colored, soft fur.

"Best we can determine, she's about twelve weeks old. So really very young." Rimmel got up and rummaged around in her bag while she talked. A few seconds later, she pulled out two small bowls, one for dog food and the other for water, and a big white pad. It was a training pad for the puppy to pee on.

"So what happens to her now?" I asked.

Rimmel shrugged. "She'll stay at the shelter until she's adopted."

"In that cold shelter all alone?" I gasped.

Rimmel laughed. "Well, we do have heat."

I picked up the fuzzy blanket I used when I studied and tucked it around her. "She can hang out with us," I suggested.

"Yeah, I hoped you wouldn't mind. I couldn't bear the thought of leaving her there either."

"No one will even know she's in here she's so tiny."

Rimmel nodded. "But not very long. She needs a good home."

I nodded. "I can stay here with her tonight, watch over her."

Rimmel gave me a look, kind of a cross between suspicion and worry. "You don't want to go out?"

I shrugged and looked back down to the puppy.

"What's going on, Ivy?"

"What do you mean?" I asked.

"You've been sort of withdrawn for weeks, since we got home from Florida actually. You seem a little down."

Of course she noticed. We shared this room. She saw me more than anyone else. And I'd been hiding out in the room a lot more than normal.

I shrugged. "School's just been busy."

"School is always busy."

Rimmel moved across the room and sat on the bed beside me. "I've been a bad friend."

My eyes shot up to hers. "What?"

Rimmel wasn't a bad friend. If anyone knew what a bad friend was, I did.

"So much has been going on. I got caught up in my own problems, my own issues and Romeo's, too. I haven't been here for you. I never really asked you…"

"Asked me what?" I pressed.

"Are you okay? I mean, after everything with Zach…" Her voice trailed away timidly.

My stomach twisted.

"I know after what he did—"

"You mean what I did?" I asked, not willing to let myself off the hook. "I slept with him. I gave him access to this room, to your stuff. And because of me, you almost got thrown out of college. You were attacked. Romeo broke his arm."

"Zach being a complete psycho is *not* your fault."

"Maybe not," I allowed, "but I didn't help things."

"The way I see it, you were a victim just like the rest of us," Rimmel said passionately.

I smiled. "You're a good friend. You give me a lot of credit I don't deserve."

"Why are you being so hard on yourself? Is there more to this than just Zach?"

The puppy chose that moment to get up and start licking my hand. I giggled and started petting her.

Rimmel smiled.

It dawned on me. "You brought this puppy home for me. You knew I couldn't resist something this cute."

"No one can resist a little puppy," Rim agreed.

"Is she really even a shelter dog?"

Rimmel nodded. "She really is. She really was found on the street today. It's just, when I saw her… I thought of you. I knew she'd make you smile."

I reached out and hugged her with one arm since the puppy was still between us. "Thank you." I sat back and looked at the light-colored Chi. "If she were mine, I'd call her Prada."

Rimmel laughed. "Only you would name a dog after a designer."

"Hey, they make some good bags," I admonished. "And besides, she's trendy. I can tell already."

Rimmel nodded once. "Prada it is."

"We can't name her," I protested.

"Sure we can. We gotta call her something. I can put her name on the tag on her cage at the shelter. Maybe whoever adopts her will keep it."

"What do you think about that, Prada?" I crooned.

She tripped on the blanket again and fell over. I rubbed her tummy and we laughed.

"You know you can talk to me anytime about anything, right?" Rimmel said. "Even Zach. No one blames you for anything he did."

"No one knows," I scoffed. Then I paused. "Did you…?"

She shook her head adamantly. "I didn't tell anyone. Romeo knows, of course, because he was part of the investigation his father launched on my laptop. But no one else."

I let out a relieved sigh. "I don't want anyone to know. I'm so embarrassed. I've been making some really bad choices lately. I can only imagine what Romeo thinks of me." I cringed. I know people always say not to care about what others think of you, but that isn't always easy. A girl wants her friends to like and respect her.

Rimmel's hand covered mine. "I promise you. Romeo doesn't think badly about you. He's actually noticed a change. I think he's proud of you."

"Really?" I don't know why that meant so much to me, but it did. I know Romeo was just a guy like everyone else. He wasn't really the big celebrity everyone made him out to be. He was a good guy. A nice guy. And he took really good care of Rimmel.

However, he was sort of the alpha of our group, the leader. This past year, we'd really formed a tight group of friendship. Sure, Braeden and I were at each other's throats all the time. Missy kind of fell off the map when her relationship with Braeden went south…

I saw a pattern here. Braeden was like dynamite to all relationships he's involved in.

Wasn't that an interesting realization?

But even through it all, I knew my friends would be there if I needed them. Especially Romeo and Rimmel. They were solid.

Rimmel nodded sagely. "He even told Trent when he asked about you."

"Trent asked about me?" I asked curiously. It was always flattering when a guy asked about you.

Prada was up dancing around on the bed again, so Rimmel lifted her down and put her on the training pad and near her food. I watched her maneuver around. She sniffed at everything and seemed curious of everything her nose touched.

"He did. I couldn't help but notice he seemed pretty interested at breakfast the other day."

As much as I wanted to deny it, maybe Trent did seem interested in me. I groaned. "Me and guys aren't a very good idea."

"You just need to find the right one."

"And you think Trent is the right one?" I asked. I couldn't help but think about Braeden.

I told myself to shut it.

"Could be." Rim smiled. "He's sweet, good-looking, and he seems to really be into you."

"Yeah," I echoed. "Maybe. But wasn't the whole idea to set him up with Missy?"

Rimmel didn't seem bothered. "Yeah, but it didn't work out that way. Missy doesn't seem interested in Trent at all."

You have no idea.

Before I decided to change the path I was on, to stop making choices that might come back to bite me later, I would have jumped on Rimmel's idea. I would have thought the best way to get over someone I couldn't and shouldn't want was by getting into something with someone else, especially if that someone was interested in me.

However, I was doing things different now. Better.

That didn't necessarily mean Trent wasn't someone I could spend time with. But he wasn't someone I was going to jump into bed with. He wasn't someone I was going to get drunk with, and he most definitely was *not* a one-night stand.

Maybe I could be into him. He did make me laugh, and he was so sweet when I cut my foot at the beach.

After Braeden jumped over the railing to make sure you were okay.

I shook my head, trying to clear the thought.

Rimmel frowned. "I don't mean to push. If it's too soon after what happened with Zach…"

"You're not pushing. You're just being a friend." And I was a liar. She had no idea I'd been with Braeden.

Of course, it wasn't all about him. I was still haunted by Zach. Still so ashamed. Did that make me half a liar?

Half a liar was better than a full liar.

Right?

"So what do you say? Screamerz?" Rimmel asked, hope in her eyes.

I laughed. "Since when did you want to go out and me want to stay in?"

She grinned and pushed up her glasses. "Maybe it's a full moon."

I slid off the bed and onto the floor next to Prada. She romped over to me, and I started petting her again. As I moved my hand, she tried to chew my fingers. Her teeth were so tiny it didn't even hurt.

"Prada can stay here. I'll call Romeo and ask him to bring Murphy's crate we use when he goes to the vet. We can line it with a blanket and she can sleep while we're gone."

"I don't know," I hedged. "She might get lonely."

Rimmel smiled. "She'll sleep. Puppies sleep a lot. She'll be tired out by us soon."

When I didn't say anything, Rimmel sighed. "I can take her to Romeo's? She can stay at the house with Murphy. I can take her back to the shelter tomorrow."

"No," I said quickly. I wasn't ready to let this little bundle of cuteness go yet. "If you think she'll be okay here."

"I really do."

"Okay. I'll come out. But only for a while. Then I'll come back and take care of Prada."

"I'd planned on staying at Romeo's tonight." Rimmel chewed her lower lip, seeming conflicted.

She always stayed with him on the weekends. I never expected her to sleep here. "I promise I'll take care of her."

"I know you will," Rimmel agreed. "Now, I better go shower and pick out something to wear."

"I'll braid your hair," I offered.

"You know I'd be a hot mess if it weren't for you, right?" she said as she gathered up all her shower stuff.

"Rimmel?" I called before she could leave. "Thanks. For bringing home Prada, for cheering me up, and for just being here."

"Anytime." She smiled and closed the door quietly behind her.

* * *

Prada was dragging around my fuzzy slipper, which was twice as big as her, and acting like she was gonna do some damage. I laughed and went back to finishing my half-done hair.

When it was done, I played with the puppy some more and then put on my makeup. The polka dot eye makeup wasn't as time consuming as I thought it would be. And it turned out really awesome. The dots accented my eyes and seemed to arise out of the smoky-gray shadow at the corners. On the inner corner, I put something shimmering and light, just enough to catch the light. I kept the rest of my face fairly simple and then slid on some pale-pink lipstick.

When Rimmel came back from her shower, we talked clothes, and I decided to wear a pair of mint-colored skinny jeans—it was spring after all—and a simple white tank top. Over the tank, I layered a big, chunky necklace with various strands of silver chains, turquoise-colored beads, and a couple white, flirty feathers.

Since it still got cool at night, I figured I could get away with a pair of boots, so I dug around until I found a pair of grey boots with big wedge heels. They would be more comfortable to dance in than stilettos, and since I didn't want to irritate the cut that was almost healed on the bottom of my foot, I figured it was a win-win.

"You're gonna freeze in that tank top!" Rimmel said when she saw what I was wearing.

"Nah. I'll wear a sweater until we get inside," I replied and pulled out a chunky grey knit cardigan.

"Well, for someone who wanted to stay in, you sure look hot."

I smiled. "Just being me."

"How about you be you over here with me and a brush?"

I laughed, and Rimmel held Prada while I braided both sides of her hair back in a loose French braid and then twisted the ends up into a knot at the base of her head. After pulling out a few loose pieces around her face, I helped her pick out a pair of maroon-colored leggings and a flowy, loose top in a black-and-white chevron pattern. The only necklace she ever wore was a gold cameo pendant that belonged to her mother and the gold bracelet Romeo gave her for Christmas.

But it worked and she looked great.

A few minutes later, Romeo knocked on the door and Rimmel ushered him inside quickly.

"What's the rush, smalls?" he asked as she yanked him inside and shut the door.

He drew up short when he saw me on the floor amongst a bunch of makeshift toys and a little puppy in the center. He laughed. "This is what you needed Murphy's carrier for?"

Prada glanced at Romeo and wagged her little tail. Her entire butt wiggled with the action. She pounced on his shoe, and I laughed because it was literally like five times the size of her body.

He set down the carrier and reached for Rim.

He lifted her off the ground without any effort and brought her up to his eye level. "Smalls, are you gonna be bringing home every animal that tugs at your heart?"

She stuck out her chin. "And what if I do?"

I couldn't help but watch them. They had like an epic love story. Just watching them look at each other was captivating.

Romeo chuckled. "Then I guess I'm gonna have to buy a farm with a whole lot of land."

"You'd do that?"

"I'd do anything for you, baby. You know that."

I turned away. Their story was beautiful, but it seemed unattainable for someone like me.

Rimmel whispered that she loved him, and then in a louder voice, she said, "Well, I didn't adopt Prada. I just smuggled her in so she could meet Ivy. I didn't want to leave her all alone at the shelter."

"Yes, I'm sure the fifty other animals there would have made her feel lonely," Romeo cracked and set Rim down.

"She sure makes me feel less lonely."

Silence enveloped the room, and I glanced up. Romeo and Rimmel were both staring at me. "Did I say that out loud?" I asked, feeling my cheeks heat.

"Yep," Romeo answered. "But we won't tell."

• • •

I cleared my throat and reached for the carrier. It was made of sturdy, thick plastic with a black handle on top. It had good-sized vents on the sides and a black iron door on the front.

"Is this too small?" I worried.

"No, it's a good size for her. She's so small she needs a space that's contained. It will give her a sense of security."

I nodded. It made sense. My blanket was too big to put inside the carrier, so I used one of my clean, soft towels I used for showering instead. After that, I put one of my fuzzy socks Prada had found and was dragging around inside as well.

I tucked the carrier beneath my desk, but not too far back so she wouldn't be able to see. Then I clicked on my desk lamp so it wouldn't be dark.

Rimmel waited and watched patiently as I set up a little space for our guest. Even Romeo didn't seem to mind my fussing. Of course, he was probably used to it with Murphy.

"Ready?" Romeo asked us after we both cuddled the dog again and tucked her inside the carrier.

"I think so," I said.

Rimmel laughed. "She'll be okay. I promise."

I peeked inside before we left, and she was already curled up sleeping with her tiny head pillowed on my sock.

"Ladies," Romeo said, motioning for us to go ahead of him in the hall—after we locked the room door.

On our way to the Hellcat, nerves started dancing in my belly… or maybe it was anticipation. I really didn't want to go out tonight.

But I couldn't deny I was looking forward to seeing Braeden.

CHAPTER FIFTEEN

#ResultsAreIn
Lots of votes. One clear winner. Seems
Alpha U has a new resident hottie.
#BraedenIsInTheSpotlight #13

... Alpha BuzzFeed

BRAEDEN

"Aww, shit." Romeo laughed.

I glanced over the rim of the Miller Light tap I was drinking as he snickered. A few of the guys around us all started doing the same.

They were all looking down at their phones.

"I miss something?" I asked.

"You tell us, Mr. Resident Hottie," one of my teammates said from across the table.

"Excuse me? I don't speak idiot. Please explain in English," I cracked.

• • •

Romeo slid his phone in front of my face. I read the newest Buzz notification was plastered on the screen.

My beer sloshed over the rim of the glass when I sat forward in surprise. "What the fuck?" I hollered.

"To the new Alpha U stud!" Romeo yelled and raised his glass. Everyone around us followed suit.

"What a bunch of bullshit!" I yelled over the wolf howls.

Romeo clapped me on the back. "Have fun with that."

I let out a string of curses. "Are you kidding me? The last thing I want is some gossipmonger on campus reporting my every move. I don't know how the hell you tolerated it, man." I shook my head.

Romeo grunted. "It's pretty damned annoying. Especially when the Boss would go after Rim."

"Labeling her a hashtag nerd and shit," I spat. "Not to mention all the other people's dirty laundry that's been aired all over campus thanks to this fool."

"I definitely ain't gonna miss that," Rome said and drank some beer.

"It's gonna be weird you not being around. Not having you on the field. We've been teammates almost as long as we've been friends."

"I'm not quitting you, B," Romeo vowed, laying a hand on his chest. Dude thought he was a comedian. "Our bromance will live on!"

"You say the word bromance one more time and I'm never speaking to you again."

Romeo laughed. "Seriously, though. I might not be around as much come summer, but we're family. That ain't gonna change."

I nodded. I wouldn't admit it, but I needed to hear that. Everything felt so out of control lately; everything was changing so fast. Knowing some things would always stay the same was reassuring.

Romeo glanced out on the dance floor where Rim was dancing—and not too coordinated—with Missy and Ivy. The ghost of a smile played on his lips as he watched her, but then he refocused his attention and sat up in his chair. His beer hit the table and he leaned in like he had something more to say.

I ducked my head a little closer because the music was so loud.

"About the other night," he began.

I knew he was talking about the night we had dinner with Mom, the night my father called like it was no big deal to ask to talk to me. The night I stormed out of the house and went to the gym where I pounded the body bag for over an hour after I ran a few miles on the treadmill.

Through it all, Rome had been there. He didn't ask me any questions or push me to talk about my feelings. Thank fuck. If I wanted to do that, I'd call up Dr. Phil. He just hit the bag with me, then hopped on the elliptical while I ran off my anger on the treadmill.

Basically, he was just there.

I did realize, however, even if I didn't want to talk about it, he had a right to know what was going on.

"Rimmel knows."

I glanced up, surprised. I was prepared for some questions, not that.

"I know it wasn't really my place, but after what happened at Mom's… Well, she and Caroline talked, and I filled in any questions she had later."

And that explained the hug I got when I walked in tonight. It wasn't like me and Rim didn't ever hug. We had. Yet it wasn't something that happened every day and never in a bar.

But even she didn't say anything. She just hugged me extra tight and then told me I better behave tonight.

That was why they were family. They got it, and I didn't have to say a word.

"It's cool. After dinner, I'm sure she was freaked."

"Nah." Romeo scoffed. "She's been through a lot. I don't think much surprises her anymore. If anything, it explained some things."

I tilted my head to the side. "What things?"

"Like why you're impossibly obnoxious." He flashed his teeth in a wide grin.

I gave him the finger.

One of the guys came up from behind, then leaned his ugly mug over my shoulder and held his phone in my face. "Resident hottie!" He chortled. "The BuzzBoss is watching!"

I dug my cell out of my pocket, lit up the screen, and hit delete in front of everyone staring. "The resident hottie has left the building!" I tossed my phone onto the table and it slid to a stop.

"To Romeo!" I yelled. "The original resident hottie!"

Everyone cheered, and a tray of those damned Smurf Balls shots appeared in the center of the table. The girls had already done more than one.

And judging by the way my little sis was dancing, she didn't need another.

The guy to my right went off in search of an easy lay, and Rome and I sat there watching the girls make fools of themselves.

Well, okay, Rim was the only one looking a little foolish. But that's why we all loved her.

And really, I wasn't watching her much anyway. My eyes kept drifting back to Ivy. I was starting to think I needed to get my eyes checked. I seemed to have a problem keeping them away from her.

The damn candy-colored pants she was wearing molded to her porn-worthy ass like a second skin, and the tank top… Good Lord the tank. If only she'd trip and fall in a puddle of water. Every guy in here would get a stiffy. There was nothing hotter than a woman in a wet white tank top.

Well, except maybe a woman in a wet white tank top and a thong.

She was flinging her long, glossy hair around as she moved, and it didn't escape my notice that she attracted too much attention. I glanced down the table at where the sweater she was wearing when she came in lay. She should put it back on.

Guys sidled up to her every few minutes, and she'd flash them a wide, seductive smile, entertain their attention for the span of a few heartbeats, and then move away, back to her friends.

It definitely didn't hurt my feelings she seemed so uninterested, but I also couldn't help but wonder why. She could have any guy out there on the floor tonight, even the ones with dates, yet she seemed to want to stay alone.

• • •

Someone slid in the vacant seat beside me, and I rolled my head in their direction.

Missy smiled, her full lips turning up at the corners. Her hair was in a high ponytail that bounced around with the beat of the music. She was wearing a pair of skintight black pants and a yellow shirt that tied around her neck. I'd been so intent on watching Ivy, I hadn't even noticed she'd left the dance floor.

"Have some balls," I said and gestured toward the shot glasses full of blue liquid.

"I'll have some if you do," she replied over the music.

"Balls aren't my thing." I grabbed a shot off the table and held it out to her.

She took it, tossed it back, and slammed it down on the table. Then with a wicked glint in her eye, she plucked my beer out of my hand and took a long sip. When she was done, her lips glistened with beer and she pressed the back of her hand to them, wiping them dry. "Thanks."

"It's what I'm here for." I shrugged.

"Dude." Romeo drew my attention. "I gotta go save Rimmel from herself."

"May the force be with you!" I yelled after him.

I was drinking some beer when Missy leaned close and whispered in my ear, "So if balls aren't your thing, then what is?"

I lowered the glass and looked at her. "I'm pretty sure you know."

Her lips pulled up into a satisfied and welcoming smile.

What. Was. Happening?

Was she hitting on me or just being nice?

Sometimes I really wished women came with an instruction manual.

I leaned back in my seat, putting a little distance between us, and tried to ignore the way she angled her legs and body toward mine. I liked Missy. I really did. But she wasn't girlfriend material, not for me.

It wasn't anything personal. No girl was girlfriend material to me.

The second I started getting the feels from her (the feels = she wanted a permanent piece of the B-man), I

● ● ●

pulled back. I made it clear we were just having fun. I wasn't trying to string her along or let her believe it was more than what it was.

I thought she accepted it. Yet sometimes, the way she looked at me during spring break and then again right now… it made a guy wonder.

"Yeah, I think I do," she agreed.

I couldn't even remember what the hell I said.

Movement on the dance floor caught my eye. Ivy was almost in my direct line of sight and so was Trent. I hadn't noticed him before, but I wouldn't have because he wasn't anywhere near Ivy.

But he sure as hell was now.

My tongue slid over my teeth as I watched with veiled interest as he approached her. Trent was a little bolder than the other guys coming on to Ivy. He was more familiar with her, more confident. Kind of like he already knew what her response would be.

Poor guy.

He and I were friends. I didn't want to see him get dissed in front of everyone.

I watched him palm her hips, pulling her back against his body so they were molded together. Ivy seemed startled and she stiffened. Trent leaned around her and said something in her ear.

And this was when she would send him packing. Buh-bye.

But she didn't.

Her body relaxed into his, and one of his arms snaked around her waist and held her close. Her hand covered his and they danced in sync with the beat.

I tossed back the rest of my beer, then reached for the pitcher to fill up my glass. I was about to chug it when Missy grabbed it again and smiled, wrapping her lips around the glass.

I grabbed an empty glass and filled up another. "Keep it," I told her.

I don't think she liked that too much, but I didn't give a fuck. I just wanted to get drunk.

"They make a good couple," Missy yelled and motioned out to the dance floor. I didn't look again. I didn't need to. I knew who she meant.

"Poor shmuck," I replied.

• • •

Missy laughed. It wasn't a joke.

I drank some more beer and my damn eyes wandered back to the train wreck in front of me. Ivy was facing him now. He had one of his legs between hers and they were moving to the beat. At least it was an upbeat song and not a slow one. The pace of the music kept some inches between them.

"You know," I said conversationally, leaning back toward Missy, "I thought you and Trent were a thing."

"Me and Trent?" she said, her eyes growing wide. "No way."

"Why no way?"

She shrugged. "I'm not interested in him like that."

"She is?" I hitched my chin toward the pair.

"Why wouldn't she be? Trent's great and he's really sweet to her."

I grunted. I didn't do sweet and I never would.

"Women like that, huh?" The beer slipped down my throat with ease, and I hoped it started mellowing me out.

"Some do. But not me." Her tone changed, became a little suggestive.

● ● ●

I focused my gaze on her. She didn't look away. She looked me over with bold interest. When she pushed her fingers through my hair near my forehead and gave it a tug, I didn't say a thing.

It would be so easy.

I could have her with barely a word. I could have her beneath me in no time, and I could bury my cock inside her until it didn't matter she wasn't who I really wanted.

I thought about it. I was close. So close to giving in.

Missy was here. She wanted me. And I did like her.

"Braeden," Missy said. I saw my name on her lips more than I heard her say it over the music. Her hand left my hair but landed on my jean-clad thigh.

"What do you want, Missy?" I asked.

"I think you know."

Just then the song went off and another one began. It was a slow one. Sexy and deep. I looked back at the dance floor, knowing exactly what I didn't want to see.

But it was there.

· · ·

Trent pulled Ivy all the way against him. Her body was molded to his and his hands were so close to her ass—*my* ass—I felt the muscle in the side of my jaw tick.

Ivy's head was tilted up so her hair fell back, creating a curtain behind her head as she looked up at him. She was smiling. He was smiling. He ducked his head and said something to her. He spoke so close I thought he was going to kiss her.

I jumped up from my chair.

Frustration welled deep inside me, making it hard to breathe. The walls of Screamerz began to feel very close. I needed some damn air. I started to walk away.

Missy wrapped her hand around my wrist. "Where are you going?"

"I gotta piss." I pulled my arm back and left her sitting there.

In the bathroom, I stared at myself in the mirror. My eyes were wild and the muscles in my jaw were stiff. I tried unclenching my teeth, but they just went right back to the same position.

I hated this feeling. This slightly out-of-control, slightly dangerous feeling.

Sometimes it scared me because I knew while this was pumping through my system, I would likely do anything, and I probably wouldn't feel bad about it.

I stayed in the men's room until I at least felt like I wasn't going to do anything stupid. By the time I exited, the slow song was over and there was a high tempo one filling the club.

Romeo and Rimmel appeared alongside me, and the three of us made our way to the table. Missy was still where I left her, drinking the same beer and seat-dancing to the music.

Trent and Ivy weren't on the dance floor anymore. I took that observation like a punch to the damn gut. I searched around frantically, like I'd lost something I couldn't find.

I didn't want to say it, but I did. The words ripped out of me before I could bite my tongue. "Where's Ivy?"

Missy grinned. "She left with Trent."

• • •

Rimmel clapped like it was some kind of victory, and black dots swam before my eyes. A burning sensation erupted just beneath my ribs, kind of like raging heartburn, but it was worse, taking over my chest.

"We're out," Romeo said. "You need a ride over to campus?"

"Yeah, that'd be great." I took a cab to the club tonight. I knew I'd be drinking so I couldn't drive.

"Missy, you too?" Rimmel asked.

"Sure!"

I had no idea how she'd gotten here, and I really didn't care.

I snatched my phone off the table and shoved it in my back pocket. I didn't even want to see if there was another Buzz.

Missy and I sat in the back of the Hellcat on the way to campus. Her eyes kept wandering over to me, and I avoided it. I wasn't in the mood for women tonight.

I think it was the first time in the history of my life.

. . .

I stared out the window as the streets went by. I wondered where Ivy was. I wondered what she was doing. What her and Trent were doing.

Flashes of the night at the beach assaulted me. Even with the beer haze over my mind, I remembered her clearly. I remembered the way she came undone in my arms and how she'd looked when I brought her over the edge.

I was the only one who'd taken her there.

Her first orgasm was mine.

I wanted them all.

Trent was probably gonna try to claim one tonight.

In my lap, my hand fisted. Romeo pulled up to Missy's building first. She lived in the same one as Ivy.

When Romeo lifted up the seat for Missy to get out, I followed. I had to get out of this car. I needed some air. I needed to stop thinking about orgasms and Ivy.

"Thanks for the lift, man. I'm gonna walk to my building."

"You sure?" he asked.

Missy shifted behind me, and I nodded. Romeo got a knowing smile on his face. He thought I was going to go in with Missy.

But it wasn't her body I wanted.

"Training tomorrow?"

I nodded. "Meet you there."

I leaned in the open doorway and smiled at Rim. "See ya, sis."

"BBFL." Her smile was loopy. How many damn drinks did she have?

"You got that?" I asked Rome, hitching a thumb at her.

Romeo grinned. "I got that," he answered.

He pulled away from the curb and drove out of the lot. I turned in the direction of my building and started walking.

"Hey," Missy said from behind. I stopped and turned.

Her hair was floating around in the cool breeze and her cheeks were flushed. When she walked toward me, the silky yellow material of her top blew back and plastered itself to the front of her body. The wind was cold and she wasn't wearing a jacket, so her nipples hardened instantly.

I looked. Of course I did.

She stopped in front of me, tipped her head back, and looked up.

"Where you going?"

"Where do you want me to go?"

Her lips curved in a seductive smile, her hand reaching for mine. Our fingers threaded together, and Missy tugged me toward her building.

I went.

She used her keycard to get us in, and I held the door open. The lobby was empty, the hallway dim. Directly in front of us was an elevator, and to its left was a doorway leading to the stairs.

"You remember the way," she said, motioning toward her dorm room down the hall.

I stopped walking, planting my feet into the floor. Because we were holding hands, she stopped as well, a look of surprise in her eyes.

I yanked her around; I wasn't gentle. Her body slammed up against mine at the same time I crushed my mouth to hers. I kissed her roughly, some of the anger inside me seeping into our kiss. She didn't seem to mind. In fact, she groaned and kissed me back.

I tilted my head for better access, wanting deeper, and she grabbed the front of my shirt to pull me closer. I kept kissing. I ground my mouth against hers.

But it just wasn't enough.

No matter how deep I went, no matter what angle I tilted my head.

It didn't even matter when she reached around and slid her hand in the back pocket of my jeans.

She gasped when I shoved her away. Her eyes were dazed as I held her at arm's length, my fingers digging into her shoulders.

Missy's lips were swollen and her chest was heaving.

"Come on," she said and tried to turn toward her room.

Anger cracked through me like a lightning bolt in a thunderstorm. "No."

She blinked and some of the fog cleared from her eyes. "No?"

"I don't want you," I growled.

"W-what?"

"We aren't gonna happen, Missy. I don't want you and I never will."

Her face fell. It was the shittiest thing I'd ever said to a girl, especially a girl I honestly didn't want to hurt.

I'd feel like a dick for this later. But it was the only way I knew how to get through to her. Hell, Rimmel was probably going to read me the riot act. I didn't give two shits about that either.

I was done with this night. Done with these feelings. And yeah, maybe I wanted to lash out because this burning sensation in my chest was slowly giving way to pain.

Fuck it. Fuck it all.

Missy yanked herself free, turned, and fled.

I watched her go.

Once she disappeared into her room, I pivoted on my heel.

I looked between the door outside and the door leading to the stairs.

One offered solace, and the other led me straight to hell.

I debated for all of one second.

And then I made a choice.

CHAPTER SIXTEEN

IVY

He danced well.

He moved with confidence and a little bit of arrogance. When he first pulled me up against him, I stiffened, totally put off by the nerve of the guys in this club.

They were always trying to cop a feel.

But then he spoke. "May I have this dance?"

The throaty quality to his voice combined with the music gave me a buzz. I looked at him from beneath lowered lashes. "I think you've already taken it."

"I've seen you giving some dudes the bounce tonight. Thought I might be next."

"Any guy who hefts my luggage around an airport for me gets a dance."

"Only one?" He flashed a smile that showed off the dimple in his cheek.

Well, he was a smooth talker, wasn't he?

"Two?" I tilted my head to the side.

"I can work with that."

And he did. Like I said, he danced well. He almost made me forget the reasons I didn't want to be here tonight.

Almost.

Despite Trent's smooth moves, sweet-talking, and dimple, I couldn't quite shake him.

He was always there, no matter where he was. I knew his location in the club the entire night. I didn't even have to look for him to know.

It's like my body was a broken compass and it only ever pointed due north. And Braeden was that exact coordinate.

As I danced, I stole glimpses out of the corner of my eye.

At first, it'd just been him and Romeo. But it didn't stay that way. The next time I braved a glance, he was sitting there with Missy. She was drinking out of his beer, and he was watching her. God, the way he looked at a woman. Like he was a hungry fox and she was his dinner.

I knew Missy was going to try and rekindle something with Braeden, something more than what they had before.

And from what I was seeing, she was getting what she wanted.

I was happy for her. Best friends always wanted their friends to have what they desired.

I hoped they'd be very happy together.

I was dancing a slow song with Trent, and his arms held me close. It was an automatic reaction that I clung to him a little tighter, seeking some kind of comfort.

His chin dropped down near my shoulder, and his lips moved against my ear. "I think my two dances are almost up."

* * *

"I should be getting home anyway," I said. I thought about Prada and her tiny furry body; she was probably lonely.

His fingers stroked my hair. "Need a ride?"

"That would be great." Riding home with him would be a lot better than sitting in the car with Rimmel and Romeo. She'd know something was up; she already suspected something. The way I was feeling right now, if she pressured me, I might crack.

The song ended and Trent pulled back. Our fingers threaded together, and he led me off the dance floor. Romeo and Rimmel were also headed off.

"Hey," I leaned into Rimmel.

She noted my hand in Trent's and squeed. I suppressed a laugh. She was drunk. "Trent's gonna give me a ride back to the dorm."

"You cool to drive?" Romeo asked Trent. I almost felt like he was asking because he cared about my safety.

"Yeah, man. I only had one a couple hours ago."

Romeo nodded, and they pounded fists. Before Trent could pull me away, Romeo leaned down. "You cool?"

I drew back enough to look in his eyes. "If I said no?"

His eyes narrowed. "I'd kick some ass."

He did care.

I smiled. "Yeah, I am. Thanks, Romeo. You looking out for me means a lot."

"Always," he replied and held out his fist. I bumped it with mine.

"Bye," Rimmel said, giving me a wave, and then tripped over her own feet. Romeo moved fast, scooping her up and tucking her against his chest.

"Call if you need anything," he said.

Rimmel petted the side of his face. "You're so pretty."

Trent and I laughed. Romeo's lips twitched. "Not as pretty as you, baby."

He carried her toward the table, probably to talk to Braeden. Trent turned to me. "You ready to go?"

• • •

I nodded, and we made our way through the crowd.

Trent drove a Mustang. It looked pretty new and was the color of steel. The interior was all black and the dashboard lit up a cool blue color.

We didn't say anything until he pulled the car in a parking spot outside my dorm.

Suddenly, I got nervous. I didn't know what he expected right now. He knew Rimmel wasn't coming home because she was with Romeo. So he also knew I was going to be in my room alone.

Was he expecting to be invited in?

I couldn't. Just the thought of it locked up my body with stiffness.

"I'll walk you to your door," he said and climbed out.

I sat there twisting my hands in my lap nervously. I sat there so long he made it around to my side and opened my door like a perfect gentleman.

I smiled sheepishly and got out.

"Hey," he whispered.

"Yeah?"

"I'm just walking you to the door. Nothing else."

Relief filled me.

He chuckled. "Am I that scary?"

"No!" I burst out. I felt guilty. Trent was so nice. Nicer than I deserved. He hadn't done one thing to make me think he just wanted me for sex.

Unlike some people who shall remain nameless.

"You aren't at all. I just…" My words faded away as I searched for the right thing to say.

"Aren't in a habit of sleeping with guys you aren't dating?"

That stung. Like a lot.

He meant no harm. He said it without knowing.

But damn, did the words cut me like a knife.

"I'm sure I have a reputation," I began carefully, thinking of all the parties I'd been to in the past year.

"Lots of people have reputations. The BuzzBoss sure likes to remind everyone of that."

I laughed. "True. But I don't think the Boss has ever perpetuated my rep." They hadn't needed to. I was who I was loud and clear.

• • •

Trent smiled. "I like to form my own opinions of people."

"And I'm trying to get back the girl who would have given you a really good opinion."

"From where I'm standing, you don't have very far to go."

I stopped in front of the building entrance. "You're a really good guy, Trent."

"Ah, that's the kiss of death."

"Definitely not. Being good isn't a bad thing."

"Don't girls usually like the bad guys?"

"I don't."

I still don't like you. The words echoed in my head.

"Maybe I didn't want to just walk you to the door," Trent admitted, looking a little sheepish.

"You didn't?" I swallowed.

He shook his head slowly. "I was hoping to maybe ask you a question."

"Okay."

"You wanna maybe go out sometime? Like on a real date?"

"A date?" I echoed. The term was so foreign to me. I hadn't been out on a date in a long time. Mostly, I just hooked up at parties or hung out with guys at football games.

"Yeah, the kind where I pick you up at the door and kiss you good night."

Something pierced my heart. I wanted that.

I wanted it so badly.

But not with him.

I told that mean little whisper to take a long walk off a short pier.

"I'd love to."

Trent seemed relieved this time. I smiled because it was so cute. "Yeah?"

I nodded. "Yeah."

"Oh," he said. "Just so you know, I made sure it was cool with Missy."

"You did?" I felt my brows shoot up my forehead.

He nodded. "I thought maybe you'd feel weird about going out with me when it was pretty obvious Romeo tried to hook me up with her. I know how much your friends mean to you."

And didn't that make me feel one inch tall?

"They do," I whispered.

"She and I are just friends. In fact, she seemed pretty excited when I told her I was gonna ask you out."

"She's a good friend." *Don't cry. Don't cry. Don't cry.*

"So I'll call you later? We can set something up, maybe for next weekend?"

I nodded. "Yeah, that sounds good."

He smiled wide and started to walk off. Then he jerked to a halt like he'd forgotten something and turned back.

He moved quick, slipping his arm around my waist and pulling me close. I thought he was going to kiss me.

He did.

On the forehead. And then on the cheek.

When he pulled away, my heart was beating a little fast.

"Next time, it's gonna be the lips," he whispered and stepped back.

I watched him walk away, hands in his pockets and the cool spring air blowing around us.

• • •

#SELFIE

I was the stupidest girl on this planet.

Like, I deserved an award for my idiocy.

Because even after that, even after the freaking panty-melting behavior of Trent just now, my panties were firmly intact.

And thoughts of Braeden were still running rampant through my heart.

CHAPTER SEVENTEEN

BRAEDEN

I paced in the space around me.

What the hell was I doing?

I knew better.

It wasn't too late.

I could leave right now. No one would ever know I

was here.

The images wouldn't leave my head. They were

assaulting me. It was like fucking torture.

I threw my arm up on the wall and leaned my head

against it. I stared down at my feet, at the carpet

beneath them.

I couldn't let her do this.

I couldn't let him touch her.

I raised my other hand and knocked.

CHAPTER EIGHTEEN

IVY

There was a knock on the door. It was just a regular knock, nothing alarming or special about it. But for some reason, my pulse began to hammer and I jackknifed into a sitting position. Beside me, Prada stirred a little, and I stroked her fur reassuringly.

As I stared at the door, adrenaline pumped through my limbs like I was in some dire fight-or-flight situation.

It was ridiculous.

I was in my dorm room. Alone. Trent went home, and I came upstairs.

Maybe that's why my body was reacting this way, because I just wanted to be alone. Because I just wanted to lie here and pout.

Gah! I was pathetic.

I flung my legs over the bed, stood, and shoved my hair back out of my face. Gently, I moved Prada off my comforter and tucked her into the soft blanket beneath it. When she was settled, I snatched the fluffy white duvet off the bed and wrapped it around me, tucking everything inside but the top of my head and face.

Hopefully, whoever it was would go away fast. I wasn't in the mood for any more socializing.

God. I might as well just go check in to a nursing home now.

When my hand closed around the doorknob, a flutter of something that felt suspiciously like butterfly wings erupted beneath my ribcage.

I shoved it away and opened the door enough for me to peek out.

The top of a dark head filled my line of sight, and I blinked.

I'd know that head anywhere. Braeden was half leaning in the doorframe to my room. His arm was flung up on the wood trim, his forearm resting against it, and his head bowed down to lean on his arm. There was something in the way he stood there—sort of hunched over, not looking up—that pierced me.

If my heart was beating hard before… now it was practically galloping. Beneath the comforter, my hands tightened in the cotton, and I tugged the blanket even farther around me. Like a coat of armor, like a shield around my heart.

I'd seen Braeden a million different ways. All of them were stupid and annoying.

Okay.

Not all of them.

Like ninety-nine percent.

I'd never seen him like this.

Whatever he was feeling was palpable. It surrounded him and pushed toward the door and wound through the small opening I used to watch him. He seemed almost forlorn, regretful… and maybe a little weighed down.

He lifted his head. His rich espresso-colored eyes looked at me but then continued past, like he was trying to see inside. Short strands of his dark hair were disheveled and sticking out wildly about his head. The faint scent of beer wafted from his breath, and I wrinkled my nose.

"He here?" he spoke, gesturing toward the room with a hitch of his chin.

"Who?" I asked, my mind literally blank. There was no room for words, for common sense, when just his mere presence crowded me this way.

Bu-bump, bu-bump, bu-bump. The sound of my heart thudding beneath my ribs was so loud I was shocked he hadn't asked about it.

With sudden clarity, I realized something. I'd been waiting for him.

Braeden straightened from the door, pulling himself up to his full, impressive height. "I'm gonna take that as a no."

I stepped back when he flattened his palm on the door and pushed it open. I didn't move any farther when he stepped in and shut the door. We stood there in a perfectly roomy enough space for two bodies, yet we crowded one another.

Braeden towered over me. And I liked it. I wasn't necessarily small, but when he looked at me the way he did just then, I felt small. I felt like the smallest star in the darkest sky.

Yet I wasn't overlooked.

Make a wish on me.

Just one wish.

The thought, however beautiful and wistful, acted as a bucket of ice poured down my back. I yanked away and walked farther into the room, keeping my back to him.

I didn't trust myself to look at him right then.

"What the hell are you doing here?" I snapped. At least I sounded annoyed. He didn't have to know I was annoyed with myself and not him. I just needed that wall to come back up. The wall that was always between Braeden and me. The one that made it so easy to hate him.

"I promised Rim I'd make sure you got back okay."

That was a lie. Rimmel knew I was fine.

My annoyance meter went into the red. "Clearly, I'm fine, so you can leave. Go type up your report."

"What the fuck are you wearing?"

I spun to glare at him. "It's my blanket. I'm cold."

"It's spring," he retorted.

"Well, not everyone is full of hot air like you."

His eyes narrowed, and my tongue slid over my front teeth.

"You sick?" he demanded. I wondered if he noticed the fraction of a step he took in my direction. I sure did.

"No. It's late and I'm tired. I was in bed before you rudely came 'a knocking."

He glanced at my bed, and I followed his gaze. Pillows were all over the place, a couple on the floor and a few scattered around the bed. The sheets were twisted up in the center, and the fuzzy blanket I used beneath the comforter was all piled up, concealing Prada. It looked like I'd been rolling around in there …

Something in his eyes sparked like the catch of a match. Before I could ask him what his problem was, he surged forward and caught the front of the comforter. I let out a startled squeak and gripped the ends together until my fingers hurt.

Braeden yanked, trying to take away my shield. I stumbled forward a bit, and a corner of it came loose, but I managed to keep hold of it.

"Hey!" I protested.

"You naked?" he demanded.

"What!" I shrieked as we fought over ownership of the comforter. "You're insane! Get out!"

"Why else would you be hiding under all that fabric?"

I panicked. He couldn't see. He couldn't know.

What had I been thinking earlier when I put on my pajamas?

"Braeden, stop!" I growled as he pulled some more. The loose corner of the blanket had fallen, and I tripped over it and stumbled forward.

He caught me. Or rather, his chest did. I fell right into him, and he wrapped his arms around me. I wasn't charmed by his hold.

Fine. Maybe I was.

● ● ●

But only a little.

Prada was disturbed by our argument and jumped up from her cocoon. She gave a tiny little bark and her big ears went up when she saw Braeden.

"What the fuck!" Braeden said, noticing my little dog. "You got a rat infestation in here, Blondie!"

I gasped, so freaking insulted he would say such a thing, and I pulled away.

Too late I felt his fingers dig into the fabric at my back and start to pull.

I yelled, but really, there was no use. He shoved me away from him but kept the blanket. I spun out of my cocoon and fell into the center of the room.

Dead silence filled the room.

I'd rather hear him insult me.

My throat felt thick when I swallowed and tucked the hair behind my ears. I was facing away from him, toward the window, and I didn't bother to turn around.

I was scared to.

He was staring at me. I felt it all the way in the deepest part of me.

Why couldn't I be naked?

#SELFIE

Being naked would have been far less embarrassing than this.

* * *

CHAPTER NINETEEN

BRAEDEN

I knew she was hiding something.

The way she clutched that gigantic blanket around her curves and hid herself from sight was just wrong. Ivy wasn't the kind of girl to hide; she was the kind of girl that wanted to stand out.

I couldn't stay away tonight. No amount of beer or sex could chase away the image of her and Trent on the dance floor, the way his hands skimmed over her body and hips as they moved to the music.

It made me crazy, and I hated it.

But I still couldn't stay away and I found myself outside her room. I tried to talk myself out of it. Obviously, I sucked at it.

When she peeked out the door, I'd known. I'd known she wasn't alone, that Trent was here and his hands were doing a lot more than skimming. It was a damned miracle I hadn't busted down the door and stormed in like a ninja on 'roids.

I deserved a metal for my downright angelic behavior.

But…

The room was empty. Trent was nowhere to be seen. And Ivy acted as if she had no idea why I would ask if he was here.

When I saw the state of the bed, spots of red tinged my vision. That was a sex bed. I'd seen enough of them to know.

The memory of Ivy trying to tug the blankets off the bed in my room that night to wrap them around herself was the final straw. She was naked, and he was hiding in this room… somewhere.

So I yanked that shit right off her body.

• • •

I wasn't going to be lied to.

Oh, hells no.

But Ivy wasn't naked.

And she had been hiding something.

Something I never in a million years expected.

She was wearing my shirt.

Oh, hells yeah.

My cock got so hard so fast it made me lightheaded.

My name was stretched across her back. Right there in Wolves' colors. It basically stamped her as mine.

Mine.

My number rode low because the shirt was so much larger on her than it ever had been on me, and the bottom of the three skimmed her firm, round ass. She wasn't wearing any pants, and her legs stretched out from beneath the well-worn blue fabric and flirted with her creamy skin.

"Turn around," I demanded, but my voice had gone hoarse.

● ● ●

I was aware of a rat with big ears watching us from the bed, but even that couldn't distract me from her.

She held herself tensely, like she was expecting me to yell. I waited her out, and finally, she slowly pivoted around to face me.

The Wolves logo slashed across her chest and blond hair fell over her shoulders.

It was criminal the way she looked in that shirt. A fucking crime against women everywhere. No one else would ever look the way she did in nothing but a shirt.

My shirt.

I never understood Rome's insistence that Rimmel wear his hoodie around. I never quite got why he seemed to get such satisfaction seeing his name plastered on her that way.

I got it now.

"I thought I told you to throw that away," I said, forcing my eyes up away from her body.

"I didn't listen."

"That smart mouth of yours is gonna get you in trouble," I warned.

She exhaled. "Look, I washed it. The blood came out. I was gonna give it to you the next time I could bear to be in your presence without the thought of impaling myself on the first sharp object I saw."

My smile was swift. "Then what are you doing wearing it?"

She blanched but recovered quickly. "It was late and dark when I got home. I reached in my dresser and pulled out the first thing my hand closed around. I didn't realize it was this shirt, your shirt, until—"

"But you left it on," I cut her off.

Oh, I was enjoying this. Her cheeks were pink with embarrassment. She kept tugging at the hem, as if she could pull it down so far it would hide her from view.

"It's comfortable, okay?" she whined.

I laughed. She totally liked wearing my shirt.

And Trent wasn't in this room.

She made a low, huffing sound and crossed her arms over her chest. "What are you doing here?"

And just like that, the tides turned. I was in the spotlight now. Except I wasn't going to fidget like a damn girl.

"I came to see Rim."

Ivy gave me a look like she just ate a dozen sour eggs. "You know she's with Romeo."

I shrugged. "I wasn't sure if he was bringing her back here or not."

"You asked if *he* was here."

"I said *she*." I lied and tilted my head. "How much you have to drink tonight?"

"Not nearly enough to listen to your bullshit."

Truth was now that I was standing in the center of her room and the image of her wearing that shirt and nothing else was singed into my soul, I'd rather eat a can of buffalo fart than admit why I was really here.

I was jealous.

I was scared as shit.

When I didn't say anything, Ivy uncrossed her arms and dropped them at her sides. "Well, you can see Rimmel is clearly not here. So you can leave." She started forward, presumably toward the door.

I was blocking her path and didn't bother to move. Her arm brushed against me when she shouldered by. I should have let her go. I should have watched her open the door and motion for me to take my sorry ass out into the hall.

I didn't.

My hand shot out and caught her forearm. Her steps halted almost instantly; she went rigid and didn't look at me. Ivy kept her face turned away, staring straight ahead, waiting for me to release her.

Catch and release.

The phrase whispered through my mind, and instinctively, I tightened my fingers around her arm. Her skin was warm and soft. She felt like satin in my palm. I didn't want to let her go. Technically, I hadn't even caught her.

But I was a twisted kind of guy. Deep down, I knew if I let her go, if I dropped my hold, it would be a test.

Would Ivy flee or would she remain rooted to the spot, so closely at my side?

The answer would be telling. The action would speak much louder than anything she could say.

I let go.

* * *

I stayed exactly as I was. I didn't move except to drop my hand.

And then I waited to see what she would do. I waited for her to put distance between us.

She didn't.

We stood there in the center of her dim room, neither of us moving, neither of us saying a word. Beneath my shirt, her chest rose and fell with every breath she took, and the scent of her hair lingered in the small space between us.

I gave her the option to move away. Yet just like at the beach when we were alone, we were in the dark, and there was nothing here to help us hide the truth.

"Do you ever think about that night?" I whispered, watching her profile.

Her teeth sank into the lower portion of her lip.

Do you ever miss me? I didn't say that out loud. I didn't even want to have the thought, let alone put it out there.

Her chin dipped a little and her eyes gazed downward. Strands of wavy blond hair fell forward and blocked her profile from sight. "I think about the sounds of the ocean and the way the stars there lit up the sky like I'd never seen before."

Her voice was so quiet, but it held me captive, even though it wasn't what I wanted to hear. It was like she was a siren just then, singing something so beautiful it didn't matter what song it was.

Ivy swallowed thickly and fell silent. Her hand slid up and palmed her hip, taking a fistful of my shirt.

Without thinking, I caught the length of her hair and brushed it back over her shoulder so I could see her face. She turned toward me, and the blue of her eyes searched my face.

"Most of all, I think about the way you looked that night with the stars overhead and the sound of the ocean drowning out all the reasons I hate you so much."

Fuck.

Her words were homicide. Homicide to every thought in my head just then.

"Why are you really here, Braeden?" Her tone was hushed.

"Why are you really wearing my shirt?" I echoed.

She started to look away. I slid my hand around the base of her neck and tugged her back. Reluctantly, her eyes met mine.

Even the expanse of a few inches between us was just too much. I guided her forward, keeping my palm firmly at the base of her neck, and lowered my face to capture her mouth.

The first touch was like aloe to a burn. It was like a drink of water to a really dry tongue. The relief that flowed through me was so heavy I drew back slightly.

Her lashes fluttered open and our eyes met.

Goddamn, I'd never in my entire life been wound so tight.

I kissed her again, this time fusing our mouths together and not pulling back. I kissed her deeply but softly, nibbling at her lips between deep strokes of my tongue. Her body went boneless. She literally turned to putty in my arms. I wrapped myself around her and held us both in place. My hands didn't roam her body. I didn't try to cop a feel. Even though my cock was raging inside my jeans, I didn't think about burying it deep inside her.

• • •

All I thought about was the way she kissed. The way I felt exploring her. She opened up to me in ways I didn't realize existed. She opened up a part of me I didn't realize I had.

The kiss went on and on. Our lips tangled together, our tongues danced, and a heavy fog settled over us both. I was in that place one only existed when they were between sleep and awake. That kind of fuzzy, heavy awareness that pulled you down and kept most of reality at bay.

I don't know how long we stood like that, but when she pulled back, it hadn't been long enough. Her lips were slightly swollen, and her eyes were dazed.

I kept my palm cupped around her neck and flexed my fingers.

"You shouldn't kiss me like that," she whispered.

"Like what?" My voice sounded as if I'd just smoked three packs of cigarettes.

"Like this is more than just having fun."

I pulled back. The haze around us was still dense, but her words cut through it just enough for some reality to seep inside. She basically just threw my own code in my face.

I didn't date women. I didn't get the feels. All I ever did was have fun.

Everyone knew it. I never made it a secret.

No girl ever had a problem with it.

And no one ever used it against me.

"Missy is my best friend." As she spoke, she backed away, like I was a poisonous snake.

"Missy and I aren't together." We never were. And after what just happened downstairs, we never would be.

"But she wants to be."

And there went the rest of the haze over the room. The statement was like a category-five hurricane ripping up every last ounce of intensity from that kiss.

"I don't want Missy," I ground out.

"What do you want?"

If that wasn't a loaded question, then nothing was. Her voice was almost desperate, imploring me to just tell her, to put us both out of our misery.

"I'm not into Missy," I ground out again. Saying what I didn't want was a hell of a lot easier than admitting what I did.

"Yeah?" Ivy tapped her foot on the floor like she was scolding a five-year-old. It was damned cute.

Wait. What? Damned cute? Scratch that. She was being annoying as hell.

She kept on yapping. "Well, you aren't into me either. You just want something you can't have."

"News flash," I retorted. "I already had you."

"You're an asshole!" she yelled at me.

"You ain't a prize either," I muttered.

"Look, I'm not going to be your next 'just for fun' fling. What happened at the beach was a mistake. You might not be into Missy, but she is into you. I won't hurt her like that." She stomped to the door but didn't pull it open. Instead, she stood there staring at the wall.

"Is there a reason you didn't want Trent to be here tonight?" she whispered after a minute of silence. It was like even after her speech, her declaration we would never happen, she still couldn't let it go.

I knew how she felt. I was standing here because of it.

Why couldn't I just say it?

Tell her you want her…

A little whine cut through the room. Ivy made a noise and rushed past me to scoop up the rat. "Oh, you poor thing," she crooned. "I'll make the bad man go away."

I guess the bad man she was referring to was me? How original.

She turned, cradling the ball of fluff in her arms. All I saw was ears and wayward strands of hair. My heart turned over, and it scared the living shit out of me.

"What the fuck is that? Should I call an exterminator?"

She glared at me. "She's a Chihuahua. Rimmel brought her home. Her name is Prada."

I rolled my eyes. Of course this was my sister's doing.

She was getting my girl all wrapped up in rescuing the helpless rats of Maryland.

I jerked. *Did I just think of Ivy as my girl?*

Oh, this was bad. Very bad.

Ivy noticed my behavior, and it seemed to draw her up short.

"You're hiding a gremlin in your room? What happens when it gets wet? This building will turn into a bad horror movie." I was good at covering up my feelings with sarcasm.

Ivy covered the dog's ears like it could understand my insult, and I rolled my eyes again.

"She's just a little baby." I watched her bend down carefully and set the dog on the ground near a bowl of dog food and a white sheet thing on the floor. I hadn't even noticed that stuff before.

"There you go, little girl," Ivy spoke softly, and the dog wagged her entire butt. Seriously, I had farts bigger than that thing. But damned if Ivy didn't seem to love it. I wasn't necessarily used to seeing her so in love with something. So in tune.

It made me jealous all over again.

Jealous of a rat.

It was a low day for me.

* * *

When she stood again, my shirt rode up on her hips, exposing more of her thigh. The need to grab her and cover her body with mine was so intense I took a step back.

"What are we doing, Braeden?" Ivy asked wearily.

"I don't know."

"Trent asked me out. On a date." She was watching me, gauging my reaction.

"So?" I growled.

"So I said yes."

She what the what? I felt my blood start to boil. It was my normal reaction to being around Ivy too long.

"Poor guy," I quipped. "He must be desperate."

"Well, at least he wants more from a woman than just sex," she retorted, but it was said without her usual heat, without any anger.

It was almost like she was just sad.

I started forward. "Ivy—"

She leapt at me, shoved at my shoulders. "Watch where you walk! You might step on Prada!"

I looked down. The dog was attacking my loose shoelace.

"Vicious," I remarked, dry.

Ivy rolled her eyes.

"She doesn't seem too concerned that I'm as bad as you say I am."

Ivy straightened but didn't step away.

"I don't think you're bad, Braeden," she whispered.

I brushed the pad of my thumb across the expanse of her cheekbone. "What do you think of me, then?"

She turned her face into my touch, and I flattened my palm against her face. After a few seconds, she pulled away.

"Missy is my friend. It doesn't matter what I think."

"What if Missy wasn't an issue? What would you want, then?"

Ivy wet her lips with the tip of her tongue. My stomach tightened. She looked into me with those blue eyes of hers, and I saw the words in her eyes. Then I watched her bury them.

"But she is."

Frustrated and mad, I turned away. The rat tried to chase after me to catch my shoelace.

"Prada," Ivy called out, worry in her tone.

I stopped walking. Even though I felt like stomping out of the room, I wasn't going to risk stepping on that damn dog.

Ivy would never forgive me. And I wasn't a dog killer, even the ones that looked like gremlins.

"Thank you," Ivy said and scooped up the puppy. Once I knew the dog was out of harm's way, I stormed to the door. Ivy followed along behind me.

I turned back just to take in the sight of her in my shirt one last time.

She saw me looking. "If you give me a minute, I'll change and you can have it back."

I laughed.

For two reasons:

I was never gonna wear that shirt again. It was hers now. Forever.

And…

If she went to change, I'd never resist the temptation of her just steps away, naked.

· · ·

I closed the distance between us in one great step. Ivy's back went up against the wall. Prada wiggled around between us.

"I don't want my shirt back," I murmured. I craved her lips. Her kiss. "I want to think about you wearing it. About it touching your bare skin and covering you at night when you sleep."

She visibly swallowed

"Tell me you'll sleep in my shirt, Ivy."

"What about Rimmel?"

"When no else is around. Sleep in it." I amended and tugged the hem. My knuckles brushed against her leg.

She nodded. The dog started making a bunch of puppy sounds and reached up to lick Ivy's chin.

She giggled, trying to steer clear of the wild licks.

The sound of her laugh squeezed my heart. The way she looked just now, with her guard down and nothing in her eyes but happiness, was so enticing.

I wanted more of this side of her. I wanted it all.

She sat Prada down, and immediately the dog took off toward her bed.

I shifted so I was just that much closer. "I don't want you to go out with him," I rasped, unable to not put my hand in the curve of her waist. "Don't go out with him, Blondie."

I know my touch was hard to resist. And I wasn't above fighting dirty.

I just wasn't sure what the hell I was fighting for.

Ivy glanced up at me. Her azure eyes were torn—one part desire, one part bleakness.

Before she could deny the request, I touched our lips together.

It was the softest kiss I ever gave.

She was still standing there when I slipped out the door. I leaned against it once it was closed. I didn't know how to feel. I was in unchartered territory.

Nearby, a door opened and a girl stepped out. She seemed surprised to see me there, and we stared at each other for long moments before I recovered to give her a smile. "'Sup," I said and hitched my chin at her.

She smiled and headed in the opposite direction down the hall.

* * *

I pushed away from the door and left the building. I felt better knowing Trent wasn't in there putting his damn hands all over her, and she was wearing my shirt.

But knowing that didn't make anything better. I didn't do relationships. I couldn't change the fact I'd slept with Missy. And Ivy wouldn't even tell me if any of that mattered. There was also Trent. I asked her not to date him, but she never listened to me. Trent wasn't going to give up. I wouldn't if I were him.

But I wasn't him. I was me, and I had a hell of a lot more baggage than Trent ever would.

Ivy and I were better off hating each other.

Problem was it was getting harder and harder to hate her.

CHAPTER TWENTY

IVY

He gave the kind of kisses a girl sank into.

The kind that robbed your body of gravity, robbed your mind of reason, and sent ripples into your soul. I never really thought much about a person's soul, but recently, it was hard not to. A human body was made up of organs, muscle, and bone. Feelings were reported to the brain, which then alerted everything else about what it should feel.

But what about the soul? What about that place deep inside you, the place that couldn't be identified on a chart or a page in a book?

• • •

It didn't have a bone or an organ.

It didn't have blood.

The brain couldn't send information to a place it didn't know was there.

So where did these feelings come from? How were they so incredibly strong?

The only thing that made sense to me was my soul.

A person's soul went beyond chemistry and brain synapses. It went beyond controlling the human body.

I pictured it like a ghost. Almost see-through, but not quite. It took any shape, molded to any form. That's the reason it fit so deep inside, because it could conform to any shape, any hollow place. In fact, it was hard to even know it was there, haunting you, waiting for that one person it would connect to.

I was very, very afraid the person my soul had been looking for was found.

I was very afraid it was Braeden.

I'd been wearing his shirt for weeks. No one ever knew. As soon as we got home from Florida, I washed it twice and every last trace of my blood disappeared.

But he remained. The way he looked wearing it. The way I used to watch it mold to his shoulders and arms.

I always wondered if it was as soft to the touch as I imagined it to be.

The answer was yes. Infinitely yes.

The first time I slipped it on, Rimmel had been at the shelter. I'd been alone in my room. I was feeling guilty for what I did with him, but even the guilt couldn't stop me from reliving it over and over again.

The second his shirt slid over my skin, a piece of me—a piece of my soul—relaxed. So I kept wearing it. I wore it every chance I got when I was alone.

It didn't smell like him, but when I closed my eyes, I sometimes pretended I was in his arms.

Of course, the reality of his arms was so much better than anything I could conjure in my head. The thunderous beating of my heart when I opened the door and saw him there was unmatched. The way he looked at me. The way he touched me. The way he whispered my name.

My hands still trembled. It had been days.

* * *

How was I supposed to go out with Trent now? How would I convince myself if I just tried, I could push Braeden out of my head?

Even if I succeeded, he would still be inside me. In my soul.

The food court was busy today, as it always was during the lunchtime rush. I was a little late getting here after class because I stayed a few minutes after to talk to my professor about the final paper.

Missy and Rimmel were already sitting down, and they both had trays of food in front of them. As I waited in line, Romeo joined the table and sat beside Rimmel. I glanced around nervously, afraid Braeden wouldn't be far behind.

Once I got my food (a Caesar salad with chicken and a Naked juice), I made my way to the table, not feeling too social, but prepared to fake it.

I took the seat next to Missy and greeted everyone.

"Girl, where's the beef?" Missy teased, pointing at my tray.

"Haven't you heard? Cows want us to eat more chikin'," I joked, thinking of the TV commercials of cows with their misspelled signs.

Missy and Rimmel laughed, and Romeo rolled his eyes.

Truth was I wasn't very hungry. I had too much on my mind to eat.

No one pressed about my appetite, and conversation went on to campus gossip, classes, and upcoming finals. People stopped by the table to talk to Romeo occasionally, which I didn't mind because it kept the topic away from me.

"So…" Missy elbowed me as Romeo entertained one of his visitors. "How'd it go with Trent?"

I set my fork down and smiled. "You didn't tell me he talked to you."

She batted her eyes. "Who, me?"

Rimmel leaned across the table. "What'd I miss?"

"Trent asked for Missy's approval to ask me out on a date."

Rimmel made a squealing sound. "That is so sweet!"

Smiling, Missy nodded. Her hair was styled in loose curls and they bounced around as she moved. "I know! He said he wanted to make sure I was okay with it since Romeo tried to fix us up."

"No, I didn't," he interjected and then went back to his own conversation. How he was able to pay attention to two different convos, I'll never know.

Rimmel nodded like that was indeed what Romeo tried to do, and I giggled.

"I can't believe he did that," I said, thinking about the other night with Trent and the incredibly sweet way he was with me.

Why couldn't I be all worked up over him?

"So you told him it was okay to ask out Ivy?" Rimmel asked Missy.

She nodded. "Of course. I encouraged it. I told him Ivy needed a good guy in her life."

I picked up my juice and took a drink.

Guilt threatened to drown me.

Braeden picked that moment to show up. He dropped his tray on the table beside Romeo and across from me. Before he sat down, he reached across the table to fist bump Rimmel.

Rimmel turned back to us. "So did you say yes?"

Missy was looking at me expectantly as well.

I smiled. "Yeah, I did. He said he was gonna call me so we could go out this weekend."

Braeden pulled out his chair a little rougher than he needed to pound it into the floor before he sat down.

Romeo's fan club took their leave, and he turned back to the conversation as well. I hoped no one else felt the tension I suddenly did.

"Yo, man, what's up?" Romeo said.

"Romeo," Braeden said. Then in one sweeping look around the table, he said, "Ladies."

I went back to playing with my salad. The pull to look at him, to take in the strong lines of his jaw, the dark hair on his head, and the way his eyes made me crave chocolate, was almost unbearable.

Because I was so lost in my own misery, it took me a minute to realize how tense Missy had become. I glanced at her. She was picking through her fruit salad with no interest.

• • •

"You okay?" I leaned over and whispered.

She smiled. "Of course."

Was something going on between her and Braeden?

The little bit of appetite I had vanished. But this wasn't about me.

"You still heading out of town, Rome?" Braeden asked.

"Yeah, we're leaving later today."

"Where are you going?" I asked, glancing at Rimmel. I didn't know they were going anywhere.

Rimmel saw my look and shook her head. "I'm not going. Just Romeo and his dad."

"I have some meetings with the Knights," Romeo added.

I nodded.

"I was actually gonna talk to you about that, Ivy," Rimmel began. "I'm gonna stay at his place while he's gone, you know, to take care of Murphy."

"Of course."

"I thought maybe you'd want to stay there with me?"

I looked up, surprised. I hadn't expected an invitation. I glanced at Romeo, trying to decide if he knew she was going to ask.

He lounged back in his seat, his arm outstretched across the back of Rimmel's chair. He kicked up the side of his mouth. "Mi casa es su casa."

I guess that meant he knew and he approved.

"Uhh." I wasn't sure what to say. I just figured I would be at the dorm alone for a few days.

"I figured it would give us a break from hiding Prada in our room."

Braeden made a scoffing sound. "That rat is still in your room?"

As soon as the words left his mouth, he seemed to realize his mistake. I glanced at him, shocked, and hoped no one else noticed his slip.

No one was supposed to know he'd been at our room.

"You know about Prada?" Rimmel asked, leaning around Romeo to look at him.

Missy shifted in her chair and was listening intently.

I wanted to climb under the table and hide.

Braeden made a sound. "You think you can drag home another stray and Rome not tell me about it?"

Rimmel glanced at Romeo, and he shrugged. "Gotta keep my boy in the loop."

They pounded their fists together.

I rolled my eyes and sank back in my chair, relief making me weak. Of course Romeo had told him. It's not like it was a huge secret among our group anyway. If I had acted anymore shocked, I would have given myself away.

Stupid.

Yet I could have sworn I saw the alarm in Braeden's eyes when he first spoke...

"Anyway, I thought it would be good for her to get out. She can play in the yard. Murphy might like the company. And you know... it'll be fun. We can have girl time."

I met Rimmel's eyes. I knew why she was doing this. Yes, because of Prada but more so because of me. She didn't want me to be alone that long. She was still worried about me.

* * *

"Girl time," Braeden cracked. "You're gonna need a testosterone bomb to clear out your place when you get back, Rome."

Romeo laughed.

Rimmel looked at Missy. "You're invited too, of course."

Missy smiled. "I have play practice every night this week. Opening night is coming, but I can come by after and hang out?"

Missy was a drama major. She had one of the lead roles in the spring production of *A Midsummer's Night Dream*. She was super excited, and I was so proud of her. She'd known what she wanted to do with her life ever since I met her. This was her first starring role, and I knew she was going to kick ass.

"Yes!" Rimmel smiled widely. Then she looked back at me.

I shrugged. "Sure. Why not?"

Rimmel clapped and Romeo chuckled.

"You gonna be back in time for the scrimmage game Saturday night?" Braeden asked Romeo.

He hadn't looked at me one time the entire lunch. I knew why, and I also thought it was better this way. I'd made myself clear the other night. There was no me and Braeden.

But it still hurt.

"You know it," Romeo replied. "I might not be able to play, but I'll be there."

I made a mental note to ask Rimmel about how his arm was doing.

"What game?" Missy asked, picking up her latte and taking a sip.

Braeden glanced her way and offered her a smile. She didn't exactly return it, but she didn't blow him off either.

What the hell was going on between them?

I glanced at Missy and gave her a WTF look.

Everybody's cell phones started going off. None of us reached for them right away because Romeo answered Missy.

"It's tradition. Every year in the off-season, the Wolves get together with the university on the other side of the state. We have a scrimmage game and a big bonfire afterward."

Braeden nodded. "It's kind of the last thing we do as a team for the year, kind of like the sendoff for the seniors"—he nudged Romeo—"or anyone being pulled into the NFL. The team doesn't get back together again for football until summer. Coach gives us time for finals and all that stuff."

"Everyone at this table is invited," Romeo said.

Rimmel bit her lip. "I don't know."

Romeo grabbed the edge of her chair and dragged it so it was right up against his and put his arm around her. "You're not gonna come watch me play, smalls?"

"You probably won't play."

Braeden leaned around Romeo. "I will. What about your BBFL?"

Rimmel sighed. "Fine. But I'm not drinking. I think I'm still sick from last weekend."

Missy laughed. "Too many balls."

I giggled.

"You ladies coming?" Braeden asked. He looked at Missy and then me.

I glanced at him and then away.

"Maybe," I echoed.

"The BuzzBoss strikes again," Missy said. She was looking down at her phone.

I groaned. "Who did they call out now?"

Everyone picked up their phones to see.

"No one really, but it's kind of an ominous notification."

When I read what it said, my stomach sank. It was about betrayal. I knew it wasn't about me, but it sure hit close to home.

"I feel bad for whoever the Boss is talking about," Rimmel said, putting down her phone. "He'll probably start calling them out."

"I'm surprised the dean allows the notifications to continue. I mean, the Boss gives, what, one or two actual announcements a month? The rest is all gossip and drama." Missy frowned.

I started picking up my lunch. My stomach was in knots and I needed to get out of here for a while. "I gotta go. I need to check on Prada before my last class."

Before I could get up, I felt something brush the side of my foot. At first I thought I just kicked the table leg, and I moved my foot away. Yet whatever it was followed.

Chills rushed up my spine. I knew then it was him. Braeden was rubbing his foot against mine.

Is this what my life was reduced to?

Wanting someone I couldn't have, someone I didn't particularly like? Waiting on stolen moments for a touch, a look, or a chance to wear a shirt no one knew I had?

I couldn't do this anymore.

I wouldn't.

I yanked my foot back and jumped up from the table.

"I'll see you ladies tonight." I picked up my tray and then hesitated. "Bye, guys."

"See ya, Blondie," Braeden said.

It pissed me off. How could he be so damn casual?

Because you feel more than he does.

Mortified. That's exactly how I felt. I kept trying to make myself better, get back on the right path, yet I kept getting in my own way.

I left without another word. I dumped everything in the trash, hefted my bag higher on my shoulder, and rushed from the food court.

My mind was a million miles away, and I wasn't paying attention, so I collided into something hard and bounced back.

"Damn, girl," a familiar voice said when he steadied me. "You gonna try out for a linebacker next season?"

"Trent!" I gasped. "I'm so sorry. I wasn't watching where I was going."

He smiled. "Yeah, I noticed."

"Are you okay?" I worried.

He grunted. "You think that's all it takes to hurt me?"

"Well…" I didn't mean to insult him.

He chuckled. "I was kidding."

"Right." I tucked a strand of hair that had come loose from my bun behind my ear.

"Looks like you've got a lot on your mind. What's up?"

I felt my shoulders sag. The weight on them was becoming impossibly hard to carry. "Just one of those days."

"Lucky for you, I got what you need."

Before I could ask what he was talking about, he pulled me close. My cheek went against his shoulder and his arms came around me. The palm of his hand pressed into the back of my head, and he hugged me tight.

It felt good, and I closed my eyes for a moment. Then I tucked my hands up beneath me, resting them on his chest.

The thing with Trent was so uncomplicated. So easy. He didn't seem to have an endgame or an agenda. He didn't seem to want anything from me other than my time. He wasn't off-limits and he was really good-looking.

What the hell was my problem? Why had I been trying to come up with ways to cancel our date?

"You eat?" Trent asked against my hair.

* * *

I nodded.

"I was just on my way in."

"Oh." I pulled back. "I'm sorry. You should get something."

"Where you headed?"

"I gotta go back to my dorm. I, uh, forgot something for my next class."

"I'll walk you," he offered.

"Aren't you hungry?"

"Woman, I'm always hungry. But I'm never so hungry I would pass up a couple minutes with a beautiful blonde." His eyes looked green today and they crinkled at the corners. His sandy hair flopped over his forehead.

I smiled. "Okay, then. Thanks."

"I'll take this," he said, slipping a hand beneath the strap on my shoulder and relieving me of my bag. "Seems like it's weighing you down."

Actually, it was just life, but I didn't bother to tell him that.

Once my backpack was on his back, Trent draped an arm across my shoulders and tugged me into his side. "Shall we?"

I felt sheltered in his hold. I liked that feeling. I'd felt so exposed these last few weeks, like a sapling in a field without protection from a storm.

Suddenly, I didn't want to get out of my date with Trent.

Maybe he was exactly what I needed.

CHAPTER TWENTY-ONE

BRAEDEN

I couldn't help but stare at the unfolding scene before me.

Ivy was so uptight at lunch I wondered if steam was going to come out of her ears. And there were dark circles beneath her eyes, like she hadn't been sleeping.

I just wanted her to know I was here. I just wanted…

Hell, I don't know what I wanted.

I didn't like seeing her that way.

• • •

So I touched her the only way I knew how. I brushed my foot against hers. It was meant to comfort her, to tell her even though I didn't look at her, the distance between us wasn't as far as she thought.

It backfired.

She freaked out even more and fled from the table, right into Trent's waiting arms.

I knew just by his body language he was flirting with her. The set of his shoulders, the way his eyes focused completely on her. She was tense at first.

Until he pulled her into his arms.

Right there.

Right fucking there in front of everyone.

In front of me.

He had no right to touch her.

I waited for her to pull away.

She didn't.

If anything, she looked relieved, comforted even.

I wanted to be the one to comfort her.

I watched him lead her out of the food court, and the entire time I wondered where they were going. Was he going back to her room with her so they could be alone?

"B." Romeo's voice cut into my inner turmoil. There was something in his tone that made me look down. The plastic fork I'd been eating with snapped in half in my hand. The bottom part fell onto my plate while the rest was being held hostage by my fingers.

The prongs were digging into my skin, but I didn't even feel it.

I dropped it and sat back.

"I have to swing by the library on my way to class," Rimmel said and started picking up her stuff.

"I'm actually headed in that direction, too," Missy remarked. "The auditorium."

"We can walk together," Rimmel said.

"Leave your stuff, baby. I'll pick it up." Romeo motioned at her tray. "Yours too, Missy."

The girls got up quickly, like they knew Romeo wanted to be alone with me. But it didn't stop Rim from fitting her small body between Rome and me to hug me. I wrapped an arm around her because brothers didn't leave their sisters hanging.

• • •

"Will you stop by tonight?" she whispered in my ear. "I wanna talk."

I groaned. Why the hell did women like to talk so much? Talking was overrated.

"Please, B?"

"Of course, tutor girl," I replied in her ear.

She pecked a kiss on my cheek and pulled back. "Bye."

"Give me some sugar, woman," Romeo said.

She laughed and kissed him. He didn't let her pull away too fast, though.

"I'll pick you up after class and drive you home before I head out of town," he told her.

After agreeing, she and Missy left.

Romeo cut right to the chase. "What the fuck is wrong with you?"

I gasped. "You kiss your momma with that mouth?"

His comeback was quick. "I kiss *your* momma with this mouth."

I laughed. If anyone else said that shit about my mom, I'd deck 'em. But Rome was different.

"Seriously." He leaned on the table. "Is this about him? Has he called again?"

"No," I growled. "And he better not."

"Mom okay?"

"Yeah, she's fine," I confirmed.

"Then it must be a woman," he surmised.

"What makes you say that?"

"Maybe the broken fork on your plate? The frustrated way you move? The way your fists clench when anything at all gets under your skin?"

I shoved my hand through my hair and cussed.

"You need to get laid or something?"

I laughed. "If only it was that easy."

Romeo laughed this time. "B, I know damn well you could have any woman in this place if you just crooked your finger. The fact that you haven't… Well, that's very telling."

"Just say what you wanna say," I spat. I didn't have time for his analysis.

"Did you sleep with Ivy?"

"Is it that goddamned obvious?" I groaned.

Romeo slapped me on the back, then crossed his arms over his chest and leaned back. "I don't think so. But I know you very well."

I grunted.

"When?" he asked.

"Spring break. Our last night."

That surprised him. I saw it right there in his eyes. "You mean to tell me you ain't had sex in over two weeks?"

Why was that so hard to believe? "Who said I haven't?"

He glanced down at the fork on my plate.

"Fuck you."

Romeo chuckled. "I always wondered when you two would combust."

"What?" My voice was sharp.

"C'mon, B. You can't say you never saw it. You two have been at each other's throats from almost day one. It's like you live to insult each other. Makes me sorry I was the one that grabbed her that night all those months ago at the bonfire."

Rage and jealousy hit me so hard and fast there was no controlling it. I leapt out of my seat, sending it clattering to the floor. I grabbed up Romeo by the shirt and pulled him toward me.

He was still in his chair. He didn't go on the defensive to my threatening moves, but his eyes narrowed.

Whispers rippled through the room, and I was aware of people staring. I didn't care.

"You sleep with her?" I growled low enough only he could hear.

"You know I didn't," he growled back.

"You fucking touched her."

"Get your hands off me," Romeo warned, and beneath my hands, his body stiffened.

That alone would have sent most guys pissing in their drawers. But I wasn't most guys. I knew how tough Romeo was, but I also knew I could take him. I was so pissed off right then I knew I could.

"You wanna do this?" Romeo intoned. "Let's do it."

I shoved him away from me and backed up a step. My chest heaved.

Romeo stood. He snagged some kid, a freshman by the looks of him, by his sleeve. "You," he said gruffly, "clean this up."

The kid looked at the trays on the table and then back at Romeo.

He nodded. Romeo dug some cash out of his pocket and tossed it on the table. "There's your tip."

He dismissed the kid and grabbed up my bag and his. "Outside."

I went, not because he ordered, but because I needed some air. I was out of control. Fuck, I'd almost just attacked my best friend.

Outside, the sun was shining and the temperature was in the seventies. It was a pretty nice day, but I barely noticed. We walked to a grassy strip alongside the food court, and Romeo tossed our shit down on the ground.

"You wanna hit me, go ahead." He shoved me.

My teeth clenched.

"C'mon, man. If that'll make you feel better, do it."

I thought about it. I felt like punching something. But not him. Not my best friend. You know you had a true friend for life when they were willing to let you use their face as a punching bag.

"Rimmel would kick my ass," I said, relenting.

"She's scary," Romeo agreed.

It was a good joke, but I still wasn't relaxed enough to laugh.

"I'm sorry," I spat, pissed at myself. "I shouldn't have lost it like that in there. On you."

He shrugged. "I get it. The thought of anyone else touching your girl, especially your best friend, can make a guy crazy."

"She's not my girl," I insisted.

"Could have fooled me."

"It's complicated."

"Missy?" he guessed.

"Are you fucking psychic?"

He laughed. "I was thinking about opening up a hotline. 1-800-I-know-your-business."

"Maybe you're the BuzzBoss," I guessed.

Rome gave me a look.

It wasn't a confirmation or a denial.

A group of girls walked by and checked out Romeo, and then their eyes slid to me. I ignored them.

"Official or not, she's your girl," Romeo said. "You didn't even give those girls the time of day. That's the first time I've seen that."

"They weren't hot," I muttered.

He laughed. We both knew they were totally hot.

"So what's up with the tension I felt between you and Missy at the table?"

"I never should have slept with her." I groaned.

"So she's still interested."

"It's like the chick can't get the message. I don't want her," I replied.

"And that's why she didn't hook up with Trent at the beach."

I made a rude sound. "So now he's hot for Ivy."

"I noticed. He asked her out."

I gave him a level glare. "You sound like a chick passing gossip."

He shrugged. "Gotta have this conversation sometime. I'm leaving in a couple hours. I can't leave you here all riled up and no one to bring you down."

That made me feel like shit. Because it was true. For years, he's been the one to anchor me. To give me an outlet for all the rage.

"Rim asked me to stop by later," I told him.

"Rim ain't your punching bag."

I narrowed my eyes. "I'd never touch her."

Romeo sighed. "Look, I know. Sorry."

I shrugged. "You're entitled. I did worse a few minutes ago."

"I didn't sleep with her. I swear to God."

"I believe you."

"We just made out."

I slashed my hand through the air. "I don't want to hear it," I growled. "It's bad enough Trent's all over her."

Romeo's brows shot up. "He sleeping with her?"

"I'll fucking kill him."

"Calm down," Romeo said. "Chill."

I paced in the grass, trying to get the image of Trent and Ivy together out of my head.

"I'm having a hard time believing Ivy's entertaining Trent when you two—"

"We aren't anything," I said, cutting him off. "It was just that one time. She insists there's nothing between us. She doesn't want to hurt Missy."

"It's a tough spot," Romeo said. "She probably feels guilty as hell."

I didn't say anything. I just paced some more.

"And that's why she's trying to start something with Trent. To make room for Missy."

"I tried with Missy," I confessed. "Last weekend. Hell, it would be so much easier with her."

"I take it things didn't go well?"

"Basically, I revved her up, then shut her down. She was pissed, with good reason. And then I ended up outside Ivy's door."

"You got it bad, man." Romeo seemed amused.

"This isn't funny."

He sighed. "Look. I've been where you are. Not in exactly the same place, but close enough. Rim and I seemed impossible in the beginning too. There was a lot between us, but we made it work.”

“I can’t.” And damned if that didn’t make something inside me hurt.

“Why not?”

I burst around and flung out my arm at the building. “Were you not just up there? I almost pounded my best friend. You know me, Rome. My temper. You know how hot I run. I can’t trust myself with her. What if I—”

Romeo cut me off by shoving me hard.

Then he shoved me again. I stumbled back. “What the—”

“Come on, then,” Romeo yelled. “Hit me!”

“You’re out of your damn mind,” I yelled.

He swung at me. The fucker actually tried to punch me. I ducked and doubled back around. My fists clenched at my sides.

“If you’re so uncontrollable, then go ahead!”

I pulled my arm back. Romeo readied his stance. Just before I delivered a blow, I slumped forward. “I’m not gonna hit you, man.”

Romeo relaxed and clapped me on the back. "I know."

I gave him and incredulous look. "You know? I could've nailed you right in the face, dude."

He grinned. "You could have. But you didn't. You're not as uncontrollable as you think, B. You're not as dangerous."

"It only takes one time," I murmured. "One hit. One moment, and then everything would be gone."

"So what're you gonna do, then? Let her go? Sleep around forever? If you're already hurting this much after two weeks, it's gonna be worse later. If she's the one you want, then you have to fight for it."

"He called, Rome," I said, my voice breaking a little. "He fucking brought it all back up."

Romeo followed the change in topic with ease. He knew what was going on. Maybe better than I did.

He stepped close, his voice low. "He doesn't own you. He never will. If shit's turned up now, then take the opportunity to bury it. Bury it so deep it won't matter anymore."

I nodded.

Romeo caught me in a hug, right there in the open. Two dudes hugging in the grass.

It was like a romance movie no one ever wanted to see.

Someone catcalled at us, and I pulled back to shoot them the finger.

"They're just jealous of what we have," Romeo said with a big cheese-eating grin on his face.

"Dude, you are not right."

"Think about what I said, huh?"

I nodded.

"And I know you got a lot going on."

I held up my hand, already knowing what he was gonna say. "You know I'll watch out for her, man."

"Thanks." Romeo's voice was genuine. "If you need anything while I'm gone, call. I might play for the Knights now, but I'll always be Team Braeden."

I grabbed my package and gave it a little shake. Romeo looked at me funny. "I'm just checking to make sure I still had this. Making sure all your sappy talk didn't shrivel it up."

Romeo roared.

● ● ●

"Better check your shit. I'm not explaining to your girl why you can't perform in the bedroom all the sudden."

Romeo grabbed his junk and grunted. "Still fucking huge."

"Shit, you know my dick is bigger than yours."

"If that's what you need to believe," Romeo said and threw my bag at me. I caught it with no problem.

"I don't need to believe nothing. I know."

We walked around the building and onto the sidewalk where people hurried to class.

"I'll see you Saturday for the scrimmage." He turned toward the parking lot.

"Don't worry about Rim. I'll make sure she's okay."

He nodded. "And you are, too. I can live with whatever you decide to do. Just make sure you can also."

I nodded and he walked away.

I honestly always thought I had it figured out. I knew where my life was going and who I was.

But now I wasn't so sure.

CHAPTER TWENTY-TWO

IVY

After my last class of the day, I went to the room and tucked Prada into an oversized bag. I walked a good ways away from the dorms, away from the main buildings, and into a large grassy area near the indoor football field.

Once we were there, I put Prada in the grass and let her play. I felt bad for keeping her in the room. I did take her out as much as I could, and Rimmel took her to the shelter when she was working.

● ● ●

Sometimes I worried she'd get adopted while she was there with Rim and she wouldn't come back. I knew I shouldn't, but I'd grown attached to the puppy. Not like it was hard to do. Seemed like it was easy to get attached to lots of things I shouldn't these days.

I watched her hop in the grass and chase after a cricket she'd somehow found.

Today had been hard. I couldn't really put my finger on why, other than the guilt I felt about what I did with Braeden and how Missy was going to feel when she found out.

I knew now that I probably should tell her. I didn't want to, but that only served as another reason I should. Lies put distance between friends, and I didn't want that. There was a big chance she'd hate me, and if she did, I was going to have to accept it, because the bottom line was I was the one who messed up.

I was tired of messing up.

I thought Zach had been my wakeup call. And then I slept with Braeden.

Funny how both haunted me but for very different reasons.

• • •

I still dreamed about Zach, and they came more frequently lately, which I think was guilt, too. I knew Rimmel said I shouldn't blame myself for what happened, but part of me always would. Beyond that, I felt guilty on my own behalf. Guilty for what I did to myself when I let him touch me.

Sometimes I still can't believe I did.

I'd never been that drunk before, so drunk I couldn't remember what happened. So drunk I just let someone like him come back to my room and had sex with him.

Inside my bag, my phone started ringing. Pulling it out, I looked at the screen. It was my brother. I hit the ignore button and tossed it back inside. I didn't want to talk to him right now either. He'd know something was off and then he'd demand to know what it was.

The last thing I wanted to do was explain to my brother about everything that had been going on in my life.

Prada barked, and I laughed. "You silly girl!" I told her and sat down in the grass. When she attacked my shoe, I took it off and let her "chew" it. I thought about the other night when she attacked Braeden's.

He didn't want me to go out with Trent. And the way he kissed me…

I forced the thoughts away.

Braeden and I were over, over before we even got started. I was going to come clean to Missy and hope she could forgive me. Then I was going to go out with Trent and give him a chance. He might not make me feel so turned inside-out like Braeden, but maybe that was a good thing.

After a while, I picked Prada up and went back to the room. When we got there, she ate and burrowed in my bed to nap. I worked on some homework and then lay down with some reading I was supposed to do.

It was boring and I fell asleep.

I dreamt about Braeden. About the words he whispered that night at the beach. I dreamt of the stars and the waves, and of his hands. When I woke up, my hands were sweaty and my breasts felt tender. How could just the memory of him arouse me?

I shook off the dream as best I could and realized the room was dark. I hadn't meant to sleep so long; I was supposed to be at Romeo's. I jumped up and grabbed a bag to throw in some clothes, shower stuff, and everything else I'd need for class the next morning.

When I was done, I packed up Prada's little things and texted Rimmel that I'd be there in just a few minutes.

As I drove, it was far too easy to slip back into thoughts of the dream I had. The sky was dark, and my headlights created the only illumination on the road. Occasionally, I passed another car, but when I turned off the main road and into the neighborhood I drove through to get to Romeo's, there were even less cars, making me feel like I was alone.

I wondered how long Missy would be at practice tonight and if I would have enough guts to come clean when she arrived. I was glad Rimmel and I would have some time alone before Missy came, because I needed to talk to someone and I knew she would understand.

Well, maybe not understand, but she wouldn't judge me.

• • •

I was almost to Romeo's when Prada made a little noise. She was in the carrier that was Murphy's. I managed to smuggle it out of the dorm without anyone seeing. I figured it would be comforting for her to sleep in since we were going to be somewhere she wasn't familiar with.

The carrier was on the passenger-side floor of the car. I glanced down and told her we were almost there.

When I looked back up, something large and fast darted out from the bushes on the side of the road.

I screamed and jerked the wheel, trying to avoid whatever it was.

But my attempts were futile.

AKA an epic failure.

Something hard slammed into the front end of my car. I screamed on impact. The crunching sound of metal was deafening, and I slammed on the brakes. The car fishtailed wildly, then came to a stop.

My hands griped the steering wheel so hard my knuckles were white. My body was so tense it hurt and my lungs gasped for air like I'd just been strangled.

After a few moments of me just sitting there in shock, I forced my fingers to release the wheel. I tried to reach for my phone, but I was trapped against the seat. I fumbled for the seatbelt release and hit it; my body sagged forward and my shoulder screamed in relief. I had no idea it locked up so tightly on me.

I made sure Prada was okay, lifting the carrier to the passenger seat and turning on the overhead light inside the car. She was okay, and I exhaled in relief. It was a good thing she'd been in this protective case.

Once the original shock of the accident passed, I was able to think more clearly. I realized I was sitting on the side of a darkened road, and I was alone. I could get out and walk over the little bridge I'd just gone over and knock on someone's door.

Or I could just use my cell.

I liked that idea better.

I was close to Romeo's. I could just call Rimmel. I'd let her know what happened and… Wait. My car was still running. I could just drive there.

But then I remembered. I hit something.

Or rather something hit me.

* * *

My brain was slow and scrambled, and I looked out the windshield to the area surrounding my car. What had I hit?

Was someone injured? Did they need help?

Oh my God, what if they were dead?

I swallowed back my panic as my eyes searched. I didn't see another car or hear anyone yelling for help.

But then I saw something.

A flickering shadow against the bright beams of my headlights. It wasn't quite in the center, but more on the edge of the light. Yet once I looked upon it, it was impossible to look away.

I unlatched my door and got out on unsteady legs. Clutching my phone in my hand, I moved around the front of the car, staring, hearing the sounds of a struggle.

Then I saw the blood.

And I started to cry.

CHAPTER TWENTY-THREE

BRAEDEN

I laughed when I pulled up to Romeo's place.

His lime-green Hellcat was parked right in its place, looking as spotless as ever.

It probably killed him to leave that car here for Rim to drive. He was probably sweating through his shirt worrying about what she was gonna do to it while he was gone.

But he left it anyway.

Said a lot about him and how he felt for Rim.

● ● ●

I sent him a text with a pic of the car.

YOU'RE WHIPPED.

A few seconds later, he replied.

SCREW YOU.

I laughed and walked up to the red front door. It swung open before I could knock. "Hey, tutor girl."

"Hey, Braeden. Thanks for coming over."

"Why don't ya call Rome? Tell him ya wrecked the Cat. I wanna see what he does." I grinned and rubbed my hands together.

Rimmel smacked me in the ribs. "I will not! You're mean."

"You love me," I told her and tugged her ponytail.

"Yes, I do."

"Why?" I asked abruptly. The words came right out, like diarrhea.

Rimmel stopped on her way to the kitchen and glanced over her shoulder at me. She was wearing a pair of sweatpants that were so big I was surprised they stayed up. On her feet were a pair of white furry-looking slippers, her hair was in a crooked ponytail, and of course, she was wearing Rome's hoodie.

"I got lots of reasons," she replied.

"Well, I am impossibly good-looking," I said, trying to make light of the question.

Rimmel snorted and went on into the kitchen. I followed along behind her. "I'm not sure if that's a good thing."

"Say what?"

She held out a soda and I nodded. The can came flying at my head, and I snatched it out of the air.

"You trying to deform all of this?" I asked, waving to my face.

"Sometimes I think you're too good-looking for your own good."

"You hitting on me?" I teased. "I'm gonna have to call Rome." I pulled out my phone, and she snatched it away and set it on the counter.

"Your jokes won't make me forget the question."

"Will beer?"

She uncapped a water and took a sip. "I assume you're asking because you somehow got it in your head you aren't lovable."

"Oh, I know I am," I cracked. But then I added, "I just wonder how long it will take for my lovable-ness to fade."

Rimmel set the water aside and crossed her arms over her chest. Murphy came in the room and slid around my legs before going over and doing the same to Rimmel.

"I talked to your mom after dinner the other night."

"Romeo told me." I popped the top to the soda and took a long sip. The carbonation burned my throat as I gulped it.

"I'm sure it's really hard to talk about, so we don't have to."

"If you got questions, sis, I got answers."

"I do have one," she said.

I braced myself. "Shoot."

"Do you think I love easily?"

I heard the question, but it took a minute for me to understand. Why would she ask me that?

I cleared my throat. "Honestly, after everything I've learned about you, I don't. Sometimes I'm surprised as hell you let Rome in."

"But he isn't the only one I let in."

I blinked.

"I let you in, too."

I was starting to see where she was going with this.

"I've been hurt a lot in my life, B. I've been lied to, used, taken advantage of. I've been attacked and made fun of… You know."

"Yeah." My voice was low. "I do know." And it pissed me off to no end.

"I planned to live my whole life alone. With animals and my career. I never wanted to let anyone in. I vowed I wouldn't. But then Romeo came along. And you know that wasn't easy either."

"Rim—"

She held up her hand. I shut my mouth.

"And then there was you. Charming, obnoxious, and frankly, a dog."

"You do like dogs."

"I have a cat," she pointed out.

I laughed.

"But that's not all you are. It isn't who you are. You might not know it, but underneath your temper—which I finally understand by the way—underneath your jokes and your charm… you're real. You're soft, and I think you feel way more than most people do."

I set down my soda. I felt like those glasses of hers had X-ray vision. I didn't like it. It made me uncomfortable.

"I think you know me letting anyone in, me loving anyone is a pretty big deal. But yet here you are. My BBFL. Big brother for life. I'm pretty sure for life implies your lovable-ness will never go away."

"But what if it does?" I whispered.

"What if it doesn't?"

"You know our talks are a lot different than mine and Rome's."

A smile tugged at her mouth and her head tilted. "In what way?"

I shrugged. "We usually hit each other."

She snorted and pulled her arm up to make a muscle. "You don't wanna take this on."

I pulled her into a hug. "You sure know how to make a guy feel better."

Her laugh was muffled against my shirt. The doorbell rang, and I stiffened. She pulled back. "I ordered Chinese takeout. I'll go pay."

I followed her to the door and then made her move back so I could answer it. It was a Chinese dude with some boxes and bags. Rimmel muttered something beneath her breath about me being an idiot and pushed me away so she could pay and smile politely at the man.

"Thank you!" she said.

He smiled at her. I slammed the door in his face.

"You have very bad manners," she told me.

Wasn't the first time I heard that.

"You hungry?" she called.

"You know I am."

"I got enough for all of us."

I remembered her telling Ivy she'd see her tonight. "You know, I'm not that hungry after all. Think I'm gonna go."

Rimmel set down the food and turned to face me. Her hands went on her hips and she glared at me. "You're eating. Wash your hands."

"You bossing me?"

"You disobeying?"

I went and washed my hands. When I came back out, she smiled sweetly and handed over all the food. "Let's eat in the living room, and you can tell me what's going on with you and Ivy."

I made a choking sound and felt my eyes nearly fall out of my head. "What makes you think there's something going on?"

She just smiled and patted my chest. Then she disappeared into the bathroom to wash her hands.

CHAPTER TWENTY-FOUR

IVY

Blood and tears stained my vision.

Pain was in the air.

My hands shook uncontrollably.

I dialed the phone.

Cambria Hebert

CHAPTER TWENTY-FIVE

#YouMightBeABadDriver

If your idea of hunting is picking up the animals you hit on your way to the store.

... *Alpha BuzzFeed*

BRAEDEN

"Is that my phone?" Rimmel called out from the bathroom, the running water muffling her voice slightly.

"Yeah," I yelled back.

"Pick it up! It's probably Romeo."

I snatched the cell off the table beside the couch and glanced down at the screen. It wasn't Rome. And

• • •

that meant it probably didn't matter if I answered it or not.

But I did anyway.

The second I silenced the ring and put it up to my ear, I anticipated hearing her voice. I tried not to think too much about that. Before I could even muster a hello or what do you want, she started talking. Words rushed out of her mouth so fast and wobbly my hand tightened around the phone.

"Rimmel? Thank God you picked up. It's bad, really bad," Ivy said, and her voice caught on nearly every other word.

"What the hell is going on?" I practically growled. Tension coiled inside me so tightly I was afraid a piece of me might snap.

"B-Braeden?" Her voice wobbled again. I heard the distinct sound of tears there.

"Are you crying?" I demanded. I started pacing, not even thinking about it, but moving quickly around the room and toward the door.

"Y-y-yes." She sniffed.

"Where are you?" I ground out. "Did someone hurt you?"

"Don't yell at me," she said pathetically.

That's when I knew she was really upset. Usually, when she thought I was yelling, she would yell back.

Pinching the bridge of my nose with my forefinger and thumb, I pulled in a breath. "I didn't mean to yell. I'm just worried. Please tell me what's going on."

A sob broke over the line, and I rushed to snatch my keys off the coffee table. Rimmel was standing beside the couch with a worried expression on her face.

"I was on my way over. It came out of nowhere." Her voice shook. "I didn't mean to hit it."

Okay, she was in an accident. She might be hurt. I needed to get there. I flung open the door and rushed outside.

Behind me, Rimmel was calling my name and ran out behind me.

I stopped and turned. "Stay here. I'll be back."

"What's going on?"

"Ivy just needs some help."

"I can—"

* * *

"No," I said harshly. "I'll be back."

My tone drew her up short. I'd never talked to her like that before. I hadn't meant to, but I was going out of my damn mind.

"Where are you?" I asked Ivy as I climbed into the truck and slammed the door.

"A few blocks away. I just came over that small bridge," she said, hollow, like she was focused on something else. She started crying again. The sounds of her soft sniffles had me pressing down on the gas and tearing out of the driveway and up the street.

I knew where she was. She was by Old River Crossing. It was a small bridge, not even a quarter mile long, that drove over Old River that ran through town.

"Ivy, are you hurt?" I tore around the corner and down the next street. I was just two blocks away now. I'd be there in seconds.

"What?" She was totally distracted. "I-I'm not sure."

My tires squealed when I took the next turn, and the sound of the V8 under my hood roared through the darkness. I hadn't seen any other cars on the road. It was late, but not so late that other people wouldn't be out. I knew I should slow down, exercise some caution, but it was physically impossible.

She needed me.

I was going to get there.

Up ahead, a car on the side of the road came into view. It was parked crookedly, and the driver's door was wide open. The headlights were on, and I could see her outline standing in the dark, beside her car.

What the fuck was she doing standing there in the dark on the side of the road by herself?

My God, this woman was going to put me in an early grave.

Slamming on the brakes, I skidded to a stop just behind her little car. I hit the END CALL button on the phone and tossed it on the seat. The truck was left running when I leapt out and rushed around the side.

"Ivy!"

"Braeden," she sobbed and rushed toward me. Her phone was still clutched at her ear like she didn't realize we could talk without it.

The second she was close enough, she wrapped her arms around my waist and pressed against me as close as she could. Her body was shaking like a delicate leaf in a windstorm.

"Hey," I murmured. Some of my fear she was seriously injured cleared because she was finally in my arms. That had been the longest short drive of my life.

"What happened?" I rubbed her back and noted she wasn't wearing a jacket. It was spring, but when the sun went down, it got cold. How long had she been out here? She was probably freezing.

She forced her head back and looked up at me with a tear-streaked face. With the harsh light from my headlights, she looked like a ghost. "It's suffering. It's all my fault." Her voice rose and hysteria started to creep in.

I brushed back the blond strands that had gotten stuck in her tears and held her face so I could look at her. "What's suffering?"

She drew in a breath and wrapped her hand around mine. I let her lead me around the front of the car, but she didn't have to point out what I was supposed to see. My eyes went right to it.

There on the side of the road, where the pavement turned to loose gravel and then gave way to grass, was a large deer.

"It came out of nowhere. I tried to stop. I tried to swerve." She started crying, burying her face in her hands.

"It's okay." I tried to pry her hands away.

"It's not!" she yelled and pointed to the animal. "Look at him! It's been struggling for minutes. It keeps trying to get up, but it can't. It's bleeding…" She stared at it, almost transfixed. "It's dying."

I wrapped a hand around her chin and forced her eyes away. "Stop looking," I commanded.

"How long is it going to lie there and suffer? Its last moments of life will be nothing but pain and panic, and it's all my fault."

A fat, glistening tear fell out of her eye and rolled down her cheek. Her eyes squeezed shut as her chest heaved, and the tear dripped onto my hand and slid across my skin.

• • •

"Aw, baby," I whispered. "I'm gonna make it stop."

Her eyes reopened and focused on me. I released her chin and walked through the beams of the headlights. The animal was definitely struggling, and it definitely wasn't easy to watch. I could almost smell its fear in the air when I drew closer. As I came forward, it panicked more, its already wide eyes going even bigger.

I talked to it softly, kindly, trying to convey I wasn't here to make it hurt.

I was going to take away its pain.

I didn't want to do this. But if I didn't, Ivy would stand here and cry until every last breath drained from its body. She would beat herself up over the way it was suffering, over the way it hurt.

Blood smeared its light-colored fur, and one of its legs was completely twisted. It was a female, something I hoped Ivy didn't realize and something I didn't plan on sharing with her when this was done. I swept the surrounding roadside for any fawns waiting anxiously nearby, but thank God this doe seemed to be alone.

"Hey, there," I murmured when I was close enough to touch it.

The animal stilled, like maybe it could fool me into thinking it wasn't there anymore.

"Sometimes life sucks, huh?" I said, taking another tentative step closer. She was watching me out of the corner of her eyes and her breathing was very labored.

Several feet away, Ivy called my name. I held up my hand so she would stay where she was.

"This isn't something I wanna do," I told the doe, "but sometimes the hard thing is the best thing. At least this way you'll have some peace."

I moved swiftly, wrapping my arms around the neck of the animal. She was already growing weaker; her struggles weren't enough to keep me back.

I took a deep breath and shut my eyes.

Then I broke her neck.

The distinct cracking sound was so loud to my ears that I stood there for long moments wondering if I'd gone deaf.

The animal was limp and lifeless in my arms, and when I realized it was over, I lowered it to the ground.

● ● ●

Because she was partially still in the road, I dragged the body into the grass, near the trees.

I hoped she was at peace.

When it was done, I turned back to go to Ivy. I faltered when I saw she was only steps away. Her rounded, wide eyes were fixed on the deer and her lower lip was trembling. I pulled off the lightweight athletic jacket I was wearing, draped it around her shoulders, and tucked it underneath her chin. She didn't seem to notice.

"There's no more pain," I whispered, palming the back of her head. "He's at peace now."

Ivy sank into me, and I felt her shoulders shake with silent tears. I held her close, as tight as I dared. Most women were full of drama; they liked to turn on the tears when they thought it would get them somewhere.

But Ivy wasn't most women.

I guess I'd never realized that until very recently.

Or maybe I had. Maybe I just hadn't wanted to admit it to myself.

She wasn't being dramatic right now. She was genuinely hurting, genuinely in pain over this animal. The fact that she hadn't kept on driving after she hit it said a lot. Instead, she pulled over, got out, and called someone for help.

Calling my sister wasn't the best form of help. I'd have to tell her that. But later, when she wasn't crying in my arms.

Rimmel was so sensitive to animals; they both would have stood here on the side of the road and cried. Two women blubbering on the side of the road, in the dark, all alone.

Damn.

I knew Rimmel needed looking after, but it was crystal clear that Ivy needed the same.

Thank Jesus I picked up the phone tonight.

"C'mon," I whispered and tucked her into my side. "Let's go. You're freezing."

"We're just going to leave it there?" she asked, craning her neck to look back.

* * *

I blocked her view with my arm. "Did you want to have a funeral for it?" I asked. I deserved an Academy Award for making that sound sincere and not snide.

She tipped her head back and looked up at me with wide, pain-filled eyes. "You would do that?"

Something in my chest squeezed, and I'm pretty sure my heart skipped a beat. "If that's what you need to feel better, then yes, baby, I would." In that second, I meant it. I would give a damn sermon over the body of that animal right then if it meant giving her any peace.

"Don't call me that." She looked down.

I tipped her face back up. "What?"

"Baby."

Shit. I called her baby?

"Why not?" I asked. I was supposed to tell her she'd been hearing things. That grief was making her cuckoo.

"Because I like it." Her voice was deep and scratched from all the crying she'd been doing.

Now was not the time to get a hard-on.

Now was not the time for a serious case of stiff dick.

I just killed a deer. I was on the side of a road. I was comforting a girl who literally drove me insane every chance she got.

But I called her baby.

And she liked it.

I brushed the pad of my thumb over her bottom lip and tucked her beneath my arm. "C'mon, Blondie. Time to go."

"Prada is in the car. I left her there. I didn't want her to see…"

"Okay, I'll get her." I promised and got the dog and the other stuff she had piled in the front of the car. I took all her stuff, including the dog, to my truck. When I came back, she was still standing in the same spot, seemingly staring off in space like she forgot where we were.

After parking her car neatly on the side of the road, I cut the lights and engine. I made sure it was locked up before I shut the door.

"What are you doing?" she asked.

"We'll come back for it in the morning."

"Just leave it here?"

Why did this surprise her? Did she really think I'd let her behind the wheel of a car right now? She was beyond upset, and it was dark. Since she'd just managed to mow down an animal when she was in her right state of mind, I wasn't about to risk what she'd do now.

"I'll come get it in the morning, and I'll look it over for damage from the accident," was all I said. I didn't think she'd appreciate my real thoughts.

"I'm gonna get a lecture from my dad. And my brothers," she muttered.

I smiled. "Maybe I can fix it. You won't have to say anything."

"You know how to fix cars?"

I stopped beside my truck and pressed a hand over my chest. "I'm a man."

She shrugged like that meant nothing.

I slapped my Ford on the hood. "I did all the work on this beast."

She eyed my truck as if giving it an appraisal. "Not bad. For a pretty boy."

"You just call me a pretty boy?" I was incredulous.

"If the shoe fits." Ivy shrugged and started around to the passenger side.

"Oh, hells no." I grabbed her wrist and pulled her around. In seconds, I had her pinned between me and the grill of the truck.

Her curves were distracting. My hand found that place where her waist dipped in and fitted itself there with unapologetic ease. "There's nothing about me that's a boy, Blondie," I drawled, stroking my fingers along her side. I lowered my mouth closer to hers so she could feel the words as I whispered them between my lips. "Everything about me is all man."

Her head fell back against the truck; the curve of the hood fit into the arc of her neck, displaying all its creamy perfection to its full potential. "Is that so?"

I pressed my lips against the exposed, vulnerable flesh. Her quiet sigh made me hard all over again. I trailed feather-light kisses upward on the underside of her jaw and then up to the corner of her lips.

She remained pressed into the truck, and I remained plastered to her front.

• • •

Our lips were so close they almost touched, but I didn't close the last centimeters. I held myself there and felt sick satisfaction when she moved restlessly against me.

"I know so," I murmured. "And so do you."

I pulled back, robbing us both of the kiss we almost shared.

When she realized I was gone, she straightened and blinked. I saw something snarky form on her tongue. I wasn't in the mood, so I slid my fingers between hers. The words died before she could speak, and I led her around to the passenger side.

My truck was lifted off the ground. It had large tires and no step rail to make getting in easy. When the door was open Ivy hesitated, unsure how to get in.

Usually, girls just whined and wanted me to lift them. I did it, just so I wouldn't have to hear them yap.

I was actually looking forward to giving Ivy a boost, but she didn't ask. I was about to wrap my hands around her waist and lift when she moved forward, took a leap, and grabbed onto the handle on the inside of the door. From there, she climbed in like she'd done it a hundred times before.

Well, that was sexy.

"You part monkey?" I cracked.

"I've got lots of sides you've never seen."

"You've got lots I have."

Ivy rolled her eyes. "There's a lot more to a woman than just sex."

I grunted and slammed the door. This conversation was heading into Nowhereville.

Walking around the front of the truck I glanced back at her car and the spot where I knew the deer was lying. The image of the way she looked when I pulled up was seared into my head. The sound of her crying and the bleak way she tortured herself over the hurt she caused another living being was also something I wouldn't soon forget.

Yeah, Ivy had a lot of sides. She was like a flower in the spring, slowly blooming and opening up her petals to reveal a stunning blossom.

* * *

I was always good—no, I had it down to an art form—when it came to keeping my dealings with women one-dimensional.

Yet the more of Ivy that bloomed, the more I wanted to know.

I wanted so much more.

CHAPTER TWENTY-SIX

#BoringBuzz
The staff would like to remind
students that finals are soon.
Studying is necessary.
#GoodGradesMakeAlphaULookGood
... Alpha BuzzFeed

IVY

I'd never been inside his truck before.

Sure, I'd seen the monster driving around campus and parked at the parties we all attended. Braeden's truck was the kind you would see on a beer commercial. It was an older model Ford, cherry red (but it was never shiny because that would mean he'd have to wash it), and had huge tires on it. I would bet money he put them on there so he could go mudding through the woods on the other side of campus.

It wasn't sleek and sporty like Romeo's Hellcat. But it was just as defining and just as attention-getting as the sports car.

This truck was macho, full of muscle in the form of what was beneath the hood, and was definitely rough around the edges. It was always dusty, there was always mud on the tires, and the fact he had no step rails for people—like ladies—to get in showed he was no gentleman.

Maybe this truck was meant to intimidate, but it never worked on me. I had too many brothers to be put off by this kind of vehicle. And I didn't need a step rail to get in it either. I might look like a girly-girl, and I was, but I'd grown up a tomboy in the mountains of North Carolina.

Inside, there was a single bench seat, and it didn't have any fancy cup holders in the center, just seatbelts. The dashboard was black and didn't have all the gadgets new cars had today. There was just a radio (he upgraded to add a single-disc CD player), the heat and

A/C controls, and the couple other necessary gauges and buttons. The thingy that put the car in drive and park was on a long black stick and stuck up out of the floor.

It was a big space in here, and it was much cleaner than the outside.

It made me curious.

Was Braeden a lot cleaner, a lot tidier on the inside than what he wanted people to believe?

My feet didn't touch the floorboards, so I swung them over the floor as my eyes snooped around the inside. His jacket was warm. And it smelled like him.

I have no idea what he smelled like; there was no signature scent to Braeden. It wasn't some cologne you could get at the mall. Yet whatever it was, I loved. It was heady, the kind of scent that when you got a lungful, something inside you instantly eased. Kind of like walking into a coffee shop after a long day and being bombarded with the rich scent of coffee.

I curled my hands in the too-long sleeves of the jacket and leaned against the seat.

"You still cold?" he asked.

I shrugged. I was, but I didn't care.

"Come here." His voice was just as enticing as his words.

No guy ever had so much power to affect me the way he did.

He lifted his arm, inviting me close. I was sort of glad there were no cup holders in the center. Their absence allowed me to slide right over and fit myself against him.

Braeden dropped his arm around me and his free hand on the steering wheel. Once he pulled onto the road, he tucked his hand into my side, pulling me a little closer.

My head felt heavy, my eyes puffy, and my stomach was slightly nauseated. The image of that deer just wouldn't leave my thoughts.

His shirt was soft against my cheek. He was so warm, so large, and I felt so safe sitting here beside him that without thinking, I turned and faced him, tucked my knees up close, and curled into his side.

He didn't say anything, but his arm tightened.

My eyes slid closed, and he slowly pulled out and turned in the direction of Rimmel's. He killed that deer… Well, technically, I was the reason it was dead and he was the reason it didn't have to suffer. I couldn't imagine how hard that must have been, to break its neck like that.

I never would have been able to do such a thing.

But I was grateful he did. The image of that deer struggling, hurt and confused like that, would haunt me for years to come. It didn't understand why it was hurting, and it only wanted to get away where it thought it would be safe.

I'd never hit an animal before. I hoped I never did again. The horrible sound it made when the body slammed into the side of my car… so deafening and frightening.

My car skidded sideways, and I'd screamed. When the car was finally still on the side of the road, I looked up and saw it. It was illuminated by my headlights, and I knew immediately it was going to die.

Driving away didn't even cross my mind. I got out and rushed toward the animal, but my presence seemed to make its pain worse. And I admit panic clawed at me, too. What if it was able to get up? Would it come at me, try and attack me for what I did?

I paced on the side of the road for a long time, trying to figure out what to do and getting more hysterical by the minute. I called Rimmel because she was always a voice of reason. She was close by and she would know what to do. Hurt animals were her specialty.

But B answered. The second his voice, urgent and demanding, flowed through the line, my body sagged with relief. I hated it, but my body seemed to have a mind of its own where Braeden was concerned. It reacted to him as if he were the most familiar thing in my life.

I mean, just now I was curled against him and drawing comfort from the even way he breathed.

And, oh momma, if he didn't stop calling me baby… It wasn't the kind of nickname a feminists would want. Hell, most of them would argue it tried to pigeonhole us into the role of a lesser equal.

But not to me. Yeah, maybe Braeden did make me feel... lesser, but not in a bad way. It's just because he was so big. He was so all-encompassing that it was impossible not to feel small. I realized I'd always felt that way around him. Maybe it's the reason I disliked him so much. I thought he was trying to make me feel unimportant, like I didn't matter.

Yet that wasn't it at all.

Lately, when he looked at me, I felt like I mattered so much.

The truck slowed and he pulled into the long driveway around Romeo's parents' and parked nearby the pool house.

I wasn't ready to move away, to pull away from him just yet.

To my surprise, he didn't try to make me.

The engine cut out and the silence of night filled the air around us.

His fingers started idly caressing my side. Even through his jacket and my clothes, the touch seared me to my soul.

"Hey," he murmured.

I didn't lift my head or open my eyes. "Hmm?"

"Are you hurt at all? Did you hit your head or anything when that deer ran into you?"

I mentally took stock of myself. How was I supposed to feel any pain when I was sitting here like this?

"I don't think so," I whispered.

"Thank fuck," he murmured and lifted his hand to stroke the side of my head.

And then he did something.

Something I never expected in a million years.

Something I never thought I'd like so intensely.

He pressed his lips to the top of my head. He kissed my hair like he really was grateful and relieved I was okay.

Intimacy filled the cab of his truck, thick enough to cut with a knife. I tilted my face up and our eyes met.

What was happening between us? How had everything shifted so much, so fast?

I wanted an explanation, but I was sort of afraid I already knew.

There's a thin line between love and hate.

● ● ●

But I didn't love Braeden. The idea was laughable. It was beyond ridiculous.

Missy had him first.

I pulled back, suddenly very ashamed of the way I was feeling. I was doing it again.

A sharp tap on the driver's-side window made me squeal. Braeden turned and looked, even as his hand found mine where it lay on the seat. He gave it a reassuring squeeze. "It's just Rim."

He popped open the door and turned toward Rimmel so he was blocking me from view. I was grateful for the few seconds of privacy to compose myself.

God, I was such a mess.

"What happened?" Rimmel gasped. "You ran out of here like the house was on fire. I've been worried sick!"

He ran out of the house when I called?

"Ivy had a minor accident."

I made a sound. "I don't think the deer would call it minor."

"Oh no!" Rimmel exclaimed. I saw her hands waving for Braeden to move out of the way. "How awful!" When he was gone, Rimmel reached for my hand. "Are you okay?"

"I will be." I smiled.

"Come inside! It's cold out here." She glanced at the jacket I was wearing but didn't say a word.

I reached for Prada but left all my other stuff behind.

We walked inside together, and Braeden followed close behind. Funny, he could probably be ten miles away and I'd still notice him as if he were right beside me.

"Please tell me Rome left some beer," Braeden groaned once we were inside as he went past us to the kitchen.

"It's behind the milk and juice. He hides it from his mother!" Rimmel called.

Braeden's laughter filled the house. "Please. Valerie knows what's in this fridge."

Rimmel looked at me and laughed. "Oh, I'm sure she does."

* * *

I giggled. Rimmel leaned forward and hugged me. "You okay?"

"Watching it die like that, it was horrible."

Rim nodded emphatically. Inside the carrier, Prada whined. I unlatched the door and she waddled out, sniffing as she went.

"Hey, girl," Rimmel said, and Prada wagged her tail and went to her.

Thinking of the training pads, I said, "I have her stuff. It's outside."

"We'll get it in a minute." Rimmel didn't seem too worried about it.

Murphy appeared and stared at the puppy from across the room. Prada saw him and went bouncing across the floor to check him out.

Murphy took off running, and Prada followed.

Rimmel laughed. "Murphy's gonna get his exercise tonight."

I smiled.

"Want something to drink?" Rimmel asked.

"Hot chocolate?"

"Of course!" She dragged me into the kitchen with her and went about making the drink.

Braeden was sipping at a beer and his eyes swept over me from head to toe over the rim of the bottle.

I remembered I was still wearing his jacket, and I reached for the zipper to tug it off and return it. He caught my eye and shook his head.

I dropped my hand. If he didn't want me to take it off, well, I didn't feel like arguing.

Yeah, that was totally the reason I was listening.

When the hot chocolate was made, Rimmel turned to Braeden. "Ivy and I were gonna watch movies. I take it by the way you're chugging that beer you're going to stay and watch, too?"

"You two need a babysitter," he muttered. "You eat all the food?"

"I haven't touched it," Rimmel said.

I was shocked he wasn't out hooking up with some random girl. "What are you doing here anyway?" I asked, disgruntled at the thought.

He gave me a weird look. "I came by to talk to my sis. I knew Romeo was gone, so I wanted to check in with her."

Of course. I felt dumb. Braeden cared about Rimmel. He never hid it, so it was only natural he'd be here to check up on her.

"You don't mind if he stays, do you?" Rimmel turned her eyes on me. Her eyes swept over his jacket.

I felt like blushing. She totally saw through me right now. She totally knew.

"Of course not." I tried to inject enthusiasm into my tone.

"Great! Why don't you guys pick a movie? I'll be right there. I'll take Prada outside for a potty break and grab the stuff for her out of the truck."

"I'll do that," I protested.

Rimmel shook her head. "No, you need to sit down. Go with Braeden."

I nodded and she went off in search of Prada.

Braeden grabbed an unopened bag of chips out of the cabinet and went into the living room. I trailed along behind him. On the way, Rimmel passed us with a wiggling puppy and slipped out the door.

"You're really gonna stay?" I asked.

"You really don't want me here?" he countered.

"I…"

He smirked. "Have a seat, Blondie. Let's watch a movie."

It was almost like a dare. Like he thought I couldn't just sit in the same room as him without trying to jump his bones or something.

What a douche!

I spied a totally girly movie on the table and picked it up. "Yes, let's."

His eyes narrowed. "Don't even think about putting that estrogen-saturated disc in the DVD player."

I fluttered my eyelashes at him.

"There's a thriller right there under it." He shoved three whole chips into his mouth.

He was so gross.

"I want to watch this one," I maintained.

"Yeah? Well, I want to see you naked and riding me, but we aren't gonna get what we want."

I gasped. My entire body flooded with awareness. The stark image of what he suggested filled my mind and my lower abdominal muscles contracted.

Wide-eyed, I gaped at him. Did he just admit he wanted me again?

He avoided my stare and tipped the beer up to his lips.

Rimmel padded into the room, the puppy at her heels and her cell in her hand. By the smile on her face, I would bet she talked to Romeo.

"How's Rome?" Braeden asked.

I still couldn't stop staring at him.

"He's good!" Rimmel replied. She sank down into a chair across from the couch and pulled the blanket off the back around her. "What are we watching?"

"This," Braeden said, getting up and snatching the thriller off the table. As he was putting it in, I noted the only other seat that faced the TV in here was on the couch, where Braeden was.

Great.

"Sit." Rimmel motioned and picked up her hot chocolate.

I busied myself setting a few things up for Prada, but when there was nothing left to do, I sat on the far end of the sofa, away from Braeden. I squished myself against the arm and pulled the only other available blanket around me like a shield. I still felt jittery from the accident. My nerves were totally shot.

The fifty hours of previews they put before every movie actually started playing across the screen and Braeden sat down once more.

"Ivy?" Rimmel said, concern written on her face. "Are you sure you're okay? You feeling sick or something from the accident?"

I felt Braeden's eyes as soon as he looked at me. The piercing dark gaze of his threatened to dissect me where I sat.

"You seem tense," Rimmel added.

I smiled at her. "I'm fine. Still just a little shaken up I guess."

"She'll be okay, tutor girl," Braeden said. The sweet nickname reminded me of what he called me not so long ago. "She just needs a distraction. Once the movie starts, she'll relax."

He reached up and clicked off the lamp beside him, and the room was plunged into darkness except for the flickering light of the television screen.

Reaching over, Braeden tugged some of the blanket down so it wasn't so tight around me. I glared at him and kicked out my foot, hoping to connect with his side.

He caught it with a silent smirk and wrapped his palm around my arch. Instead of shoving it back at me, he tugged it into his lap. Then he adjusted the blanket so it covered my foot and his hand.

I stared at him, my pulse kicking up. His thumb caressed the underside of my foot and chills raced up my spine. Even through my sock, I could feel his warmth.

I didn't pull away.

I left it there, just as his hand stayed where it was.

And I barely paid any attention to the movie on the screen.

CHAPTER TWENTY-SEVEN

BRAEDEN

The sound of soft whimpering aroused me from sleep.

I ignored it at first and burrowed farther down in the position I was sleeping in.

But it persisted, and it turned into a sound I couldn't ignore.

My eyes snapped open and I blinked against the darkness. I didn't know what time it was, but I knew it had to be very early in the morning. The room was nearly pitch black; the only illumination came from the dim light left on in the kitchen.

Rim had gone to bed hours ago, and I promised her I'd stay. Partly because I'd had a few beers and partly because I wasn't sure leaving both girls alone was a good idea. Especially after what Ivy had been through.

The sound cut through the silence again, and I jerked up out of the chair I was sleeping in. I thought maybe it was from the dog, but it wasn't. It was coming from Ivy.

From across the room, I could see her body shaking on the couch. Her blond hair was like a beacon in the dark, and her head tossed from side to side as she made whimpering noises of someone who was very frightened.

I pushed out of the chair and moved across the room.

"Don't touch me," she murmured. "Please, don't."

My blood ran cold. Clearly, she was having a nightmare, but just the sounds she was making and the words she was saying made it feel all too real to me as well.

"Ivy," I whispered. "Wake up."

She thrashed around a bit more, not hearing me. I took hold of her arms and spoke her name again.

She gasped and her eyes flew open. I knew right away she wasn't fully awake, that she didn't see me, but she felt my hands and she panicked. "No!"

I released her right away but knelt down beside the couch. "Ivy, it's Braeden. You're dreaming."

Her body stilled. I saw her blink and awareness slip in.

"Braeden?" she whispered.

"You were having a nightmare."

Her eyes squeezed shut and she shuddered.

"Hey," I murmured and reached for her again. This time she didn't panic when I touched her arm. "Wanna talk about it?"

"No." She rolled away from me, burying her face in a pillow. Her body was still trembling.

I cursed and stood. I started to walk away, but then I stopped and turned back. In one fluid movement, I picked her up off the couch, blanket and all.

Ivy gasped as I lay down on the cushions, taking her with me and tucking her along my body. She trembled a bit more, so I pulled at the blanket until it covered us. I thought she might protest or try and get away.

She didn't.

She curled her arm around my waist and sighed.

This was way more comfortable than the chair I just left.

"Thank you," she whispered.

"For what?"

"For everything you did tonight. Coming to get me. Helping me."

"If you need me, I'm gonna be there."

Her hand tightened at my side.

I pulled my fingers through her hair. The trembling in her limbs stopped and her breathing grew even. I thought she'd fallen back to sleep when she spoke.

"I wish things were different between us."

"I want you, Ivy," I confessed. It was like the words just wouldn't stay in anymore.

She lifted her head off my chest, and in the dark, I could see the whites of her eyes pointed right at me. "I want you, too," she whispered.

I lifted her so she was draped across my chest and took her face in my hands. She met me halfway, our lips pressing together.

It wasn't tentative at first. I knew exactly what I wanted. I kissed her like I'd been longing to do since we got on that plane in Florida. It was the kind of kiss I knew would lead to sex. She seduced me with her lips, so full and pliant. She yielded to me in every perfect way but gave it all back, matching my desire. When her tongue slid over my teeth, I growled like a lion and ripped my mouth away. I kissed down her neck, dragging my teeth as I went and sucking her supple flesh into my mouth.

She moaned quietly and her hands fisted in my shirt.

I released her face and slid my hands over the small of her back, pushing her T-shirt out of the way

● ● ●

and exploring the smooth skin of her lower back with my fingers as we started kissing again.

My hands caressed higher, beneath the fabric of her top, and I noticed she wasn't wearing a bra. My fingers glided down her sides and brushed against the side of her breasts where they were pressed against me.

I ripped my mouth away and tugged at her shirt. Because we were so plastered together, it wouldn't come off. I swung my legs over the couch and sat up, leaning back and allowing her to sit facing me in my lap.

When I started to pull the shirt over her head, she stopped me. "Rimmel," she whispered, looking toward the bedroom.

"We'll just have to be quiet," I murmured.

She dropped her hands, and I swept the top over her head to reveal creamy, perky breasts. Her nipples were hard already when I filled my hands with them and jolted forward to take one into my mouth.

Her head fell back, and I sucked her deeper. As her hips rocked a little on my lap, I grabbed her hip with one hand to encourage the movement.

I lavished attention to her breasts until she started panting and her nails dug into my shirt. Ivy started ripping at the fabric, so I tore it over my head and threw it beside us. She shoved me back against the couch and came forward to draw one of my nipples in her mouth.

Sighing, I buried my hands in her hair while she kissed and licked every inch of my chest. As she nipped at the underside of my jaw, her fingers deftly unfastened my jeans.

She pulled back, her hand caressing the bulge in my open pants. "I've never wanted anyone the way I want you."

"God, baby," I moaned. "Me either."

Ivy slipped off my lap and onto the floor between my legs. I helped her pull off my jeans and boxers, and when they were gone, she reached for my shaft.

The second her hand wrapped around the base, my stomach muscles spasmed. I tried to think of something else, something that might cool me down just a little so I didn't explode just then.

But I couldn't. Her lips wrapped around me and slid down, taking all my inches deep.

My fingers tangled in her hair as she worked my cock. The way she licked and sucked made me whisper a prayer. And her teeth… Most women would be too afraid to use their teeth to lightly run along a man's pulsing cock.

Yet she wasn't. She dragged them right over the tip and to the bottom, making me shudder.

When I seriously couldn't take it anymore, I pulled her up and yanked down the pajama bottoms she was wearing.

She glanced over the back of the couch, worrying if Rimmel was going to come out and catch us.

I pulled her into my lap. "It's just me right now. Only me."

"Oh, Braeden," she sighed. "It's been just you for a long time."

"Wrap your legs around me, baby," I whispered and sat up a little so she could do just that.

We were both completely bare, her slick, warm center teasing my hard and ready dick. She rubbed up against me, and I marveled in the bare contact for a moment before reaching for my jeans and pulling out a condom.

I slipped it on quickly, then lifted her hips so she could position herself above me. She looked like a fucking goddess on top of me; her curves were insane and her skin was so smooth. Ivy was perfection personified. I'd seen a lot of naked women, but none of them looked like her.

I fit my hands in the dips of her waist and guided her down over me. Inch by delicious inch.

Her teeth sank into her bottom lip and her eyes latched onto mine. I sat forward and tugged a nipple between my lips, sucking it deep. Her fingers dug into my back as she rocked a little, taking me in the rest of the way. I pulled back, unable to breathe from pleasure.

We stared at each other while I was buried inside her. Her inner walls clenched me tight, like she wouldn't ever let me go. Still holding her gaze, I reached between us and found her clit. It was already swollen and exposed. I used some of her juices to wet my finger and then circle around her the hardened bud.

● ● ●

Ivy shuddered.

She stroked my cheek unexpectedly, and I turned my face to kiss her palm. Grabbing the blanket beside us, I draped it around her shoulders. I wanted to see all of her, every last inch, but since we weren't really in private, I thought it was best to give her some modesty.

She started moving against me, and my head fell back on the couch. She licked up my neck as she rocked, making small, almost silent sounds of satisfaction as we made love.

Yeah, made love.

This wasn't sex. It was far too intense for that.

When I thought I might tumble over the edge, I grabbed her hips to stop her from rocking. "Not yet, baby. Not yet."

I sat up to kiss her, to tangle our tongues in an impossible puzzle. Twisting my hand around her hair, I kissed her until I felt lightheaded from lack of oxygen.

When I finally released her, she fell against my chest, spent.

But I wasn't done with her yet.

* * *

With one arm holding her close, I pushed the other down between us again. She trembled when I found her clit, and I smiled against her hair.

I rolled it between my finger and thumb, teasing it until she moved against me restlessly. Just when I knew she was at the edge, I drew back, grabbed her hips, and surged upward, pushing as deep as I could go. Her mouth opened, but no sound came out.

Ivy bore down on me and rode me until an orgasm broke over us both.

Her teeth sank into my shoulder as we shuddered, and when the tremors turned to deep breaths, her body was boneless in my arms.

I wrapped her up, holding her as tight as I dared.

"I always feel so safe with you," she whispered. Her voice sounded drunk.

My stomach tightened, but I pushed that feeling away. I wouldn't let anything come between us in that moment. Not even me.

"I'll always protect you, baby. I swear."

I wondered what I was gonna have to do to keep that promise.

She made a contented sound that made me feel like the most powerful man on Earth. Is this what the other side of just sex felt like? Is this what it was to have all this… emotion wrapped up with our bodies?

Well, damn.

There was no going back from this. This was the standard to which everything, everyone else would be measured. She was the one that no one else could compare to.

I held her for a long time. Until she drifted to sleep with me still inside her. Since I didn't know what time it was, I finally made myself lift her off. She made a sound of protest and tried to grab me back.

I chuckled and laid her on the couch, taking a moment to pull her shirt over her naked form. After I cleaned up, reluctantly I pulled on my boxers and jeans. I'd love to spend an entire night with Ivy in a bed with no clothes at all. All night. All naked.

She stirred and saw me looking at her and reached out a hand. I couldn't resist; I fitted myself on the couch with her practically covering my body. Her lips brushed over my jaw and then my cheek.

My heart turned over.

A little scratching sound and a mini whine came from the floor. Ivy giggled. "Prada."

"Hells no," I said. That rat was not coming up here.

"She's used to sleeping with me." She kissed the underside of my jaw again.

Picking up the tiny ball of fluff, I put her on the couch, and she wagged her tail. I told her to go to sleep.

Ivy giggled when Prada plopped herself in the center of my chest and lay down.

"Rat," I whispered.

The rat licked me.

Ivy giggled again. "She likes you."

"What about you?" I asked. "Do you like me?"

She thought for long minutes. "I think I still don't like you."

I grunted and palmed her ass. "Me either."

"Can we stay like this? Just for a little while?" she whispered.

"I'm not going anywhere."

She snuggled closer and sighed.

● ● ●

This was when a man knew he had it bad. I never cuddled. I never held women after sex. And I never let a rat dog plop its ass on me and go to sleep.

But here I was, smooshed and smothered by both.

Oddly, I'd never liked anything more.

CHAPTER TWENTY-EIGHT

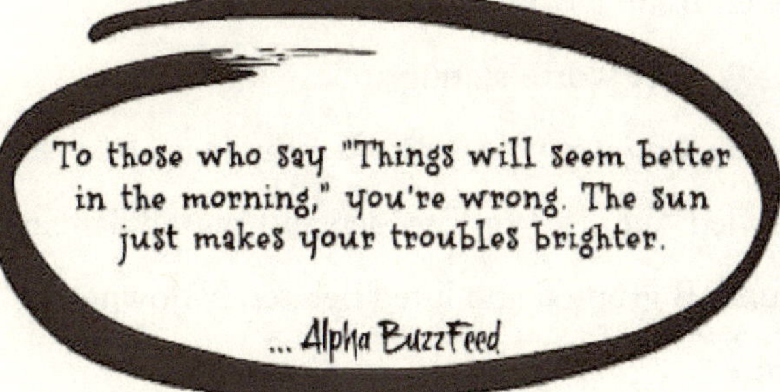

IVY

The sound of someone moving around in the kitchen woke me. I stretched a little and realized I wasn't alone. I cracked one eye open. Then the other.

Braeden was lying so close he was partially beneath me. His jaw was shadowed with stubble and his long black lashes swept against his cheeks as he slept.

I did it again.

● ● ●

I had sex with him. But it wasn't just sex. It was more, and it had been incredible. I lay there and stared at him, taking in his jaw, his neck, and the feel of him breathing beneath me.

"You're staring," he whispered. His voice was deeper in the morning.

"You're worth staring at."

Hearing our voices, Prada jumped up from her sprawled-out place on Braeden and started dancing around. B grunted and lifted her gently down onto the floor.

His hand slipped beneath the blanket and up the side of my leg. His fingertips flirted with the bare skin of my butt, and desire slammed into me hard.

Braeden lifted his head and came forward, capturing my lips in a soft morning kiss.

"I like waking up to you," he murmured.

Rimmel laughed from around the corner in the kitchen, and we both stiffened at once. How could we forget we weren't actually alone?

"Hang on, Murphy. Geez. You act like I never feed you," she said, laughter still in her voice.

"Ohmigod." My words rushed together.

He smiled and kissed my forehead. "Relax. She's in the other room."

"She's gonna see us. She'll know."

"Know what?" He turned his head, and dark eyes searched mine.

I knew he was asking something more than what I'd been implying. I wasn't ready for that yet.

"She'll know we did it," I whispered.

His chest vibrated beneath me with silent laughter.

"I have to get up." I rolled over him. I would have fallen on the ground, but his arm caught me. Instead, my feet swung around and I sat up beside him.

"Ivy." Braeden caught my hand when I tried to dive for my pants.

I stopped and looked over my shoulder.

He rose up onto his elbow. "You're beautiful."

I basked in the unexpected but totally welcomed compliment for a moment before rushing to throw on my pants and run my fingers through my hair.

I was standing near the couch (fully dressed, thank goodness) when Rimmel rushed by the doorway for the

* * *

room. She saw me there and stopped. If she seemed surprised Braeden was on the couch where I'd slept last night, she didn't say a thing.

"I'm taking this little girl out in the yard. Coffee's on!"

"You're my favorite sister!" Braeden yelled after her.

When she shut the door, it cut off her laughter. I blew out a breath. Braeden caught my hand. "I'll talk to her, okay?"

I knew he meant Rimmel.

I sat down on the coffee table in front of him. "I'm telling Missy."

"Good."

I was sort of surprised he was so nonchalant about it. He noticed and chuckled. "I told her there was never gonna be an us. I was kind of a douche about it."

My mouth fell open. "Why would you do that?"

"Because it's the truth." He shrugged and sat up. "And because I was in a shitty mood."

"When?" I demanded. Why hadn't she said anything to me about it?

"The night at the club. The night I thought you went home with Trent."

I gasped. "You did say he!" I knew it. But I hadn't realized he was there because he thought Trent was too.

He picked up his shirt and pulled it on.

"You were jealous," I whispered.

"I told you I didn't want you to go out with him."

"I told you I was."

He paused and pinned me with a dark, ominous stare. "And after last night?"

I looked away.

He caught my chin and made me look at him. "The thought of him touching you makes me crazy, Blondie."

I was secretly thrilled by that.

"What about you, Mr. Just For Fun?" I snapped.

He looked smug. "You jealous?"

I crossed my arms over my chest. "I don't like getting orders." I sniffed.

He flashed his teeth when he laughed. "I haven't been with anyone else since you."

"You know what they say…" I scoffed.

"No, what?"

"Once you go Ivy, you never go back."

He threw his head back and laughed. Then he caught me around the waist and tossed me on the couch. "Well, I really don't want him touching you then."

"We aren't together," I told him, all playfulness gone from my tone.

His jaw clenched and he rolled off me before standing. "I know that."

I shouldn't have said that. But it was the truth.

Rimmel stuck her head back inside the door, and Braeden grunted. "It's safe."

Prada barreled in the room and barked at me. Laughing, I scooped her up. "Let's get some coffee," I told her.

I gave Rimmel a sheepish look on the way into the kitchen.

She just smiled.

I heard them talking in the other room but didn't hear what they said. Glancing at the clock, I noted I had two hours before I had to be in class.

● ● ●

Braeden walked in the kitchen and grabbed the coffee I'd made for myself out of my hand. He took a sip and smiled. "Thanks, Blondie."

I narrowed my eyes.

"Rim's gonna drive me over to get your car. I'll bring it back here and then look it over."

"You mind if I use the shower while you're gone?" I asked Rim.

"Extra towels are on the counter," she replied.

I reached for my coffee, and Braeden snatched his hand away. "Get your own!"

I glared at him, but he didn't mind. He and Rimmel slipped on some shoes and left. The entire time, he was teasing her about driving the Hellcat.

When they were gone, I made myself another cup of coffee and went to shower.

I wondered what Rimmel would say to me when we were alone.

Funny, I wasn't worried about it anymore. Last night had been so satisfying I didn't have it in me to regret it.

• • •

CHAPTER TWENTY-NINE

BRAEDEN

"So you and Ivy?" Rimmel said the second we got in the Hellcat.

I was in the driver's seat because I figured I could spare the Cat some torture and at least drive one way to get Ivy's car. Rim would have to drive it back because I wasn't letting her drive a car I needed to make sure didn't have anything wrong with it.

I took a sip of the coffee—a woman who made good coffee and was good in bed? It might as well be Christmas!—then handed the mug to Rim.

I backed the Cat out of the driveway, aware of her staring daggers at me through her glasses the entire time.

"There is no me and Ivy," I finally said.

"Yeah, that looked like nothing this morning." She snorted. It was the most obnoxious sound. So obnoxious it was cute.

"You couldn't have seen much." I scratched the back of my head and silently replayed the sex we'd had last night on the couch. We'd been quiet… right?

"When I got up this morning, I walked into the living room. You two were wrapped around each other and Prada was in the center." She sighed. "It was so adorable. I almost took a pic."

"Tutor girl, you better not be taking pics of me when I ain't looking."

She gave me a sly smile. I wasn't sure I liked it. I thought about the weird Buzz notification that was on my phone when I looked this morning. Seemed the

Boss was gonna start plastering pics everywhere. I felt bad for the poor schmuck that was gonna be in them.

"Rimmel," I growled.

"Tell me!" she demanded.

I turned the corner, and Ivy's Corolla came into view. I had a flashback of how she looked standing there crying, tears soaking her skin. I'd driven this road a thousand times in my life and never realized how ominous it could look at night. Of course, it was daylight now and everything appeared peaceful and the way it always had.

I stopped the Cat near Ivy's car, reversed it, and turned it around—just trying to make it easier on my sis—and then shut off the engine.

"Be a good girl and put your books on the seat so you can see while the big kid goes and checks out Ivy's car for damage."

Rimmel stuck out her tongue at me.

Laughing, I tossed her the keys and got out. I heard her muttering about being too short to drive, and I smiled to myself as I rounded Ivy's car. Rimmel's bickering faded away as I focused solely on the car and the body. I checked the tires over first, mainly the front passenger one because that's where the deer hit the car. The tire seemed fine, the air level was stable, and the car sat level on the ground. The hazard light on that same side was cracked; it would need to be replaced. I could switch that out with just a simple trip to an auto store.

A dark smear of dried blood was on the broken part. I made a mental note to clean that off before I gave Ivy back the keys.

There was also a dent in the front quarter panel. I could probably pop that out as well with the correct tools. There didn't appear to be any scratching or damage to the paint. Her windshield wasn't cracked, and everything else seemed to be fine.

It was pretty much what I expected, but even so, I got in, started it up, and listened to it run. All the gauges looked good; the engine seemed to be running strong. She was almost out of gas, and I didn't like it. What if she stalled out somewhere? What if she got stranded? I mean, seriously, she needed to be more responsible.

I was gonna have to fill up the tank before I brought it back.

It was the only responsible thing to do.

I left it running and jogged over to the Hellcat where Rimmel was sitting in the driver's seat. "Aww, aren't you cute on those books," I teased her.

"Ha-ha."

"You good to go? You can make it back to Rome's, right? I'm just gonna drive this a few miles before I bring it back, make sure it's good."

Rimmel tilted her head. "She hit a deer, right?"

"Technically, it hit her."

"So I'm thinking the worst is a dent. Why wouldn't her car be running good?"

"I'm just making sure. You guys drive around in that thing a lot."

She smiled a smile I didn't like. I started shaking my head. She nodded. "You like her," she sang. "You're worried about her safety."

I glowered down at her and crossed my arms. "You done?"

"Are you kidding?" she cracked. "I could go for months on this."

"Rimmel," I growled, a large note of warning in my tone.

She didn't seem very threatened.

She sighed. "I'm happy. My BBFL and my best friend together? It's perfect."

"We aren't together," I said through clenched teeth. "This isn't a fairytale or some soap opera on TV."

"Because of Missy," she surmised.

"And because of me."

It took a couple minutes for her to connect the dots. When she did, she leapt out of the car. "That's why you never date girls? You're afraid—"

I cut her off. "Don't you have class?"

She narrowed her eyes. "I'm prepared to miss it."

You know it's serious when Miss Studious herself is willing to miss class.

"Look." I scrubbed a hand over my face. "Last night was…" *Really fucking hot,* my mind supplied, but this was my sister. I wasn't talking about my sex life with her. "It was."

Rimmel put me out of my misery. "I understand. You guys are still working it out."

I nodded because I didn't want to talk anymore.

"Can I just say one thing?"

"You will even if I say no," I pointed out.

She shrugged because she knew it was true. "Even before I saw you guys this morning, I knew something was up. I've seen the way she looks at you. I know you try to hide it, but I've seen the way you look at her."

"Rim,"

"I support you."

"What?" I don't know why, but that surprised me. First Rome and now Rim. I thought everyone would be against Ivy and me. Not only because of Missy, but because they all knew I would just screw it up and hurt her. Then our little group would fall apart.

"You both have been through some stuff. Some more recent than others. But I think you two can understand each other, maybe even balance one another out."

• • •

All I heard was we've both been through some stuff. "What stuff?"

"What?"

"What stuff has Ivy been through?" I demanded. I wanted to know.

Behind her glasses, Rimmel's eyes widened a bit.

"Some more recent than others. We both know my shit is long gone. So that means she's been through it recently. What the fuck don't I know?"

"It's really not my place to say."

I laughed, but it was a harsh, ear-splitting sound. "Are you kidding? You can't say that then tell me never mind. Might as well hand me a million dollars and tell me not to spend it."

"You could put it in the bank? Save it for later?" she offered meekly.

I gave her a look and clenched my jaw.

She started to wring her hands and fidget.

I relented. "Hey," I said gruffly, "I won't hurt you."

"I know." She smiled weakly. "But I don't like it when you get mad at me."

• • •

"I've never been mad at you before."

"Well, I don't like it."

I groaned. "How the hell does Romeo keep up with you?"

"I'm not telling someone else's secret," she maintained.

So it was a secret? Must be bad if Ivy didn't want anyone to know.

"It's cool, tutor girl." I motioned for her to get in the car, and she did quickly. She probably wanted to get away from me.

I shut the door and leaned in the open window. "You know I love ya, right?"

She smiled. "I know."

"I'm not mad at ya."

"I know."

"Don't rip the transmission out, okay?"

She snorted. "This car likes me."

I stepped back and watched her drive away. The poor Cat was practically crying as it went down the road.

• • •

I climbed back in Ivy's ride and adjusted the seat. Damn, she was short. I needed me some legroom. I drove the car to the nearest gas station and jogged inside to put some cash on the pump. As the tank was filling, I wondered about what Rimmel said.

Ivy's secret.

What the hell was she hiding?

CHAPTER THIRTY

IVY

The day dragged by.

Probably because of what I had planned once classes were finished for the day. It was something I dreaded, something I tried to talk myself out of every hour upon the hour. You would think I would welcome the way the day seemed to go on forever.

But I didn't.

I wanted to get this over with. I wanted to know where the pieces of my friendship with Missy would lie.

• • •

I was going to tell her about Braeden and me. That I somehow developed feelings for him. I was going to leave out spring break… and probably what happened last night. I didn't want to hurt her. I was also prepared to tell her—to promise—I wouldn't date him. I wouldn't act on the way I felt.

Okay, yeah, I guess it was kind of a lie.

But the way my stomach twisted the entire day, I knew looking her in the face and telling her I slept with him would just be too hard. I wasn't prepared for the look of betrayal on her face. I wasn't prepared to hurt her that way.

Still, I would be as honest as I could and hopefully she wouldn't hate me.

I had no idea if what I was doing was the right thing, the best thing. Yet in this moment, it was the only thing that felt right, and I had to abide by the way I felt.

However, if Missy asked me not to date him, I wouldn't.

Buds before studs.

It's the way it was going to be.

● ● ●

When my last class finally let out, I stepped out into the sunshine and pulled out my phone to text her.

WHERE U AT? NEED 2 TALK.

She replied seconds later.

GOING 2 DORM TO GET READY FOR PLAY PRACTICE.

OK. I'LL BE THERE IN A FEW.

☺

My last class was on the other side of campus from the dorm. I usually walked for the exercise, but today I'd driven. I didn't bother lying to myself about why. It's because Braeden drove my car this morning. He sat where I was sitting now.

Yes. I know. I was a total lame-o.

When I started the engine, I glanced at the fuel needle immediately and watched it rise all the way to the full line. He totally put gas in my car. When he brought it back to Romeo's, he tossed me the keys and said it was good to go. Then he promised to go get the

• • •

new light cover I needed so he could fix it this weekend.

Before he left, he gave me a hard look and told me… No, he ordered me to pay better attention to the gas levels and not let it get so low.

I told him he was stupid.

I didn't realize he filled it until I got in and started it up. Most girls got flowers, candy, and jewelry.

I got gas.

But damn, if it didn't feel like the most romantic thing anyone could ever do.

Missy opened her door almost the second after I knocked and waved me inside. I looked around the standard dorm room even though I'd seen it a thousand times.

"Where's the roomie?" I asked. Her roommate, Janelle, kept her side of the room neat and tidy. The bed was draped with a white spread with multi-colored flowers all over it. Her bookshelf and mini desk near her headboard were organized and all the books were lined up by size. Her pink tote full of shower supplies was in its own little space, and not even one shirt was lying around on the bed.

"Still at class," Missy replied. "Hey, would you mind braiding my hair back? I want to keep it out of my way tonight at rehearsal."

"Of course!" I replied and plopped down on her bed. It was made, but not as meticulously as Janelle's.

Missy had a gray comforter with white polka dots and yellow sheets. She had a ton of furry white and gray pillows and a few yellow-and-white chevron-patterned ones. Her desk and bookcase were cluttered with papers and pictures. In the center was her closed MacBook that was also gray with a yellow apple in the center. The walls on her side of the room had movie posters and playbills from plays she'd watched all taped up. And of course there were clothes thrown around. Every girl who truly loved style had clothes tossed about. It made it easier to put outfits together.

A brush appeared before me and so did a couple hair ties. I set them beside me and motioned for Missy to sit on the floor. She was wearing a pair of flowy, wide-legged pants with a blue-and-white paisley design all over them. Near the hem, the design changed to something thicker, creating more interest around her ankles. I loved pants like that. I looked at them all the time on the Internet, but I didn't own any. I wasn't tall enough or thin enough to wear them. In fact, when I tried on a pair, I looked like a clown.

Since I had no plans to join the circus, I sent them back.

Her simple white top was tucked in, and she accessorized with an oversized white watch, blue earrings, and a long silver chain with a lime-green glass pendant on the end.

"So how's rehearsal going?" I asked as I brushed through her silky, dark hair.

"Really great. I think the play is going to be awesome."

"Of course it will, because you're in it." I separated her hair into three thick strands to begin the braid. "I already bought my ticket for opening night."

"You're a good friend," she said, and I felt like I swallowed a bunch of fire ants.

As I braided I added in more hair to each section, weaving the strands together to create a tight, neat braid.

"So what do you want to talk about?" she asked when I said nothing.

"Um," I hedged.

"Is everything okay?" she pressed.

"I'm not really sure," I admitted. "I'm actually really worried you're going to be upset with me."

She gasped and tried to turn, but I held her head tightly to stop her. "Almost done," I murmured as I braided the length down her back. When it was done I secured the end with a hair tie and then made sure I had all the hair braided back.

"Okay." I tapped her shoulder when I was done.

"Thanks." She turned around on the floor, still sitting so she could face me. "Why would you think I'd be mad at you?"

"Because I violated the girl code."

Her phone went off on her desk. My phone went off in my bag.

"I'm sure whatever it is isn't as bad as you think." Missy leaned up and grabbed her cell to pull it down into her lap.

Just blurt it out! I told myself.

"Missy, I have feelings for B—"

She gasped before I could even get the sentence out. I winced, because if she was this mad before I said it, I could only imagine…

Wait.

She wasn't looking at me. She acted like she wasn't even listening. Her eyes were downcast as she stared at her phone. I noticed the tight grip she had around it.

"What is it?" I asked.

Slowly, her eyes lifted to me. "The notification."

I groaned. "Who did the BuzzBoss tattle on now?" I dug my phone out of my bag and lit up the screen. I read the words and winced. "Well, that's harsh," I muttered as I tapped the *view image* icon.

My blood ran cold.

Like my body temperature dropped from all the ice in my veins. I sat there frozen, so beyond horrified that my body went numb.

But my eyes still worked.

It was the only time in my life I would wish I was blind.

Memories, dreams, nightmares assaulted me. It was like finding a missing piece of a puzzle or thrown-out footage from a bad horror film.

"Ivy," Missy gasped.

I blinked, hoping the picture wouldn't be there when I looked again.

It was.

There I was, filling up the cellphone screen. And I wasn't alone.

Zach was with me.

We were both naked, bare-chested and in bed. I didn't remember this. And now I was glad I never had.

His dark, overly styled hair still looked perfect, like maybe he'd fixed it for the picture. He was wearing a smug smile, like he was thoroughly satisfied.

I wasn't so camera ready.

I looked almost passed out. But my eyes were open, so I must have been awake. I was looking up at the camera, almost with no expression. My hair looked a mess, like we'd been rolling around in the bed for hours. Who knows? Maybe we were.

My makeup was smeared and… I shut my eyes. I couldn't look at it anymore.

He took a picture.

A selfie.

How could I not have known about this? And how did the BuzzBoss get it?

"You slept with Zach?" Missy asked, getting up from the floor.

"Oh my God," I moaned, wrapping my arm around my stomach. I felt like I might throw up.

"When was this?" Missy pressed.

"A while ago. It's how he got access to Rimmel's laptop."

Missy gasped. "Does Rimmel know?"

"Yes. She doesn't blame me."

"Of course she doesn't." Missy wrapped her arm around my shoulder. I stared down at the floor, trying to make sense of what I just saw.

"Is this what you needed to talk about? I can't imagine carrying around such a big secret for so long."

"It was a mistake. I was so drunk."

"I'm so sorry. I should have been a better friend that night." Missy hugged me.

"This is no one's fault but mine."

"And the BuzzBoss," Missy added. "I can't believe he posted this! The dean is gonna go postal."

Oh God. Practically the whole campus would see this. They would all know.

I leapt up, panic surging through my body. The whole thing with Zach had been huge gossip around campus. Everyone followed the story because he was relentless in torturing Romeo and Rimmel. Everyone was so relieved when he got sent away.

But obviously, he wasn't far enough. Because he was still wreaking havoc.

This time it was on me.

Braeden was going to see this. He would know.

"I have to go," I said, frantic.

"Where are you going? Want me to come with you? I'll skip rehearsal."

I shook my head. "No. I need to be alone." I rushed to the door, the phone still gripped in my hand.

I was on the verge of hysteria. Everybody on campus was going to see me half naked in bed with Zach.

Yet I wasn't worried about everybody.

I was mostly worried about one.

CHAPTER THIRTY-ONE

BRAEDEN

The campus was buzzing about something.

Everywhere I looked, people were holding up their phones, pointing at the screens, and laughing.

But it was the catcalls that got me really curious. I reached for my phone to see if I could figure out what everyone was looking at just as it went off in my hand.

I glanced down to see a text from Romeo fill the screen.

PLEASE TELL ME YOU DIDN'T SEE IT.

The back of my neck prickled a little. Jolts of warning shot down my spine.

SEE WHAT?

B, TAKE MY ADVICE. DON'T LOOK AT YOUR NOFICATIONS.

WAVE A RED FLAG WHY DON'T YA? I typed back.

I mean, really, you can't tell a guy not to look at something and expect him to listen.

I'M SERIOUS. LOOK, I'M ON MY WAY BACK. WILL BE THERE IN A FEW HOURS. JUST… HOLD IT TOGETHER.

Now that got me worried. Why did he seem so concerned I was here and he wasn't?

You know what I had to do.

I backed out of the messages and pulled up the latest notification.

Aaannnd that was why Rome was freaking out.

Ivy was naked.

Ivy was in bed.

Ivy was with the fucking lowest life form on this planet.

She fucking screwed him.

I took in her messy hair, her smeared makeup, and that shit-eating grin on Zach's face. It was almost like he was taunting me. Only me.

Rage consumed me so wholly I lost a few minutes. When reality came crashing back, I was standing in the parking lot near my truck with a heaving chest.

I glanced down and saw blood. My knuckles were ripped open and raw. I had no idea how they got that way.

And where the fuck was my cell?

I glanced around, noting that people were watching me from a safe distance and a car alarm was going off not too far away.

The window was shattered.

I glanced back at my hand. There was glass in it.

Well, that explained that.

And my cell phone? It lay at my feet, shattered into a million unusable pieces.

Someone was hurrying by me, trying to go unnoticed, but they didn't succeed. I grabbed him by the book bag and hauled him close.

He muttered something pathetic, but I didn't hear him. My head was filled with deafening noise.

"You know who I am?" I growled.

The kid nodded.

"Good. Tell the owner of that car to bill me."

He stared at me with fear in his eyes.

"You hear me?"

"Y-yes."

I shoved him away, and he took off running. I left my cell lying on the pavement and got in my truck. I don't remember the drive to the dorms. I knew I shouldn't be driving at all, but fuck, I shouldn't be doing a lot of things. Like punching in windows, breaking five hundred-dollar phones…

And I definitely shouldn't be storming into the girls' dorm.

As I stalked to the door, one of the girls who lived there took one look at me, rushed to open the door, and cowered until I was through.

I took the stairs three at a time and landed in front of Ivy's door. I beat on it, not even feeling the pain in my glass-littered hand. "Open this door!" I yelled.

• • •

People in the rooms nearby opened their doors to stare.

"So help me God, I will kick it in!"

The door swung open, but no one was in the doorway.

I walked in and slammed it behind me.

Ivy was pressed up against the wall so she would be behind the door when it opened. Just looking at her made me want to hit something again.

"Where's the rat?"

"At Romeo's still." Her voice was gravelly and low. I barely noticed.

I barely noticed anything. All I could see was her naked body in bed with Zach.

"This where it happened?" I spat and pointed at the bed. "You bring him back here and let him touch you?"

"Braeden, stop." Her voice quivered.

I jolted forward and slammed both hands against the wall on either side of her head. "You were naked. With him."

She started crying. Her chin dipped on her chest and hid her face from view. Her body shook and trembled as she tried to keep the sounds of her sobs inside.

But I could hear.

"How could you do it?" I demanded. "How could you let that scum into your body?"

She ducked under my arm and rushed away from me. Even though her back was turned, I saw her wiping furiously at her face, trying to get the tears to stop.

I sucked in a deep breath, trying to calm down, but I just couldn't.

"Say something!" I demanded.

She swung around. I noticed for the first time how terrible she looked. Pale, blotchy skin, bloodshot, puffy eyes, and red lips from chewing them. "What do you want me to say, Braeden?" she cried. "You want me to deny it? I can't."

She dashed a tear off her face.

"Everybody can see it happened." Her voice quaked. "No one was supposed to know."

I rubbed a hand over my face. "What must Rimmel be thinking?"

"She knows."

I glanced up. "What?"

"Romeo too."

There came the rage again. I paced the room, tearing around in circles. Romeo knew. He knew about Ivy and Zach. He knew about Ivy and me, yet he still said nothing. I felt betrayed on all fronts.

Family.

Friends.

The girl I—

"Fuck!" I yelled.

"What happened to your hand?"

"I punched a car," I growled.

"You're an idiot." She started rummaging around her desk for something.

"You're a slut."

She jerked like I slapped her. Her entire body locked up and she swung around woodenly. She had a first aid kit in her hand. It fell to the floor with a soft thud.

• • •

"Get out," she growled.

"Ivy," I began and stepped forward.

She took a step back. "Get out right now or I swear to God I will start screaming bloody murder."

I stormed out into the hallway, shocked it was empty and silent as a tomb. Bitches were probably all standing around with their ears pressed to their doors.

I slammed Ivy's door so hard the door to the room next to hers rattled. As I started to leave, the pain in my hand finally starting to sink in.

A low sound stopped me in my tracks.

She was crying again.

Deep, wrenching sobs muffled by the walls.

I put my hand on the door, suddenly feeling like the world's largest ass.

The bloody mess that were my knuckles caught my attention. It served as a reminder.

Of why exactly I shouldn't be here. Of why exactly I never should have gotten involved with Ivy at all.

I walked away and didn't look back.

CHAPTER THIRTY-TWO

#EveryoneWantsToKnow
How low do your standards have to be to sleep with the campus crazy?
#HopeSheGotTested
... Alpha BuzzFeed

IVY

People stared.

They whispered.

They laughed.

I thought this stuff only happened in high school.

In the movies or in books. I was too old for this kind of thing, wasn't I?

Weren't we all?

Yet here I was in the center of a terrible hate campaign, an Alpha U scandal no one could get enough of.

I was ashamed.

I was embarrassed.

I wanted to hide in my room.

But mostly… mostly I was pissed off.

How dare anyone judge me? How dare someone take a nude picture of me and put it up for the world to see. It was easy to judge others when their own skeletons remained safely locked away.

I had no idea how the picture got to the BuzzBoss, but I guess it didn't matter. The damage was done. I was the campus pariah. I was a slut.

Oh, and I probably had some raging STD.

And did you hear (Gasp!)? I got pregnant, then had a horrific miscarriage when Zach found out and pushed me down a flight of stairs.

No matter how badly I wanted to hide in my dorm or at Romeo's place—away from campus entirely—I didn't.

I still went to every class. I grabbed food at the food court but took it back to my room. I still went to the gym, and I held my head high.

Most of the time, I felt like the only thing that held me together was sheer will and a little dollop of not wanting to let the haters win. Most nights, I cried myself to sleep. When I did manage sleep, I'd dream about Zach, that horrible picture, and what we'd done.

Rimmel was behind me one hundred percent. People wondered how she could be. I mean, technically, I was the reason she was almost kicked out of school. And while Rimmel might be labeled a hashtag nerd, she was a popular one. She was number twenty-four's choice. She suffered incredibly at the hand of Zach. Her and Romeo both.

You think people would see she was still friends with me, that she was on my side, and it would make them stop and think, *Hey, maybe there was more to the story than we know. Maybe if Rimmel and Romeo could forgive her, it's not that big of a deal.*

But Rimmel was way too nice, and Romeo hadn't really come out and said he supported me. It would go a long way if he did, but I wasn't going to ask. I didn't deserve it. I made a choice, and now I was living with it.

Raging STD and all.

(Note: I really don't have an STD. I got tested after it happened. I'm clean and healthy.)

I actually hadn't seen Romeo at all since the picture went viral. I knew he was back. He actually came back a little early. Prada was still at his place with Rimmel. We thought since I was being scrutinized and watched so much on campus, it would be better if Prada wasn't here. The dorm room could be surprise inspected at any time.

I missed her.

I told myself it was better this way because I wasn't going to be able to keep her anyway. Maybe it was better if I just let her go now instead of getting more and more attached.

In fact, I was starting to think maybe it was time to move on from Alpha U entirely. Finals were almost here, the semester almost over. Summer break would be here, and I could go home, enroll in a college in North Carolina, and start over.

No Alpha Buzzfeed, no party girl reputation, no Zach.

No Braeden.

I had no idea how he was. I didn't see him. He didn't call. I didn't ask Rimmel about him.

The way he'd looked at me like I was so, so disappointing… That hurt worse than him calling me a slut.

Thank goodness it was the weekend. Since I didn't have class, I could hide for a couple days. Maybe by Monday, this whole thing would blow over.

I snorted (I learned it from Rimmel). Yeah right. This would blow over when money grew on trees.

I threw myself onto my bed and stared at the wall.

A knock sounded at the door.

At first I thought it was just for the girls next door, but then the person knocked again. So far, everyone had been leaving me alone when I was in my room. I hoped that wasn't about to change now.

I opened the door cautiously, like on the other side was some brain-eating zombie.

When I saw who it was, my mouth dropped open.

"Hey," Romeo said, shifting his bag on his shoulder.

"Hey."

The corner of his mouth kicked up. "You gonna let me in?"

"Rimmel isn't here."

"I know. I'm here to see you."

I opened the door and motioned for him to come in. Before I closed the door, I noticed several girls watching curiously. Out of spite, I waved and then shut the door.

Romeo had his bag on Rimmel's bed, and when he turned around, he was holding Prada. I rushed forward and scooped her up. She wiggled and wagged her tail happily, peppering my face with kisses.

I talked to her in a baby voice for a while, until I realized Romeo was watching me in amusement.

I set Prada on the floor and she rushed to my slipper, the one she loved to attack, and started pouncing on it.

"Thanks for bringing her to see me," I said, awkward.

"You know you can come to my place and see her."

"I wasn't sure…" My voice fell away.

"That you were still welcome?" he asked, lifting a brow.

"Well, yeah."

"You are."

I nodded and sat on the edge of my bed. "Thanks."

"I'm just gonna cut to the chase here, Ivy. Talking in circles isn't my style, and from the looks of you, you ain't up for it either."

"Gee, thanks," I muttered.

"You've looked better." He shrugged like it was no big deal.

Prada came over and sat at my feet, looking up at me expectantly. I lifted her onto my lap.

"I know things with us kind of started out awkward," he began.

"You were suspicious of me. You thought I was using Rimmel."

He looked me in the eye. "Yeah. I did. But I was wrong."

I gasped. "A man who actually admits when he's wrong? Is today the apocalypse?"

He chuckled and flashed his perfectly white teeth. "You've been a good friend to Rimmel, and I appreciate that. But beyond that, I've noticed you've changed. Like you decided you didn't want to be who you were anymore."

"No, this is who I am," I said, then grimaced. "Well, not this right here." I motioned to myself. "I can look better."

He laughed.

"On the inside, I've always been this girl. But I was posing as someone different. Someone I wasn't proud of and don't want to be."

"I get it," Romeo said. "I can understand how people are defined by labels. How they get caught up in their image and it gets out of hand. I've been there. Rimmel is the one who sort of pulled me back from that. She showed me there are more important things in life than being who everyone wants you to be. Who everyone thinks you are."

I nodded.

"I respect you, Ivy, and I like you. Not just because of Rimmel, but because I've gotten to know you."

Tears pricked the backs of my eyes and I blinked them back, focusing on Prada and stroking her fur. "Thanks for telling me that."

"You've got my support. Anyone gives you problems, you call me. I'll take care of it."

I smiled wistfully. "You gonna beat up everyone who calls me a slut?"

His bright-blue eyes narrowed. "If I have to."

"Even your best friend?"

"Braeden runs hot, Ivy. He says shit sometimes he don't mean."

"Oh, I think he meant it."

"You're wrong."

His voice was so sure that it gave me hope.

"The fact you got him so out of control says a lot about the way he feels about you. I'm not saying its right, because it isn't. But that's just B."

* * *

I couldn't not ask. I had to know. The image of his bloody hand still bothered me. I wanted to clean it up, bandage it, but when he said that word, when he basically agreed with the BuzzBoss, I couldn't. "How is he?" I whispered.

"Just like you, he's looked better."

I nodded and stood, cradling Prada. "Thanks for coming over."

"Why don't you come to my place, hang with us tonight?"

"Oh, no—"

"Get your stuff," he said, talking over me so I didn't have a choice. "You can get up at three a.m. and put this dog out to pee." He scrubbed a hand over his face. "My life is overrun by animals and women," he muttered.

I laughed. He was a good guy. A lot better than most people realized.

I never realized it, but he and I had more in common than I ever would have guessed. "I think he needs you more than I do right now," I whispered.

He knew I meant Braeden.

• • •

"You should talk to him."

"No."

"His head is messed up. I can't fix it this time. Only you can."

I hesitated.

"Come to the scrimmage tomorrow night. Talk to him. Show him and everyone else the BuzzBoss is an asshole."

Going around all those people was the last thing I wanted to do. It was asking for rumors and nasty looks.

"He needs you, Blondie."

It wasn't lost on me he used the name only Braeden ever called me.

"I'll think about it."

"Works for me." He motioned for me to get moving, so I did. After he tucked Prada back in his bag, we went out into the hall.

Girls were standing around, looking like they hung out in the hall all the time. Uh-huh. Sure they did. A whisper rippled through the group, and I lifted my chin.

• • •

"Ladies," Romeo said, sounding charming as ever, and pushed his hand through his blond, messy hair. "Y'all are looking fine."

They giggled.

I mentally rolled my eyes. They gave a bad name to women everywhere.

"Better not get too close," one of the bolder girls warned him. "Word is she's got some nasty cooties from Zach."

I stiffened.

Romeo draped an arm across my shoulders and pulled me to his side. "What is this, kindergarten? I'm pretty sure I've seen half of you doing the walk of shame all over this campus. I'm sure if I tried hard enough, I could find some pictures as proof."

Suddenly, the room grew uncomfortable.

"Ivy's family. You know what that means?"

They shifted around nervously.

"It means she might not bite back, but I will, and my bite is a hell of a lot deeper." Romeo had this way about him. This quiet intimidation he emitted without even having to try. It's one of the reasons he earned the title of campus alpha.

A couple girls went in their rooms and shut their doors.

Romeo kept his arm around me all the way until my car came into view. Now I knew how Rimmel must have felt, because everyone stopped and stared. Of course, maybe it was at me and not him.

"I can drive you," he offered, but I shook my head.

"Thanks, but I'll drive myself." In case I needed to leave.

I walked around the side so I could put my stuff in the passenger seat.

I noticed right away and stood their rooted in place.

The damage to my car was completely fixed. No more cracked light cover, no more dent in the side. I glanced at Romeo. "You fixed my car?"

"Not me," he said, a knowing tone in his voice.

Braeden fixed my car. Even after everything, he fixed it.

I glanced at Romeo again. He clapped me on the shoulder. "Talk to him, Ivy."

I wanted to. I wanted to hear his voice desperately, even more so now.

But what if Romeo was wrong? What if he didn't want to see me?

What if he did?

CHAPTER THIRTY-THREE

#InterestingFact
Romeo has put his protection on the #slut.
His threat is real. I'm not worried. Can't
retaliate on someone you don't know.
#SecretIdentity

... Alpha BuzzFeed

BRAEDEN

I called her a slut.

And then I fixed her car.

Was it my way of apologizing? I wasn't sure.

I was so twisted up inside I could barely think.

After I left her dorm that night, I drove around for

hours. I knew Rimmel was probably worried, but I was

scared to be around her in the mood I was in.

I went back to my dorm and picked the glass out of my hand. It was pretty fucked up, but I barely paid attention to it. I passed out on my bed while my roommate tiptoed around like he was scared I would go off again.

I might.

I felt it simmering just beneath my skin.

It was like a sickness my body was trying to fight off, but it didn't matter how high my fever got, the threat remained the same.

This was what I was always afraid of. Losing control like I did. Taking my anger out on people who didn't deserve it and hurting someone.

I hurt Ivy. I saw it on her face and heard it in her voice. There she was, destroyed and crying, but she thought of me. She picked up a first aid kit, fully intent on cleaning out my hand.

I opened my big fat mouth and ruined it.

I slung the most hurtful thing I could at her. How did I know that word would scratch like no other? I just did, just as I knew if I saw Zach, I'd kill him.

It was good the little pecker was locked up.

* * *

I woke up early the next morning to someone beating on my door. I covered my head with a pillow and rolled over, but my roommate answered.

The pillow was flung off my head and hit the floor. I blinked and saw Rome standing over me with an angry expression on his face.

"Why haven't you been answering your cell?"

"Busted it."

"Do you have any idea how worried sick Rimmel is?"

I turned my back.

His hands were rough when he yanked me off the mattress. I came up swinging and caught him in the side.

"That's the only free hit you'll get from me," Romeo growled.

"You knew," I snarled and swung at him again.

I hit him in the jaw, and his head snapped back on his shoulders.

"Why didn't you tell me!" I demanded.

He nailed me back, hitting me in almost the same spot. We both stared at each other with chests heaving and rubbed at the spots on our jaws.

"Because it doesn't matter," he spat.

"You know better than that," I ground out between clenched teeth.

I prepared to deliver another punch, not worried about the cost. Romeo snatched my wrist in the air and looked at the mess I'd made of my hand.

"Goddammit, B."

After that, he forced me into the Cat and drove to his place. Rimmel alternated between lectures and hugs the entire time she cleaned it up and bandaged the worst of the cuts.

Rome and I didn't talk. We went to the gym and worked out. I ran as the image of Ivy and Zach spurred me on. I ran until I was too tired to run anymore.

After I showered and promised Rome I wouldn't do anything stupid, I went and bought a new phone. I'd lost all my contacts, all my pics.

I didn't care.

But I did think about that selfie. The one of Ivy and me. How was I any better than Zach? I'd slept with her too and took a pic to prove it.

It was gone now. I should have deleted it in the first place. Sometimes I looked at it. Late at night when I was lying in bed and my thoughts wouldn't let her go.

I heard the rumors flying around campus, knew the BuzzBoss was dragging Ivy through the mud. I wanted to go to her, but I didn't know what to say or how to say it.

Instead, I drove to my mom's. I didn't know how to make things right with Ivy, but I could make things right with her. I hadn't been back since the night we all had dinner, the night my father called and I stormed out.

I'd been doing a lot of that lately.

Mom tried to call a couple times. I either let it go to voicemail or picked up and shut the conversation down.

No more. I parked in the driveway, the entire time staring at the strange car parked at the street in front of the house. It was a black BMW, one that wasn't familiar. I keyed in the code on the garage door and walked in.

The second I stepped into the kitchen, I felt my upper lip curl.

There was a man sitting at the table. Someone I'd never seen before. Mom was at the stove, cooking something that smelled pretty damn good. When she heard me, she turned with surprise on her face.

"Braeden. I wasn't expecting you."

Well. Obviously not.

"Who the hell are you?" I barked.

"Manners!" Mom cracked. I felt like a little boy all over again. "You do not speak like that in this house, young man."

"Sorry," I muttered.

The man at the table smiled jovially, like we were entertaining. When I glared at him, he wiped the smile off his face and stood. "Braeden, I'm John Turner. I'm a friend of Caroline— uh, your mom's."

He held out his hand, and I stared at it.

Mom cleared her throat.

I shook it. When I pulled my hand away, she noticed my bandages. "What happened to your hand?" she gasped.

"Nothing. Just an accident." My eyes never left John. I measured him as we stood there. I was bigger. I'd be lying if I said that didn't make me a little giddy.

"John, would you mind if I talked to Braeden alone for a few moments?" Mom asked.

"Sure. I'll just go in the other room and watch TV." He glanced at me. "Nice to finally meet you."

Finally?

When he was gone, I looked at Mom with a raised brow. "Are you sleeping with him?"

"Braeden James Walker, I will wash your mouth out with soap!" She waved the spatula around in the air between us.

I amended my previous statement. "Are you dating?"

She deflated and moved the pan off the heat before sitting down at the table. "I could never find a right time to tell you."

"How long?" I asked. I wasn't sure how I felt about this.

"For several months now. I was going to tell you when you came home from spring break, but then your father started calling and it seemed like a bad time…"

"So that's why you had so much food when I came over. It was for him."

"For you, too," she said gently. "I do know how you love your sprinkles."

I grunted. "I do."

She smiled and busied herself by putting some huge scoops of vanilla ice cream in a bowl. When she was done, she dumped half a bottle of chocolate sprinkles on top. In the other room, the TV was loud. He was watching *SportsCenter*.

At least he had that going for him.

"You look like you could use this." She set the bowl in front of me.

It definitely wouldn't hurt. I picked up the spoon and shoved a huge bite in my mouth. The sprinkles were a little crunchy, a little soft, and added some flavor to the vanilla. "Oh yeah," I murmured and ate another huge bite.

"Why don't you tell me why your hand looks like you've been punching stuff?"

"Because I have."

"Is this about your father?"

I dropped my spoon. "He call again?"

She glanced away. I braced myself and ate another bite of sprinkles. "I won't lose it."

"He's called several times. He's very anxious to speak with you."

"I don't want to talk to him."

"I know, and I don't blame you. And normally, I would tell you not to, but I think you should."

I gaped at her.

She laughed lightly. "Not for his benefit, but for yours. This is clearly holding you back, Braeden. You need to look this in the face so you can move on, or it will haunt you for the rest of your life."

"How can you sit there and be so calm about him?"

"I made my peace with your father a long time ago. He took so much from me in the past, from both of us. I refused to let him have my future." She looked at me intently. "He's taking your future, son."

She was right. He was destroying my future, and I was allowing it. I rubbed a hand over the back of my neck. "How the hell do you know all this?"

She smirked. "I'm your mother. I know everything."

"After everything he did…"

"I know." She sat forward and placed her hand over mine. "I know better than anyone. And you were so small. I'm very afraid it scarred you for life." Tears filled her eyes. "That's the one thing I will never forgive myself for."

"You didn't do anything wrong, Mom."

"It was my job to protect you."

"And you did. Way more times than I wish you would have."

Mom wiped at her eyes and then touched my cheek. "You are truly the best thing that's ever happened to me. I'm so proud of you. I hope you know how much I love you."

"I don't think you'd be too proud of me lately." I pulled away and sat back.

"I'll always be proud of you. But I really hope you didn't punch something that can't be fixed."

I laughed. "It was a window. I'm paying to have it repaired." I was gonna have to work extra hours this summer at whatever job I managed to get to put the money back into my savings.

"Is this about a girl?"

"Why would you think that?" I asked.

She smiled. "Because men only get that riled up about two things. Women and money."

"I screwed up," I admitted.

"Can it be fixed?"

"I got involved with friends. Best friends."

"And you like one better?"

"I don't like her," I muttered.

Mom smiled. "I see. Well, she sounds very special."

I laughed.

"Sounds to me like you ruined a good thing before it could get started."

I listened and wanted to disagree, but maybe she was right.

"You are not your father, Braeden. I know it as well as you love chocolate sprinkles. Get out of your own way and bring that girl here to meet me."

The thought of Ivy and my mom ganging up on me made me groan.

"That guy in there…" I cocked my head to the side. "He makes you happy? He's good to you?"

"He makes me very happy. I hope you won't try to run him off."

"I thought about it."

She smacked me. "John is a good man and he's been wanting to get to know you, but I wasn't sure if you were ready."

"I just want you to be happy."

"I am, but I won't ever be totally happy until you are."

I shoved the rest of the ice cream and sprinkles in my mouth as she watched. A few minutes later, John appeared around the corner. "Is it safe?"

"Yeah, come on in." I pushed away from the table and stood. "I gotta go, Mom, but thanks for everything."

"You want to stay for dinner?" she asked.

"Can't. Scrimmage tonight."

"Maybe we can come watch?" she asked.

I glanced at John; he was nodding.

"You like football?" I asked.

"Does a cow have tits?"

"John!" Mom gasped.

I grinned. "It's at the outdoor field later on. I won't be able to come by after because we have the bonfire."

"We'll cheer you on from the stands."

I kissed her cheek and then held my hand out to John. I gripped it firm. "I have a shovel," I said. "There's lots of places a body won't be found around here."

"Braeden James!" Mom yelled.

John just nodded. "Understood."

The minute I got in the truck, my phone went off. I tensed, wondering what it would say this time. When I got my new phone, I was sorely tempted to not download the Alpha App, but I did. I hated the stuff being spread around, but I needed to know so I could be prepared.

This Buzz was about Rome. Apparently, he was now protecting Ivy.

Oh, hells no.

No one protected my girl but me.

CHAPTER THIRTY-FOUR

IVY

It was the first time I'd ever been to a bonfire sober.

Now I kind of understood why Rimmel never came to these things when I asked her. I was surrounded by drunk idiots. I used to be just like these people. It also didn't help that I was totally uptight about everything.

I didn't want to be here. Just like I hadn't wanted to go to the scrimmage game. But Romeo and Rimmel asked, and well… I wanted to see B.

Even if it was from afar.

The game had been fun, probably because I got to sit on the sidelines with Rimmel and Romeo. He didn't play because his arm was still healing, and his therapists and Knights trainer didn't want him to risk messing up the healing that was going so well. Because he was the quarterback, and because this was his send-off from the Wolves, he of course sat on the field.

But Rimmel and I did, too.

No one seemed to think anything of it. Not the team anyway.

I got some looks from some of the cheerleaders and from the people in the stands, but I ignored it. Rimmel and I laughed and tried to have fun as we watched the game. It was a beautiful spring night, barely a chill in the air at all.

The team played awesome—as usual. Of course, there was one player I watched more than the others. Okay, I watched him the entire time. Braeden had always been a good football player, and tonight was no different.

I did notice he was a little rougher, he acted a little more on edge, and some of the guys on the other team gave him a wide berth.

I knew it was my fault.

Missy wasn't at the game. She was at rehearsal but meeting us here at the bonfire. I still hadn't told her. With the picture of Zach and me, I just couldn't bear it. I was already ashamed enough. I knew I was gonna have to say something soon, but maybe not tonight.

Just being at this bonfire was enough to fray my nerves. A drink would likely mellow me out a little, but I didn't dare. I wanted a clear head because I never knew when mud would be slung at me.

I wasn't foolish enough to think Romeo's protection would keep all the wolves at bay.

Besides, I needed all my wits about me when I talked to Braeden. I had no idea if he would even talk to me or if he'd brush me off and humiliate me in front of everyone. But Romeo was right. I had to try. If anything, I could thank him for fixing the Corolla and then leave.

I was standing near the orange glow of the fire, staring at the way the flames danced, when Rimmel sidled up to me. She dangled a red SOLO cup in front of me, and I shook my head.

"It's water," she whispered in my ear.

I took it and looked at the liquid. It was definitely water.

"Mine, too." She tilted her cup toward me to see. "I figured even if we weren't drinking, we could look like it."

"Here comes the team," Rimmel said, motioning toward a large group of guys practically appearing out of the night.

The huge crowd cheered and roared. The players howled and dispersed around the party.

We were in the large open field on campus, the one where all the bonfires were held in the fall. The faculty knew about this one, though. Because it was for football, it was sanctioned.

Clearly, men made the rules.

• • •

Music started pumping through the dark, making my pulse drum to the beat. A couple girls walked by and pointed at me. Then they laughed.

Maybe I should just leave now, find Braeden tomorrow.

"Hey," a familiar voice said from just behind me, and I spun. Trent was standing there with sweat-dampened hair and a smile on his lips. His dimple was in full view and his eyes reflected the fire behind us.

He was dressed in a pair of jeans, sneakers, and a Wolves jersey. There was a can of beer in his hand.

"Hey," I echoed. "You played great tonight."

Really, I had no idea if he had or not. I was too busy staring at Braeden.

"Can we talk a minute?" he asked, his voice dropping a little.

My stomach clenched. I knew exactly what this was. It was the *it's not you, it's me* speech, only we both knew what he really meant was *it's totally you because you slept with Zach and your naked pic was passed around the university.*

"Um, sure," I answered, trying not to sound horrified.

• • •

I glanced at Rimmel and frowned. "I can't leave her here alone," I told Trent.

"She's not alone," Missy said, approaching the group.

Normally, I would have been thrilled to see her and called out a loud greeting, but not tonight. I hadn't talked to her much since the Buzz about me went out. I was afraid she was mad because I never told her what happened. "How was rehearsal?" I asked.

"So good!" she said and waved at Trent. "Hey, Trent."

"Hey, Missy."

"Go ahead. We'll stay here," Rimmel told me. Missy nodded.

I followed Trent away from the fire and the crowd. We stopped just before the trees grew closer together and forest seemed to take over. It was colder over here away from the fire and also much darker.

I clung to the SOLO cup like it was a shield and reverently wished there were alcohol in it. Hell, even Boones Farm would have been welcome at this moment.

• • •

"Look," I began before he could say anything. "I know you wanna call off our date. I get it. I'd probably call it off, too."

"Actually, I wanted to apologize." There was a smile playing around his lips.

I drew back, surprised. "For what?"

"For not coming to see you as soon as everything happened. I'm sure it's been pretty intense for you."

I laughed. "That's one way to put it."

He shifted his beer into one hand and reached for mine with his other, giving it a squeeze. "Fuck 'em."

"What?" I smiled.

"You're just the newest victim of the Boss. Although, I gotta say, he seems to really like letting you have it."

"I noticed."

His dimple made an appearance. I saw it even in the dark. "Everyone makes mistakes. You don't deserve this, and I wanted you to know I don't judge you for what happened."

"You mean for sleeping with Zach," I stated bluntly.

It was sort of rude, but he was being too polite about it. I wanted to see his reaction to the stark truth. Let's see if he really meant what he said about being non-judgey.

"Sometimes when I get drunk—really drunk—I drunk dial my grandma and tell her she's hot," he admitted.

"You do not." I laughed.

He held up his hand. "I swear. Seems when I get really drunk, I also speak in a Scottish accent. Granny thinks she has a secret admirer from Scotland. Since I started calling, she's had quite the pep in her step."

I covered my mouth with my hand and giggled uncontrollably.

"See?" he said. "We all do dumb shit when we're drunk." He made a face, then added, "Either that or you and I are just seriously messed up."

"You're not messed up," I said, looking at him.

I loved Romeo and Rimmel, but when they said they supported me, I kind of knew they would. Like it was expected. It's what family does. But Trent didn't have to say any of this. He didn't have to be so kind to me tonight. He could have acted like I had some terrible disease and blown me off completely, yet he didn't.

And that made me feel better than I had in days.

"Thank you." My voice was sincere.

"Don't thank me yet," he said and took a long swallow of beer.

"Uh-oh."

"I have to cancel our date."

I guess I expected that. Trent was awesome, and some girl was going to totally win the jackpot with him, but that girl wasn't me.

"And it's not because of Zach," he hurried to say. "That guy is a class-A douche, and it was an awesome day when I got his ass tossed out of the frat."

"Then why?" I whispered.

"I think we both know you have your eye on someone else."

I sucked in a breath.

He chuckled. "At first, I thought maybe I was just imagining it. You two seemed to thrive off insulting each other. Then I saw the way he stared after you in the food court that day. And it's no secret he went postal when that Buzz came out about you and Zach. But what really convinced me," he went on, "was the way you watched him tonight. And the way your eyes scan the crowd even now, just waiting for him to show up."

I was doing that? No way.

Trent nodded.

"Trent," I said, feeling incredibly guilty.

"Spare me the friendship speech, okay? It's totally cool. Maybe if I'd gotten there before B, things would be different."

I didn't say anything, and he laughed under his breath.

"Yeah, I didn't think so. It's always been him, hasn't it?"

"I think maybe so."

He nodded. "You're a cool girl, Ivy, and he's a lucky guy. If he don't treat you right, give me a call and I'll beat his ass for ya."

I wished for a second things were different and Trent and I might work out. But that wish evaporated with my reoccurring thought of Braeden.

I reached out and hugged him. He hugged me back.

"Can we all still hang out?" I asked when we pulled away.

"For sure. Just not tonight. Tonight, I gotta get my drink on. Granny's due another call from her secret admirer. It's been a while. Wouldn't want her to think he lost interest."

I laughed as he walked away, saluting me with his half-empty beer.

I stood there for long moments, not quite ready to be swallowed by the crowd, but also doing exactly what Trent called me on.

Looking for Braeden.

I'd yet to see him here tonight, and he was the only reason I'd come.

This whole thing made me realize something. I did want him. I'd wanted him for a long time. I just wouldn't admit it because he'd been with Missy from almost day one. I wasn't a bad friend, but I made a bad choice. Not a mistake, because what I felt in B's arms could never be a mistake. I just wished I'd talked to Missy first, admitted to myself how I felt before everything snowballed out of control.

This whole time I was trying to get back on the right track, be the girl I knew I was… it was a joke.

I couldn't totally do that with this hanging over my head.

All I could do now was undo what I could of my damage. I would find Braeden, lay it all bare, expose my heart, and pray he didn't annihilate it. Once I knew where he stood, I would talk to Missy and do the same.

I had no idea what I would gain and who I would lose. It didn't matter anymore. All that mattered was doing what I needed to do for me.

It felt right, and for the first time in days—maybe even weeks—I felt stronger.

I just needed to find Braeden.

I scanned the crowd again; it was dense and seemed to grow every second. I still couldn't find him, but I knew he was here somewhere.

* * *

After a few more minutes I spotted Rimmel and Missy. They were laughing and surrounded by a bunch of Wolves. Braeden was probably nearby, especially if that's where Rimmel and Romeo were.

I took a step toward my friends, but someone tugged me back.

I glanced over my shoulder, hoping maybe it was B.

"Where do you think you're going?" slurred a voice I didn't know.

It wasn't B.

I had no idea who this was, but he wasn't alone. He had three friends with him. They materialized out of the trees like ninjas in some karate movie. They reeked of booze and cigarettes.

"Someone is waiting for me," I said and tugged away.

He tugged me back. "I'm sure they won't mind waiting a few more minutes."

"I will," I growled, doing my best to sound intimidating.

He let go and held up his hands, drink and all. "Whoa, we got a feisty one, boys."

I spun away and took off.

But he was faster.

He caught me around the waist, and I kicked and cursed and yelled.

"No one's gonna hear you, slut," he whispered in my ear. His voice was ominous, and I shuddered. "Party's way too loud."

I started to yell again, but he clamped his meaty paw over my mouth as I was dragged into the concealment of trees.

CHAPTER THIRTY-FIVE

> The scrimmage game was #epic!
> Romeo looked hot on the sidelines.
> #13 was hot on the field.
> #FootballInTheSpring
>
> ... *Alpha BuzzFeed*

BRAEDEN

I managed to keep my head on straight during the game.

Even if I did play with more frustration and unnecessary roughness. There was no ref at this game, so I couldn't get thrown out. It wouldn't be the first time I used football to work through my personal demons, and it might not be the last.

* * *

I knew before I saw her that Ivy was there. Her presence was sort of like a double shot of caffeine straight into my veins.

Almighty, she looked hot.

She sat there on the sidelines, her shapely ass in a collapsible chair, jean-clad legs stretched to the ground with a pair of cowboy boots hugging her calves. Her blond hair was loose around her shoulders, and every time the wind blew, strands of it would float out around her head like a halo.

I couldn't take it anymore.

I knew exactly how I felt. Denying it was futile. If loving Ivy were a battle, then I would lose the war. Talking to Mom earlier clicked something inside me. It was as if her permission that I was able to feel like this was the catalyst that finally gave me acceptance.

If she could move on and find love, then I had a chance, too. And she was right; giving up my future to the man in my past was stupid.

I was a lot of things, but stupid wasn't one of them.

● ● ●

By the time the team arrived at the bonfire, it was raging. Music was thumping through the night so loud I was shocked the cops weren't here. Beer and liquor was flowing, and the fire had to be at least ten feet tall. Cars were parked everywhere, bodies crowded the grass, and large groups of people danced—or what they liked to think of as dancing—and it made searching for a single girl very hard. It was like trying to find a needle in a haystack.

"You see her?" I yelled to Romeo.

He shook his head as he scanned the area. "There's Rim," he said and pointed around the fire. "Missy too. She's probably there."

We picked our way through the crowd, my patience wearing thin. But she wasn't standing there with Rim. I didn't even have to ask where she was. My sis knew I would want to know. She glanced across the field, toward the line of trees where two people stood close together talking.

I watched Ivy and Trent laugh and smile. Funny, I wasn't as jealous anymore. I didn't like what I was seeing, but I no longer felt the urge to kill Trent.

• • •

It was progress.

Trent walked away, leaving Ivy standing there alone. I leaned in to Romeo and said, "Don't wait up."

He held out his fist and we pounded it out. "You got her?" he asked.

"I got her."

He turned back to the crowd as I separated from it. I rebuffed anyone who tried to lure me from my path, solely focused on getting to Ivy.

She started to head this way when four guys materialized out of the trees. I knew right away they were drunk as shit.

They were probably fucking on something, too.

My steps picked up when I watched him grab her, saw the fear in her eyes. I saw her call out, but no sound made it to my ears.

They laughed as they dragged her into the trees.

I started running.

CHAPTER THIRTY-SIX

Be careful out here tonight, ladies.
The drunk pigs are out in force.
#UseTheBuddySystem
#SomeGirlsRJustEasyTargets

... Alpha BuzzFeed

IVY

"We know who you are," said the guy who dragged me away.

It was much darker here beneath the trees without the glow of the fire. Adrenaline and fear warred inside my body as I frantically searched for a means of escape.

There was only one reason a woman was dragged into the trees by a bunch of drunk strangers.

It wasn't a good reason.

• • •

"You're the slut of Alpha U." One of the other guys snickered.

"You shouldn't believe everything you read," I snapped as I tried to get out of the arms holding me.

"Seeing is believing, and it was all right there in color," he quipped. As his friends laughed, he threw me on the ground. I landed with a hard thud, and for a few precious seconds, my vision swam before my eyes.

"Hold her!" the leader ordered.

"No!" I yelled, trying to scramble up.

Two guys pinned me down, holding my arms into the hard, cold ground. "Your tits look as good in real life as they do in that picture?"

Oh. My. God.

I screamed bloody murder. I screamed so loud it hurt. A hand came over my mouth.

I bit it.

"Ow! She bit me!"

The leader watched me over the rim of his cup as he poured more alcohol down his throat. One second, his eyes were gleaming with vile thoughts, and the next, they were rolling back in his head as he slumped to the ground.

"You got two seconds to get your hands off her!" Braeden roared and leapt forward.

The men holding me let go instantly, but one got tackled to the ground. I scrambled up and stood against a nearby tree as Braeden took on three guys at once.

They were drunk and sloppy.

He was sober and athletic.

He was also clearly infuriated.

He could have grabbed me and gone, but he didn't. I knew he wouldn't.

Instead, he left all four would-be rapists in a heap on the ground. None of them were moving. Or conscious.

"Just can't stay out of trouble, can ya?" he said and stepped up close.

I wanted so badly to fire back something smart and sassy, but all my lower lip would do is tremble.

"It's all right now," he murmured and stepped a little closer. "I got you. You're safe."

• • •

I collapsed against him, but I didn't cry. I'd done so much crying the past week I didn't have any tears left. Instead, I shook and wobbled.

Thank God he was there.

Braeden swept me up against his chest, cradled me in his arms. I listened to the rapid beat of his heart as he carried me around the edge of the party—staying in the trees—and to his truck. I slumped in the seat as he drove.

The ride was short, and soon he parked in front of my dorm.

"Key," he demanded, holding out his hand. I pulled it out of my pocket and handed it over. Instead of coming around to the passenger side, he slid me across the driver's seat and helped me down to the ground.

Quietly, we went inside, thankfully passing no one (everyone was at the party), and straight up to my room.

I didn't bother with the overhead lights. I went right to my bed and collapsed. What almost happened was so frightening I couldn't think. I just lay there, replaying over and over the things I should have done or if there was anything I could have done to keep them away.

I should have walked away with Trent.

I shouldn't have stood there alone to think.

I should have stayed home.

I shouldn't have slept with Zach.

"Ivy," Braeden whispered from nearby.

Suddenly, all I could think about was being pinned down. Their rough hands and appraising eyes. The sheer terror I felt when I realized I was outnumbered and it probably wouldn't matter how hard I fought.

I jolted off the bed, onto my feet, and started tearing at my clothes. "Get off me," I sobbed. "Off!"

My hands were rough and insistent as I tugged at the clothes those men touched. I couldn't bear to have them on me anymore.

"Hey," Braeden spoke; his voice was gentle but held a note of alarm. He moved forward and I moved back.

"I'm not gonna hurt you, baby."

"You already have." I slumped. "Everybody has."

● ● ●

"Shit," he swore and stepped up close. "Tell me what you want right now," he whispered.

"I want these clothes off. They touched them. They…" My voice broke.

Slowly, Braeden took my hands and pulled them away from myself. "I'll help you. Is that okay?"

I nodded, numb. It was scary how numb I felt. My mind was freaked out, but my body was entirely disoriented and unfeeling.

His fingers latched onto the hem of the flutter-sleeve tee. I'd probably never wear this shirt again. It was such a shame. The lace detail was so beautiful.

It was tugged away and tossed somewhere out of sight. "These too?" he murmured, grazing his finger across the buttons on my jeans.

I nodded.

My body started shaking when he peeled them down my legs. He paused in motion and looked up at me from his crouched position on the floor. "Are you scared? Want me to back up?"

Oh no, I wasn't scared.

I shook my head slowly, and he finished pulling off my boots and jeans. When he was done, he stepped back, putting some distance between us.

"Is that better?"

No. It wasn't. I sort of felt like I'd been out in the cold for too long. You know when your entire body goes numb from the low temperatures? But once you step back in the heat and your skin begins to thaw, everything starts to shake and tingle as awareness seeps back in.

That's how I felt.

My body was finally beginning to catch up with my mind.

I couldn't stop the tremors from rocking my limbs. I felt like someone flipped a switch inside me to vibrate.

Braeden went to my dresser, pulling open drawers and rifling through the clothes. He seemed to be searching for one thing, but I didn't ask. My teeth were chattering too hard.

A sound ripped from his throat when he found what he was after. He came back with his shirt gripped in his hand. I looked between him and the fabric.

"It doesn't smell like you."

He tossed it away, and it landed on Rimmel's bed. In one swift motion, he pulled the shirt he was wearing over his head and then down over mine. His unique scent swirled around me as the warmth from his body heat seeped into my skin. I pulled my arms in the oversized sleeves to unhook my bra and let it fall down at my feet.

Only then did I sigh and start to relax.

The hard contour of his bare chest wasn't to be denied. His smooth, olive-toned skin stretched wide across the strong set of his shoulders, and his waist came down into a V. The definition in his abdominals was so sharp he looked carved in stone.

And his arms.

His arms were strong and thick. They looked like the perfect place for shelter.

I stepped toward him and those arms came out, inviting me in. I fit against him easily, and the safety he always made me feel was so welcome.

My fingers dug into the muscles of his back, but he didn't seem to care. I felt his lips in my hair, and a sensation of cleanliness washed over me.

"Make love to me, Braeden. Right now." I stared up at him.

His arms flexed around me. Desire pooled in his eyes, but his mouth turned down in a frown. "I'm not sure now is a good time."

"It's the perfect time," I whispered. "I still feel their intent on my skin. My body still hums with what they wanted to do. Take it away. Take them away."

A low groan rumbled in his chest as his hands slid under my arms and lifted. I wrapped my legs around his waist and settled against him.

Usually, his kiss was eager, hot, and insistent. This time was different, but it was no less devastating. He kissed with painstaking deliberation, like he thought about every single movement, every single stroke of his tongue just before he made it.

He touched me like he'd found the manual for my body's ultimate pleasure and was following it to a T.

Everything else fell away.

• • •

The woods, the drunk guys became obsolete.

The rumors, the picture, the shame…

None of it mattered anymore.

Maybe I'd feel different when he wasn't so close, but I didn't care. Even if Braeden never touched me again, the effects of how he was making me feel right then would never fade away.

He carried me to the bed, moving like he was going to keep me on top. I knew it was so I would feel safe, but it's not what I wanted.

"No," I murmured, breathless. "I want you over me."

He pulled back and looked in my eyes. "Are you sure?"

I nodded. I'd never wanted anything more.

I wanted to be boxed in by him. I wanted to feel caged in by his arms and see nothing but his body when I looked up.

He laid me out across the mattress and came over me. His hand glided up the inside of my shirt and he kneaded my aching breast. I purred and pushed myself farther into his hand.

The buttons of his jeans proved a worthy opponent for my trembling fingers, but eventually I made a sound of defeat and pulled them away. B chuckled and pulled back. I watched him through half-closed lids as he removed all his clothes.

His cock stood out proudly from his center, and my core clenched with desire. He laid a condom on the mattress beside me and reached under my shirt to pull my panties away. I started to pull at the shirt, but he shook his head.

"Leave it. You have a beautiful body, Ivy, but seeing you in my clothes is even more so," Braeden told me as he ripped open the foil packet.

He entered my body inch by delicious inch, and my eyes rolled back in my head. Being with Braeden was almost an out-of-body experience; nothing or no one could ever compare to this.

The buildup was heavy because of his unhurried pace. By the time an orgasm crashed over me, I moaned in relief. Braeden wrapped himself around me, holding me so tight. He kept moving, kept thrusting inside me until I gasped, on the brink of another climax.

"Come for me, baby," he whispered in my ear, nipping at my earlobe.

This time we both plummeted together. It almost felt like we merged as one.

When at last I could think again, Braeden rolled to the side but pulled me with him, keeping me close. I laid my cheek on his chest and fitted one of my legs between his.

Neither one of us spoke a word.

There wasn't anything I could say, not a single word in existence that could match how he made me feel.

I just hoped he felt the same.

* * *

CHAPTER THIRTY-SEVEN

BRAEDEN

Talking.

I had every intention of talking to Ivy tonight.

I had no intention of stopping her from getting raped.

But it happened.

Just like what just went on between us in this bed.

I could have easily killed all four of them, and I probably wouldn't feel bad. Men like that deserved a lot worse than death. But Ivy deserved more. So I settled for beating the shit out of them and leaving them there to rot.

I hoped they remembered everything when they finally came to.

I sure would. If I ever saw their faces on campus, they wouldn't get a free pass again.

I was partially responsible for what happened tonight. If I weren't such a colossal asshole, she wouldn't have been vulnerable tonight. Even if she had walked off to speak with Trent (what was that about?), I would have been close by. Those guys never would have been able to lay a hand on her, but at least I stopped them before they could do too much damage.

Still, the carnage of the past few weeks was high, but I was gonna make it right. She was here with me now, and that meant I still had a chance. That's all I needed, a chance. I might have screwed up in the past, but I wouldn't this time.

This time I was going to make sure she knew exactly how I felt. How I was always gonna feel.

Ivy was it for me. She was my forever girl. For so long, I thought she didn't exist, but now I saw I wouldn't exist without her.

She was there even when I didn't want her to be. A constant. Just like the beat of a heart.

Ivy wouldn't take my crap, but she also wouldn't try to change me either.

I wasn't foolish enough to think our relationship would be perfect. In fact, it would probably be as far from perfect as two people could get.

But it was real.

And it was right.

I caressed the side of her cheek with the backs of my knuckles, and she smiled. Quickly, her smile turned to a grimace, and she grabbed my hand. "You split your hand open again."

I looked down; some of the bandages were gone, and others were ripped. There was dried blood smeared across my skin, and what bandages were left were saturated, too.

"I had faces to punch." I shrugged against the mattress.

● ● ●

A sound of distress filled the room, and she climbed over me and tumbled off the bed.

"Where you going?"

A few seconds later, she came back with the first aid kit, the same one she was going to use on me before. Except this time, I wasn't going to say something stupid to stop her. She sat down beside me and pulled my hand into her lap.

I caressed the inside of her thigh (what? I'm a guy) as she used my stomach as a table for everything she pulled out of the kit.

"Does it hurt?" She picked it up again and cradled it in her palm.

"Didn't even notice it."

She worked carefully, peeling away the rest of the bandages. When they were gone, she cleaned my hand with shit that stung like a bitch—but I acted like it didn't hurt 'cause I'm a man—and then blew across the scrapes and cuts with gentle pressure. The gesture drew attention to her lips and made me want to kiss her all over again.

• • •

"How did you even play tonight with your hand like this?" she murmured, working meticulously applying some kind of cream and clean bandages.

"It's not that bad."

Once it was clean, dry, and bandaged, she lifted it to press a soft kiss to the center.

"You know, I really intended to talk to you tonight," I murmured.

"That's why I was there, too."

"What's this shit about Rome throwing his protection behind you?"

Ivy shrugged and packed up the kit. "Some people said some stuff, and he was standing there. He said something."

I was glad he was there. I'd do the same—and had—for Rimmel. But I finally got why Romeo always got so testy when he thought I was being too protective over Rimmel. That was his job.

"I'll protect you."

"I don't need protecting."

"You seriously gonna say that shit to me after what just happened tonight?" I spat.

Her shoulders slumped as she climbed off the bed to put away the kit.

"Hey." I captured her hand, and she looked over her shoulder. "I don't mean it in a bad way. I know how strong you are. Shit, you freaking handle me like no one else does."

"I'm not sure that's true either."

She placed the kit down, and I wrapped my arms around her waist, pulling her back onto the mattress. "I didn't handle it well." I brushed the hair out of her deep-blue eyes and stared into them. "I saw that pic and pretty much exploded. I fucking hate that guy, what he did to Romeo and Rimmel." I paused and took a deep breath. "The thought of him touching you makes me insane. Just looking at Trent talk to you makes me want to punch someone, so seeing you half naked and in bed with the biggest piece of scum I know makes me—"

She ducked her head. Too late, I realized I shouldn't have said that.

"You have no idea what it's like to live with what I did," she admitted. "From the very second I woke up

• • •

that morning and realized what I'd done… It haunts me."

"Nightmares," I murmured, thinking of the night at Rome's when she was calling out in her sleep. *Don't touch me.*

"What?" She glanced up.

"Do you dream about it?"

"More than I'd like. It's like I can't get away from it. Just when I thought I was going to be able to move on, it shows up on the stupid Buzzfeed."

And it almost got her raped.

There was no excuse for that. None. There wasn't one solitary reason that could justify that Buzz about her.

"How'd you know?"

"Know what?" I asked.

"I had nightmares about Zach."

"Because that guy is a walking nightmare," I quipped.

"They're just dreams. To be honest, I really don't remember that night. I was so drunk. I've never blacked out like that before, you know?"

I frowned as she talked. I should have been there that night. I should have been watching out for her.

"It's the reason I don't drink so much anymore. It's scary, not knowing what you're doing. Clearly, when I drink, I make very bad decisions." Pausing, she shivered. "I'm glad he's gone."

"Me too," I answered. Even more so now. If they ever let him out of that fancy cage he was in and I saw him again, I had no idea what I'd do.

Her fingertips traced light circles over my chest, and just the brush of her skin over mine made the back of my neck tingle.

"I'm not good at pretty words." I admitted.

Her fingers paused.

"I'm not good at saying what I feel, and I don't know a thing about romance."

"I don't need romance, Braeden."

All girls wanted romance.

But even if she didn't, Ivy deserved it. The fact that she was even lying here in this bed with me right now was a freaking miracle. I'd never treated any girl so horribly in my life.

• • •

Wasn't that a sobering thought?

The one woman I wanted above all others was the one I treated the worst. That needed to change. Immediately.

"I want you, Ivy." I cupped her jaw.

"You have me, B. I'm right here."

"Not just for tonight."

"Missy still doesn't know about this." She gestured between us. "With everything that happened with the BuzzBoss, I've been hiding out."

I nodded. "Why don't we talk to her together?" I was afraid after what I said to Missy the last time we were alone she would still be angry. I didn't want her taking out that anger on Ivy.

Ivy shook her head. "I think I should do it alone. Friend to friend. I don't want her to think we're ganging up on her."

"If you need me, you'll call?" I rubbed my thumb over her lower lip. It was happening again. Desire pooled in my stomach and my cock stirred between us.

"Yes." She promised.

• • •

"This talking stuff is hard work." The corner of my mouth kicked up when she giggled.

I really meant it when I confessed I didn't know what to say to her.

"You know," she began, her fingers tiptoeing up my chest. "This is the first time ever we've had all night together."

"All naked. All the time." I wagged my eyebrows.

She laughed. "Maybe we could talk some more later." The suggestion in her tone was not to be missed. By my brain or my already stiff cock.

"I might be up for that."

She wrapped her hand around my shaft. "Yeah, I noticed." She leaned up to kiss me, but I pulled back.

"One more thing?" I asked.

"You sure you aren't a girl? Seems like talking is coming pretty easily."

"You watch your mouth, woman," I warned.

"Okay, what?"

"What were you and Trent talking about tonight?"

"You saw?" Her delicately shaped brow arched.

"Oh, I saw."

• • •

"You jealous?"

"Nah. I'm secure with how you feel about me." I scoffed.

"Or maybe you just feel that way right now because I'm stroking your big cock."

"Ooh, talk dirty to me, baby."

Her giggle was throaty and sexy as hell. When she tried to kiss me again, I held strong. She made a sound of frustration. "We cancelled our date. He knows I want you."

"He does, does he?" Pride fluffed up my chest.

Her blond head nodded. "Apparently, he notices the way I look at you."

"And which way is that?"

Beneath the sheets, her stroking was turning bolder and this conversation was getting much less important.

"Like I want to be naked with you. All night. All the time."

There was no more talking after that. Well, okay there was a little. Like when I made her cry out my name.

Over and over again.

• • •

I might not be good at talking, but I knew how to move between the sheets.

When we were finished, she fell asleep in my arms. The soft sound of her breathing and the feel of her body draped along mine were satisfying in ways I never thought it would be.

When my phone went off somewhere on the floor beside us, I almost ignored it. But then I thought it might be Romeo, just checking in. Maybe someone had found the pile of garbage I left in the woods, and he was worried.

If I didn't answer, he'd be over here beating on the door at five a.m. because Rimmel was upset. I managed to fish my phone out of my jeans without disturbing Ivy, and the second my back hit the mattress, she automatically gravitated toward me.

Once I had her tucked in close, I lit up the screen and glanced at it.

My blood ran ice cold.

What. The. Fuck. Was. This.

The selfie I took of Ivy and me that night on spring break was now public knowledge on the school

● ● ●

Buzzfeed. That photo was gone, lost with my shattered phone. How the hell did the BuzzBoss get ahold of it?

I held myself still even though I wanted to pace the room. Why was the Boss doing this? What did they have to gain? Popularity? Notoriety?

An ass-kicking?

I didn't care that everyone saw me like this. Everyone knew I liked a good time. But dammit, this was going to crush Ivy. Not only would it continue to feed the ridiculous rumor that she was a slut, but now everyone would know we'd been together.

Including Missy.

And honestly? I was tired of people staring at my girl.

This was the kind of shit that gave drunk, lowlife perverts the inspiration to take what they couldn't get for free.

This was a dangerous game.

That night at Romeo's, I promised Ivy I'd keep her safe.

• • •

She stirred in her sleep. Dropping the phone on the mattress, I rubbed the curve of her hip until her breathing returned even and deep.

I lay there a long time, thinking.

I came to a conclusion.

Maybe the reason I was having so much trouble saying to Ivy what I really wanted to say was because this wasn't over. Because we still had a lot to work through before we could truly be together.

I was tired of waiting. Wanting. Life was happening now. And I wanted all the time with her I could get.

So all the shit in our way?

I was gonna take it down.

First on my list? Stopping the selfie parade the Buzz

Boss was so fond of posting. Why? Because the best way to deal with a problem with many branches was to go for the root.

If the Boss stopped dragging Ivy through the mud, the students on campus would, too. They'd forget, move on, and she could go outside without threat of ridicule or rape.

But who was the BuzzBoss? No one seemed to know.

It was time to find out.

CHAPTER THIRTY-EIGHT

> The #BuzzBoss is being shut down.
> #ButNot4Long
> Send your number 2 BuzzBoss@yahoo.com to stay in the know.
>
> ... Alpha BuzzFeed

IVY

I went to bed in Braeden's arms.

I woke up alone.

I was beginning to think our relationship—or lack thereof—was a vampire.

It only came out at night.

CHAPTER

THIRTY-NINE

BRAEDEN

I've heard the most dangerous people are those who have nothing to lose.

But where I'm sitting?

The most dangerous person is a man who thought he had nothing and then found everything.

I wouldn't go back to nothing ever again. I'd protect what was mine until my very last breath.

And Ivy was mine.

Figuring out who the BuzzBoss was should have been harder. But just like a woman, a pissed-off man does better research than the FBI.

Lucky for me, I didn't need research this time.

The Boss made a mistake. One that many people wouldn't catch, but this was personal. As I lay there in the dark with Ivy so close against me, I had some time to think. I could see now why no one caught on before. The genius of the Boss was the notifications kept on coming. There was always something to talk about, something new to read.

No one had time to really stop and think about it because they were too busy talking about it.

Shut up and listen.

That's what I finally did.

My oh my… what I heard.

Once I knew, I couldn't just lay here. I had to act, to put an end to all this fuckery.

It was explosive, and part of me hoped the hell I was wrong.

I knew I wasn't.

And honestly, the betrayal would be worse for some others than me. The friendship I thought I knew was gone… All that remained was shock.

#SELFIE

The sun was just beginning to rise when I slipped out from under Ivy. I snuck to the communal bathroom down the hall and hoped no one saw. I had to piss like a racehorse and sneaking around with a full bladder wasn't my idea of a good time.

While I was in there, I noticed how much cleaner girls were than guys.

They always told us, but I never believed it was true. Even now that I knew the truth, I still would never admit it.

Ivy was still sleeping peacefully when I walked back in. I watched her for a while because she was so goddamn beautiful. I wondered what was going to happen when I blew the lid off the truth. I prayed it didn't ruin what was finally starting to feel real between us.

She was still wearing my shirt, and I wasn't about to take it off her. My bare-chested trip to the bathroom was one thing, but busting a badie was another thing entirely.

I needed me some cotton.

I spied my old Wolves shirt lying on Rimmel's bed, where I tossed it last night. I didn't think I'd wear it again, but unless I planned on strapping on a bra and tank top, I figured this would be my best option.

Besides, she wanted it to smell like me.

Who could blame her? I was like a big piece of man candy.

I made sure my phone was on silent, locked the door from the inside, and crept away.

I decided a little recon—just to be sure I was right—was a must, so once I made my way to where I thought I'd find some damning evidence, I waited around for a bit, trying to concoct a plan.

But I didn't need one.

A short time later, the suspect left, leaving all their secrets ripe for the picking. I walked down the hall like I belonged here and knocked on the door.

Several minutes later, someone with raging bedhead answered. I turned up my charm and smiled sheepishly. "I was sorta in here last night… right before you got home. I left something here." I pushed a hand through my hair and tousled it around. Bitches loved messy hair.

The door opened a little wider.

"You mind if I come in and grab it? I'll be out of that sexy hair of yours in a few."

I was invited inside.

I shut the door softly behind me and looked at the rumpled bed. "My bad, you were sleeping."

"I think I'm still drunk."

"Well, go pass out again. I swear I'll be quiet when I let myself out."

"You're lucky you're so hot."

See, before Ivy, I would have taken that as invitation and immediately tried to tap that ass.

But my random ass-tapping days were over. Now I tapped one ass exclusively.

Thank goodness for alcohol, because my accomplice started snoring—and drooling—the second she hit the pillow.

I spied a laptop on a paper-ridden desk and pulled out the chair to have a seat. The damn computer was locked with a password.

• • •

I rotated my head as I thought.

On the fourth try I got in.

DRAMA QUEEN.

Go figure.

At first glance, it was just a regular computer with regular files. I had to dig around, but then I hit pay dirt.

Seems the Boss hadn't signed out of their email account. And computers had this habit of saving passwords.

Oh my, BuzzBoss, what full folders you have.

I started with an email near the top of the inbox. It was a letter from the dean, stripping away all access to the school Buzzfeed effective as soon as the school web system rebooted. There was also a threat to find out who this student was and have them expelled.

I had to hand it to the Boss if they were able to keep their identity from the campus staff.

Guess that explained the late-night notification that the Boss was being removed. But they had another system already in place. Seems they knew getting the boot was inevitable because the new account and the new texting system was all set up. It even appeared they were in the process of developing their own app.

I poked around a while longer through the emails of people sending in tips and reports of everything drama on this campus. It was amazing to me how eager people were to rat out one another.

I took pictures of the screens I thought would be good for evidence and then started backing out of a few open tabs. That's when I saw it.

The folder of pictures. It was labeled *#Selfies*.

I clicked in. There was a ton of photos. Some were stupid and some were pretty damning. This was the kind of shit people got ruined over.

I scrolled all the way to the last row, only stopping once to make sure my drunk friend was indeed passed out. I almost missed it, but the fact it was different than the rest caught my eye. It was a folder simply labeled *Zach*.

What I saw inside made me sick.

Flashbacks from the night I interrupted Ivy's dream, her calling out, "Don't touch me!" in her sleep, flooded my mind. Those weren't manifestations of her subconscious. Those weren't nightmares just trying to ruin her rest.

It was her mind's way of working through everything it was trying to protect her from.

There were over ten photos. All of them starred Ivy. She was half naked in a lot of them and passed out in even more. They told a story, if lined up properly. A story that would haunt me for the rest of my life.

It started out with one at a party; it looked like the frat he used to be president of. He was taking a selfie of a group of people behind him. Ivy was in that group. She was laughing at something someone was saying.

Zach was in the corner of the pic, much closer than everyone else, and the empty way his eyes looked was disturbing.

Hell, that wasn't a #selfie. That pic was a #stalkie.

Then there was another pic, this one also featuring Ivy. Zach wasn't the one taking this pic, though; he was in it. Much closer to Ivy, watching her like a lion watched prey.

The next pic showed Zach pumping beer into a cup while dangling a white pill over the liquid.

• • •

Another pic showed Ivy drinking out of a cup that looked just like the one in the pic before, while Zach stood beside her and smiled.

He was good at looking friendly. He was good at pretending he wasn't rotten to the core.

The rest of the pics were harder and harder to look at. They all showed Ivy in various forms of unflattering positions. Her eyes were glassy in all of them, almost vacant and unaware.

They moved from her being fully clothed to her being fully naked. In a lot of the naked photos, she appeared to be passed out. And judging from the way he was posing her and beside her, I'd say she was.

I pressed a hand over my mouth to keep from yelling. I knew I'd find some dirt on people in the Boss's archives, but I never thought I'd find proof of assault.

The disbelief, wonder, and confusion in her voice last night when she talked about what she'd done with Zach all made perfect sense.

This wasn't consensual sex.

Ivy was drugged.

* * *

And she was assaulted.

I shoved back in the chair, resting my palms on the desk but bending at the waist. Staring at the floor, I sucked in air. My girl was given the date rape drug. My girl was fucking used by a spineless, sick bastard.

I know I said death was too good for guys like that, but I amend my previous statement. Sometimes death was the only option. Zach needed to die.

He needed to die by my hands.

How was I supposed to tell Ivy what really happened to her? Wouldn't rape be so much worse to recover from than what she thought was just a bad mistake? Should I tell her or just let her live in peaceful bliss?

This made me sick.

Utterly sick.

I hated men who took advantage of women. Men who thought they had more power than God. Men who had no idea what kind of carnage they left behind and how many pieces they left for their victims to pick up.

Put a lid on it, B, I told myself. This wasn't the time or place to lose it over this. There would be time for that later. Right now, I had other shit to deal with.

I sat back in the chair and stared at the images, thankful one of the worst ones wasn't the one that ended up on the BuzzFeed. But then again, there was always next time.

I wanted to delete the entire folder so badly. I wanted nothing more than to pretend it didn't exist. But it did and I wasn't about to delete the proof that could keep Zach locked up forever.

So I emailed the folder to myself.

Then I deleted it. I went through every program on that computer to make sure those photos were really gone.

It took longer than I hoped to be in here, but I wasn't going to leave it to chance.

Still fuming and slightly nauseous over what my girl had been put through, I decided it was time to end this.

I pulled up the program I'd already found.

I typed out a message and hoped the campus system had yet to update.

I hit send.

The notification went through.

I wondered how long I would have to wait for the explosion.

CHAPTER FORTY

IVY

Not long after I woke alone, I got a text.

I KNOW WHO THE BUZZBOSS IS.

I read it twice and double-checked the name of the sender. Braeden knew who the BuzzBoss was?

WHO?

IT'S BETTER IF YOU COME.

WHERE?

He gave me a place to meet, and I frowned.

NOW? I asked.

First he makes me wake up alone, and then he sends me weird texts. It was far too early for all this.

• • •

BLONDIE. GET YOUR ASS HERE!

I stuck out my tongue at the phone but typed out,

FINE.

I pulled on a pair of yoga pants and left B's shirt on. On my way out the door, I pulled my hair up into a bun.

When I arrived at the place, I stood there wondering what the hell all this was about. My stomach twisted a little because this all seemed so weird. I thought about last night, about the way we were together.

We were together now, right?

If so, why did I wake up alone? Why was he here now?

Had only one night with me already sent him packing? Geez, talk about an ego boost.

Not.

I lifted my hand to knock, but before I could, the door opened and I was yanked inside.

"Braeden!" I whisper-yelled. "What the hell is going on?"

He grabbed my face in his hands and searched my eyes. Even in this strange and slightly worrisome

* * *

moment, I got a little lost in his eyes, and some of the doubt I was feeling just seconds ago vanished.

"Shit's about to hit the fan, Blondie," he rumbled. "Remember something for me?"

"What?"

He kissed me. It was a deep, thorough kiss. My heart beat faster and my insides loosened. But then it was over.

I gasped and pressed my lips together, staring at him for some kind of explanation.

"Remember that. And remember I'm only doing this because I want to protect you."

"Braeden, I don't understand what's going on."

"Hellooo," a familiar voice yelled from across the room. "Trying to sleep over here!"

I jumped, startled. We weren't alone in here?

From the door, the handle jiggled as someone let themselves in. Braeden wrapped his arm around my waist and half carried me farther into the room, away from the opening door.

• • •

Missy stepped in, her grey eyes searching frantically around the room. Her cheeks were flushed and her hair was windblown like she'd been running.

"I see you got my message," Braeden said. The unkind, almost underlying anger in his tone had the hairs on the back of my neck standing up.

Missy looked between the two of us and then made a face at B. "I should have known it was you."

"Funny," Braeden drawled, and I glanced between them as they practically stared each other down, "you were the last person I would have suspected, Boss."

My hand flew to my mouth. It couldn't be…

"What. The. Hell?" Janelle, Missy's roommate, sat up in bed and flung off her covers.

Missy glanced behind Braeden. "Sorry, Janelle. Do you mind if we have a couple minutes to talk? I'll buy you breakfast."

"I could use some coffee," she said begrudgingly and got up.

Missy handed her a ten-dollar bill and she left. She didn't even comb her hair.

Ew.

"Don't want anyone else to find out your dirty little secret?" Braeden goaded.

Missy shrugged one of her shoulders.

I stared between the both of them. They seemed locked in some kind of staring death match. Missy had never looked at him like that, but something had changed. Something major.

My phone went off. I usually would have just ignored it, especially after all the rumors that were circulating about me.

But something inside me had my hand reaching for my phone before I even thought of it.

Then I realized I didn't have my phone. I had no pockets in these pants, and I left it sitting upstairs. It was Braeden's phone I heard go off.

"Let me see your phone, Braeden." I stared at Missy when I talked. She slid her eyes to me, and I thought I saw some sort of emotion pass behind them. Regret… then anger.

He handed me his phone, and I lit up the screen. The school notifications were all pulled up. I felt the blood drain from my face as I read the one that went out late last night.

Another selfie. Another man everyone knew I'd gone to bed with. There it was in color, Braeden looking at the camera and me staring at him. I remembered that moment so clearly. I was staring at him, thinking about how gorgeous he was and how amazed I was by the way he made me feel.

It had been a secret moment. One that only he and I shared.

Until now. Now everyone knew. And now Braeden was just another man who slept with #Slut Ivy. I glanced up at Missy. The anger I thought I saw in her eyes was now totally explained.

How hurt she must be.

"Missy—" I began.

"Keep reading, Ivy. Read them all up until a few minutes ago," Braeden instructed, cutting off the apology forming on my tongue.

I did.

I realized the reason I was alone when I woke up.

• • •

I realized the reason we were standing in this room and he'd been in here without Missy until just a few minutes ago.

He hacked the BuzzBoss.

The BuzzBoss just called out her hacker.

Braeden called her Boss when she walked in.

I felt lightheaded.

I looked at Missy, hoping she would tell me everything I was thinking was so wrong.

She didn't.

Missy was the BuzzBoss?

"It's you?" I whispered. "You're the one…"

The phone fell out of my hand and hit the carpet with a soft thud. Disbelief and the echo of betrayal were so strong I actually swayed on my feet.

Braeden was there. He wrapped an arm around my waist and anchored me into his side.

I wanted to speak. To hear her admit the words… to ask her why.

Why? Why would she do this to me? To all of us?

My tongue felt thick, and I couldn't speak. Yet, once again, Braeden was there and he did the talking for me.

"How could you do it, Miss? How could you set the entire campus against Ivy like that?"

"How could you sleep with her?" she fired back. "Oh, wait. It's because she's a—"

He pulled away from me as the sound of a feral growl echoed through the small room. A low gasp cut off Missy's words. "Don't even say it," Braeden intoned. "If you so much as look at Ivy cross-eyed ever again, I will out you so far and wide your grandchildren will feel it."

"So you aren't going to tell anyone?" she asked, hopeful.

I was having a hard time wrapping my brain around this. It's like everything around me was moving a thousand miles a minute, but every cell inside me processed it at a quarter of the speed.

"That ain't my call. I'm gonna leave that up to the best friends you knifed in the back," Braeden replied, and he crossed his arms over his chest.

• • •

"Best friends don't sleep with each other's men," she hissed.

"I was never *yours*," he spat.

"Didn't seem like that the other night when your tongue was jammed down my throat."

"Shut the hell up," he yelled.

It snapped me out of the sludge clogging my brain.

"Wait?" I said, and they both turned heated eyes to me.

"You're the BuzzBoss?"

"Haven't you been listening? I think all the hairspray you use has fried your brain," Missy said unkindly.

"I don't use too much hairspray," I muttered and fingered my hair. It wasn't crunchy or stiff. It was soft.

How rude.

"Babe," Braeden whispered and brought me back to the topic at hand.

Missy snorted.

It pissed me off. I propped my fists on my hips and pinned her with a stare. "You mean to tell me you did all of this because I slept with Braeden?"

"Did you think I wouldn't find out?"

I averted my gaze. "It was a one-time thing. Before you told me you wanted him back."

I felt B's eyes narrow on my face, and I gave him a sad look.

"I stayed away from him for weeks. I felt so bad. You don't even understand. When it happened again…"

Missy laughed, harsh. "Oh, yes, you felt soo bad. So bad that you did it again."

I lifted my chin. "I'm not making excuses for myself. Yeah. We were together again. I was going to tell you. I planned on talking it out."

"Funny, I don't remember that conversation." She glanced down at her nails like she was checking them for chipped polish. I knew she was trying to act all nonchalant.

But I wasn't buying it. All the notifications, the pictures she posted, the rumors she started—she did all of that because of what I did and because it hurt her.

"Because we never had it," I snapped. "You posted that sick picture of me and Zach."

"The Boss has never received so much traffic. It almost crashed the school's website." She was proud of what she did.

"Were you ever my friend?" I tilted my head and stared at her. "Because I can't believe if you ever liked me at all, you'd do something so insanely hurtful."

She dropped her hand and glanced away, guilty.

I pressed on. "Do you have any idea the kind of cruel comments and snide jokes I've had to endure? The rumors? The humiliation? How did you even find out?"

Missy glared at me. "One more thing you never told me."

"Are you kidding me?" I yelled. "I was so mortified. I got so drunk that night, Miss. I don't even remember the shit that happened."

Braeden shifted like my words bothered him. I worried maybe hearing about my sexcapades with another guy would send him packing, but he didn't move away. He moved closer, angling his body slightly in front of mine like he suddenly felt he needed to shield me.

• • •

The truth in my words seemed to get through at least a little, and Missy looked at me.

"I slept with him. I let him into our room. Because of me, he hacked Rimmel's laptop. Not only did I degrade myself by having sex with him, but I gave him unfettered access to hurt Rimmel. I didn't tell anyone. Only Rimmel, because it pertained to her court case against Zach. I was so afraid of what people would think. I mean, if I thought so low of myself, then what would everyone else think?"

Her posture slumped a little.

Braeden was so tense I swear I heard his muscles vibrating.

"Guess I found out though, didn't I?" I said. "You made sure everyone knew, and I became the campus slut. Riddled with undiagnosed diseases—so not true, by the way—and an easy lay."

Missy looked up sharply.

Braeden's voice was hard as stone when he said, "I stopped four guys from gang raping her in the woods last night."

Missy's face paled.

• • •

Is that what it took to get a reaction out of her? A little bit of regret?

"They wanted to know if her tits looked the same as in the picture you plastered all over campus. She might have slept with Zach, but you turned her into a woman every guy thought he had the right to abuse."

He turned his head like the sight of Missy made him ill. The muscle in the side of his jaw ticked. I laid a hand in the center of his shoulder blades.

"Men who abuse women are the fucking scum of this earth. Women who help them? Who know about it and use it for their own benefit?" He glanced back at her, a very hard, almost knowing edge to his tone.

Missy flinched under his impenetrable gaze.

"Those bitches are a waste of space."

My hand tightened in his shirt. That was really harsh. As mad as I was, I didn't want to stand here and insult Missy. I knew too well what insults felt like.

I stepped around him to look at the girl who I once considered my best friend. "I lied to you, and it was wrong. But it's the honest truth when I tell you I never meant for anything to happen between me and

Braeden. I didn't do it maliciously. I wanted to tell you before you found out." I paused. "How did you find out?"

Braeden answered, "She took the selfie of us off my phone. I stupidly left my phone on the table at Screamerz and went to piss. You went through my phone, didn't you, Missy?"

"I saw the way you looked at her. The way you watched her dancing with Trent. I know that expression on your face. The one of interest. It made me curious." She shrugged. "I really didn't expect to find what I did."

"So why not say anything? Why not confront us?" I asked.

"Because I wanted to see how long you'd lie to me. I wanted to see how long you'd string along Trent." She laughed, a hollow sound. "Two men that were both originally for me. You just couldn't stand it, could you, Ivy? You couldn't stand to be second best."

"Watch your mouth," Braeden snarled.

I touched his side to let him know it was okay.

"I never felt like second best," I replied honestly. "I felt like third best."

Braeden jerked, and Missy's eyes shot to me. "What?" she asked.

I smiled. "Are you kidding? You're so gorgeous you could be a Victoria Secret's model. And Rimmel, well, she's so quirky and unconventionally beautiful that she draws eyes whether she wants to admit it or not. I'm the plain one. The one who had to try the hardest to look the part. I never fit in with you two. I tried so hard."

I felt Braeden's eyes on me. He'd completely turned his back on Missy and was staring at me.

"Baby, is that true?"

I nodded. "It's no big deal. I was fine with it." Then I decided to just lay it all out there. "Okay, maybe not fine with it. It's the reason I clung so hard to Rimmel when Romeo first started showing interest in her. Not because I wanted Romeo, but because I didn't want to be left behind."

"Ivy," Braeden whispered, his voice heavy. "No one's ever gonna leave you behind."

Tears pricked the backs of my eyes. I didn't realize how weighed down those feelings made me. Now that I spoke the truth, I felt lighter than before. Why did so much have to happen to get me to finally let some of it go?

"Listen to me," he demanded and tilted up my head so he could stare into my eyes. "You are *not* second best. Or third best. You aren't plain. You're fucking perfect. You're number one's Mom."

I laughed. "What does that mean?"

He smiled. "It means when people look up *number one* in the dictionary, there's a picture of you with a caption that says: *this girl set the standard for number one.*"

I giggled and glanced away.

He pulled me back. "Look at me."

When Braeden talked, I listened.

It was something I was gonna have to work on.

"You're the kind of girl that people leave others behind for. If your so-called friend can't see that, then she's not worthy. You sure as hell got my attention."

There was a sharp sound behind us, the loud slamming of a door.

It slammed so hard, the walls rattled.

• • •

I jerked back, and Braeden reacted instinctually, spinning around and tucking me behind him.

Missy was gone.

She stormed out of the room and practically ripped the door off in the process.

Braeden and I were left standing here alone. He glanced over his shoulder at me. "I'm thinking she didn't like the things I said to you?"

I'd waited my entire life for someone to say those things to me—and for me to let myself believe them—but I never wanted my gain to be someone else's pain.

"I should go find her." I wiped at my eyes.

"Hells no."

"Excuse me?"

"Are you forgetting what that damn she-devil did to you? To Rimmel and Romeo?"

I deflated like a balloon stabbed with a pair of scissors. No. I didn't forget. I'd probably wear the scars of this betrayal for a very long time. Yet some habits were hard to break, and it was ingrained in me to not want my friends to hurt.

Though, the truth was after this morning, it was painfully clear Missy wasn't really my friend.

I wasn't sure she ever was.

CHAPTER FORTY-ONE

BRAEDEN

How do you deal when you find out your girl was assaulted, then basically bullied by her best friend?

You go out for pancakes.

Let me be clear. This was not my idea. I wanted to skip. Hell, we were already late. But the second we stepped out of Missy's room, my phone blew up. Apparently, Rimmel had been texting and calling Ivy to no avail.

She thought we were dead.

Or at the very least on the side of the road. She told me she wasn't ready to attend her brother's funeral and she never would be.

Ivy heard her shrieking into my ear and relieved me of the phone. I certainly didn't put up a fight to give it to her.

Next thing I knew, we were on our way for pancakes.

"Really, Blondie?" I asked when I opened up the passenger door of my truck for her. She didn't need help, but I helped her up anyway. By palming her ass and giving her a boost.

I liked touching her ass.

It was my happy place.

"I think Rim would understand if we bailed," I finished once I was in the driver's seat. "You've had a rough morning. Hell, a rough couple weeks."

"We have to tell them," she replied. I could hear the anxiety and sadness in her voice. It pissed me off. I didn't want to see her hurt like this. She cleared her throat. "The sooner the better. We might as well do it over coffee and sugar. I definitely need something covered in syrup. I think I might be in shock."

I turned sideways in the seat and faced her.

"I feel like I don't know her at all…" she whispered. "It's like the person I thought I knew, the one I was best friends with for years, was just a façade."

"I'm sorry I just sprang it on you like that this morning." I reached for her hand and entwined our fingers. "I didn't know what else to do. I was afraid if I just told you, you might not believe me."

"It's definitely unbelievable," she murmured, staring at our linked hands. "But I know you wouldn't say something like that unless it were true."

I lifted our hands and kissed hers.

"I know why she did what she did to me, even if it was totally off the deep end." She stared out the window to collect her thoughts. "But I don't understand all the notifications. All the drama she fueled between Romeo and Rimmel. I mean, she leaked that whole thing about the plagiarism. Rim almost got kicked out of school."

"She's done some really shitty things to a lot of people the past couple years," I agreed.

"Rimmel never did anything to her. I just don't understand why she does this. Any of it."

I turned in the seat and started up the truck. I held her hand as we drove; the ride to the diner wasn't a long one. I didn't know the answer to Ivy's questions. Hell, I wondered them myself. But the truth was sometimes people just did shitty stuff. I'd known that from a very early age.

Sometimes there is no rhyme or reason. Sometimes they do it because they can.

If there was one thing I learned throughout my life, it was people don't do things because of other people; they do them because of what they get out of it. They do it for the way it makes them feel.

Once we were parked and the engine was off, I got out, tugging her across the seat behind me. When I was on the ground, I reached in for Ivy and lifted her out. I set her close and kissed the tip of her nose on impulse.

"I don't think what Missy did was about you. Or Rimmel. Or any of the people she outed. I think it was all about her."

We walked hand in hand toward the diner, until Ivy froze in her steps.

"What's wrong?" I asked, skimming the area around us, looking for some kind of threat.

She made a sound of panic.

"Ivy?" My heart was starting to beat faster.

"I'm still wearing your shirt!" she hissed.

"Is that all, woman? Please." I started walking again. She refused to budge. I turned back and lifted an eyebrow. "What now?"

She stepped up close and whispered dramatically, "I'm not wearing a bra either!"

I matched her tone to whisper back, "Good thing the girls are perky!"

"Braeden!" She gasped.

I threw back my head and laughed. "C'mon. I'm so hungry I could eat the rotten end of a pig."

"Oh my gosh, that's disgusting!" she burst out as I towed her along behind me.

• • •

"Aw, baby. That hurts my feelings."

She made a rude noise, and I grinned. I opened the door to the diner, and she walked in first. I had to hold back a smile when she crossed her arms over her unleashed girls.

This chick was fucking hilarious.

Rimmel waved wildly from a booth near the window. Ivy hurried to the table and slid in across from Romeo and Rimmel. I followed with a lot less hurry in my step and slid in right next to Ivy.

Romeo looked at Ivy, then at me. We exchanged a look. He held out his fist to pound it out. I obliged.

"About damn time," he grunted. Then he glanced at Rimmel, who had her hair piled on the top of her head and a pencil sticking out of the mess. "Can we order now, smalls? I'm so hungry I could eat the ass out of a skunk."

Ivy and Rimmel both made gagging sounds.

"Good one," I congratulated him.

The waitress came and we all ordered pancakes. I ordered some eggs and bacon, too. So did Rome. And juice. Ivy got coffee. When the waitress walked away, I saw Romeo looking at my girl. My eyes narrowed.

"I assume she's been crying because of the mini-porn you two put on that the Boss blasted out?"

Rimmel smacked him. "Seriously? You couldn't have worded that nicer?"

He shrugged. I wasn't mad at him. Hell, there was no nice way to word what the hell Missy had done.

"You're never gonna believe it," Ivy said wearily. I draped an arm across her shoulders and moved closer.

"It affects you guys, too." I directed the words to Rome. His gaze sharpened.

"Braeden figured out who the BuzzBoss is," Ivy announced. "It's Missy."

The name flat-lined the conversation. It took a few minutes for what Ivy said to actually sink in. Once it had, the many questions started.

Our coffee and juices came. Ivy barely touched hers because she was so busy talking. Then our hotcakes came. I'd plowed through half my plate when I noticed she'd not touched hers.

She was still talking. She and Rimmel were being a bunch of women and analyzing every single thing Missy had ever done and said.

Frankly, it was giving me indigestion.

I dropped my hand across her thigh. Her sentence faltered and she looked down. "Food's getting cold."

"I'm not as hungry as I thought."

I grunted. "It's because you're still yapping about Missy. Let's give it a rest, huh?" I directed my last sentence to the entire table. "You've been through enough the past twenty-four hours. Take a breather."

"Did something else happen?" Rimmel asked, pausing mid-bite.

Beneath my hand, Ivy's thigh clenched. I gave her a reassuring squeeze. "Nah, what Missy put her through was enough."

Rimmel nodded and glanced down at her plate. She was upset, too. Betrayed and sad. I couldn't blame her, and it pissed me off all over again.

How could the two women I cared about most— besides my mom, of course—have been hurt so badly?

Rimmel started talking about Prada and the funny shit she did this morning before she and Rome left for breakfast, and Ivy was totally drawn in. I never thought I'd be thankful for that little rat, but here I was... thankful.

Romeo leaned across the table. "What else aren't you saying?"

I glanced at the girls. "Later, okay?"

Reluctantly, he nodded. We left the girls to their conversation and started our own about the scrimmage last night. I was totally paying attention to our convo, but it didn't stop me from noticing when Ivy picked up her fork and actually started eating.

I finished off my plate of eggs and bacon and was making a damn good dent in the stack of pancakes in front of me when a change came over Romeo.

I glanced up at him.

He was staring at something off behind me. Something over in the direction of the door. "What's going on?" I asked, starting to turn around.

Romeo caught my arm and shook his head. "B..."

Something was wrong. I knew it instantly.

He blinked and jerked his eyes away, back to me. "Keep it together, okay?"

What the fuck was he talking about?

I was beyond pissed about Missy, but I wasn't about to lose my shit right here in the diner.

"I'm fine," I replied.

Romeo's eyes drifted back behind our table once more. It was almost like he'd seen a ghost. I yanked my arm out of his grip and started to turn around.

Before I could, the solid wall of someone approaching our table got in my way. The feeling of being stung by an angry bee came over me.

Suddenly, it was hard to breathe.

The man stopped beside our booth. He looked a lot like I remembered. Except he didn't seem quite as big.

My fork clattered onto the table as I stared. The man's dark eyes studied every inch of me like he'd never seen me before.

Beneath the table, my hands clenched into fists.

"I realize this is rather sudden," he spoke.

"Sudden?" I scoffed. "You're not welcome here."

#SELFIE

"Braeden?" Ivy said, leaning in and tucking her arm around mine. She could probably feel the tension in my body and it was probably freaking her out.

She should be freaked out.

I fucking was.

"Who is that?" she whispered.

"Ah, you must be the girlfriend." The man smiled, his eyes now roaming every inch of my girl.

I jolted up out of the booth so fast he took two stumbling steps back. I stood so my body was blocking all view of Ivy and crossed my arms.

"What the hell are you doing here?" I growled. How dare this S.O.B look at Ivy?

"You wouldn't answer my calls or any of my messages," he said, calm. "I've been in town a while, waiting… I know you eat here every Sunday, so I decided if you wouldn't come to me, I'd just come to you."

"Have you been watching me?" So many emotions warred within me. So many memories.

Almost every single one was bad.

"I just want to talk to you, son."

● ● ●

"Son?" Rimmel and Ivy gasped at once.

"That's right," he answered, trying to look around me again. He couldn't see Ivy so he glanced at Rimmel instead.

"Yes, son. I'm Braeden's father."

CHAPTER FORTY-TWO

IVY

Braeden never mentioned his father. Not in passing, not in general comments, not ever.

Judging from the way he was acting right now and the mirrored look on Romeo's face, I would guess there was a reason.

I was curious, not because of the very cool reception this man was getting, but because this was part of Braeden's life.

● ● ●

For all the time I've spent with him—even when we fought all the time—he played things very close to the vest. His just-for-fun approach to women also extended into the rest of his life. He was always cracking a joke, an insult, or being sarcastic. I knew his mother lived near campus and he went to see her often, but that was about as much as I knew.

It seemed unfair all the embarrassing crap he knew about me, and I knew nothing at all.

"If I wanted to talk to you, I would have called you back," Braeden snapped.

His father didn't seem to be surprised or even offended at the way B was acting.

"I'm only asking for a few minutes of your time."

"I don't have a few minutes for you. Leave." The steel in his voice made the hair on the back of my neck stand up, and Rimmel and I shared a look.

For some reason, she didn't seem as intrigued. If anything, she seemed a little sickened and worried about this man's presence.

I slid forward and peeked around B to get a better look at the man.

He was tall like Braeden and had the same wide-set shoulders. He was a lot thinner than Braeden; he lacked the hefty muscle mass his son wore. His hair was dark but peppered with a lot of gray and was cut incredibly short.

He had strong facial features, a sharp nose, and eyes the same shade of deep brown as B. He also had lines around his eyes and mouth and circles under his eyes. He was older than I thought Braeden's parent would be and a lot more stoic, too.

"Hello," he said, catching my stare. "My name is Mark."

"Don't talk to her," Braeden snapped.

People from the tables nearby stopped to stare.

"Now isn't a good time," Romeo said, getting up from the booth.

Mark looked at him. "Roman. I hear congratulations are in order for the Knights."

Romeo didn't smile or say thank you.

"I'm afraid time isn't really something I have a lot of," he said, turning back to Braeden. "I've been wanting to talk to you, son. To let you know how deeply sorry I am. I want to make amends, hopefully give you some peace."

"And for yourself," Braeden said.

Mark inclined his head. "Yes, for me, too." He paused and quieted his voice. "I'm dying."

The words settled like a heavy fog in the middle of a rainstorm. It was thick and ominous, and I was shocked he would just drop that news out there like that.

Braeden didn't outwardly react. He stood there with the same rigid posture and protective stance in front of me.

"Not the first time you lied."

He smiled sadly. "I wish I were lying. It's my liver. Been sick for a long time now."

"Guess you shouldn't have drunk so much back in the day."

"I think it's karma," Mark said. "And I think you might agree."

"The day I agree with you is a day I don't wanna see."

Even though I saw no change in Braeden, I felt it. I felt it all the way to my bones. I slid my hand up to the small of his back, slipped it beneath the shirt he was wearing, and laid my palm flat against his skin.

I wanted him to know I was here for him.

"Can we go outside?" Mark asked. "Just for a minute."

Seconds stretched by and turned into a minute. Braeden seemed to honestly debate with himself about what he should do. Finally, he gave his answer.

"I can't do this right now. Not here. Not now."

Mark nodded, his face a little sad. "I understand." He reached into his pocket and pulled out a slip of paper. "This is my number. Please call me. Anytime. I have no right to ask, but all I want is one conversation."

Braeden stared at his outstretched hand with the paper for long seconds. Reluctantly, he took it. "I'll think about it."

"Thank you."

He hesitated before he left, then glanced over at Rimmel. Both Braeden and Romeo stiffened, and Mark took a step back.

* * *

"I'll look forward to your call." He left the diner without another word or glance.

Everything in the room seemed to buzz back to life, everything but Braeden. He was rooted in place like a tree in a storm. He stood there and stared out the window for a long time.

All of a sudden, he burst into action. He shoved away from our booth without a word, stalked through the diner, and banged out the door. Through the window, I saw him place both hands behind his head and stare up at the sky.

Romeo started after him. I grabbed his shirt and hurried to slide out of the booth.

"Let me go this time," I said.

Romeo seemed torn on what to do. He clearly knew what this kind of visit would do to Braeden, and I clearly did not. He wasn't sure if he could trust me to handle this the right way.

"Please," I whispered.

He relented and nodded once.

I rushed out of the diner and into the sunshine.

CHAPTER FORTY-THREE

BRAEDEN

I was leaning against the side of the building when she approached. "Go back inside, Blondie."

Her steps faltered, but almost as fast, they started up again. Ivy leaned up against the building beside me, mirroring my position.

"I take it you don't send him a Christmas card every year?" she asked.

I laughed. I couldn't help it. It was damned ridiculous. "Fuck, no."

"How long's it been since you've seen him?" Her voice was much more timid and serious.

"I was ten years old." The day was clear as a cloudless sky, and I would likely remember it forever. It didn't matter how much time passed; that day never faded.

I was sitting in a hospital, solemn and scared by my mother's bed. Standing at my side was an officer of the court, a woman who smelled like mothballs and wore an ill-fitting suit.

He'd beaten her.

He'd beaten her so bad she was in a coma for two days.

I watched, helpless, frozen with fear and unable to help her.

When she finally woke up, her first visit was from child services. I'd been taken into custody while they waited to see if she'd live. When it became clear she would, the child service rep gave her a choice: him or me.

She could press charges and have my father thrown in jail, serve him divorce papers, and get out from under his abuse.

Or…

Or she could give me up. Let me become a ward of the state while she went home and waited for the day when my father would finally beat her until she died.

She chose me.

The second visitor to her room was the police. Her injuries, previous hospital records, and testimony were enough to have him arrested that day.

But they couldn't find him to bring him in.

As my mother healed, they allowed me to visit her for short periods of time. It was during these visits when I last laid eyes on him. He stormed onto the hospital floor, drunk and yelling. I guess he felt like hitting something, and his punching bag wasn't home.

The cops were there, and I watched as they arrested him.

I never saw my father again.

Until today.

* * *

I snapped back from the memory, the day I'd never forget, to Ivy, who was in my arms. Or maybe I was in hers.

Her arms were wrapped around my neck and her head was tilted to the side. My face was buried in her neck as I hugged her to me.

"I didn't know," she whispered. "You were just a little boy."

I started to pull back, but her arms tightened. She drew lazy circles on the back of my neck, and I shuddered. She smelled good, so I tugged her that much closer.

"I said all that out loud?" I murmured. I thought I'd been thinking. I didn't realize I'd poured it all out.

"Yes. But it's okay. I wanted to know. I want to know everything there is to know."

I pulled back and carefully set her away from me. "I can't do this." Panic clawed at the inside of my throat.

"Do what?" she asked, gently.

Damn, I wanted to hug her again.

"Whatever it is we're doing." I motioned between us. "I don't do relationships."

"And now I know why."

I swung around. "What?"

"You're afraid."

"I am not." I growled. That was fucking insulting. I wasn't scared of shit.

"I can't blame you. After what you saw of relationships in your own house, frankly, I'm surprised you aren't more screwed up."

"Did you come out here to make me feel better? 'Cause you're doing a piss-poor job."

She smiled and took a step forward. "I don't think I can do anything to make you feel better. What just happened in there was intense. He comes back after all this time and expects you to have forgotten everything he did. You can't do that, and you shouldn't have to either. But there he was, and he's dying."

"He just thinks I'll hand him over a pass for what he did to Mom and me." I shook my head. I was angry, but not as angry as I thought I would be.

● ● ●

I was too tired to be angry. I was sick of all the drama. Plus, seeing him made me realize I had a lot more power now than I did back then. He couldn't hurt me or anyone else I loved anymore, and I was strong enough to make sure of that.

Maybe Mom was right. Maybe seeing him would help me move on. I looked at Ivy. She smiled. I wanted to move on. I was ready.

"Whatever you decide, B. Call him or don't call him. It doesn't matter. Just do what you need to do for you. I'll support you no matter what. I'll always support you."

"You know, if I was ever gonna do a relationship, you'd be the only one I'd do it with." I pulled her in and wrapped my arms around her.

"You sure know how to make a girl feel special," she quipped.

"I know." But in reality, I could do better. I needed to do better. I was either gonna be all in or all out with Ivy.

She deserved no less.

• • •

"If you decide to see him and you want me to come, I'll be there. Okay?"

I kissed her on the forehead and pulled back. "Thanks, baby."

Romeo and Rimmel came out the door, Rimmel carrying Ivy's bag. "We sort of figured breakfast was over," she said and handed it to Ivy.

"I'll go pay the tab."

"Taken care of," Romeo said.

I held out my fist for a bump.

"You solid?" he asked afterward.

"Yeah, I think so."

"You gonna talk to him?"

"I'm not sure yet."

Romeo nodded. "I got your back no matter what you decide."

"Me too!" Rimmel said.

I smiled.

Ivy slipped her hand in mine.

"Are you two official yet or what?" Rimmel interrogated.

• • •

Ivy didn't answer right away. In fact, the question seemed to make her slightly uncomfortable. "With everything going on, and now with Missy's big reveal, we haven't really…"

Romeo stepped in. "Don't hound them, baby. They'll figure it out."

On our way toward the truck, I glanced back at Rimmel, who was watching us walk away. I held out my thumb and pinky to make the phone sign and mouthed the words *call me*.

Her face broke into a sly smile and she nodded.

If Ivy wasn't sure of the status of our relationship and didn't know where she stood with me, then I sure as hell was gonna fix it.

CHAPTER FORTY-FOUR

> **ATTN: Students**
> Due to the misuse of the Alpha U app the university is shutting it down. For updates on campus policy, etc., see the school's website.
> Signed, Dean of Alpha U
> ... Alpha BuzzFeed

IVY

Missy was nowhere to be seen.

It's like she fell off the face of the campus. But I know she didn't because the BuzzBoss was still blowing up everyone's feed with mostly random posts.

I still had questions, still had things to say to her. The loss of our friendship and the way it ended wasn't something I could just forget.

I wasn't the only one. Rimmel wanted answers, too.

But as the days went by, I began to wonder if we would ever get them.

People on campus still whispered when I walked by, but I ignored it. Really, it didn't matter what they said. It wasn't as bad as it first was, and I knew it would fade from memory. With finals almost here, the semester would be over, and when fall finally came around, no one would remember my name.

I still dreamed about Zach sometimes, but now it wasn't always just him. Sometimes I saw the faces of the men who dragged me into the woods that night, and I'd wake up sweating. I hoped every day they'd finally go away. If not for my sake, for Braeden's. My dreams seemed to upset him almost more than me.

Basically, after all the chaos, despite Missy being MIA and Braeden still struggling with whether he wanted to talk to his father or not, life was settling down. It was welcome, because lately life had definitely been too eventful.

Now all I needed was to be sure where I stood with Braeden.

Yes, he said he wanted me, he slept in my room more often than his, and he didn't so much as look at another girl, but I still sometimes worried.

I worried his demons would chase him away, or when summer came, we'd drift apart.

I trudged up the stairs to my room, ready to kick off my shoes and play with Prada. I was still smuggling her into the dorm. Who was I kidding? I loved that dog. I'd probably take her home with me this summer. I'd even bought her a little pink tutu that Braeden thought was ridiculous. Secretly, I think he thought it was cute.

I pulled out my key to open the door. Rimmel wouldn't be here tonight; she was at Romeo's. Braeden was training and wouldn't be here until later, and after the day I'd had, I wasn't sorry to have some quiet.

It took me longer than it probably should have to realize something wasn't right in here. The door was already shut behind me, and I'd taken several steps in the room.

My steps faltered and I blinked.

● ● ●

It was bright in here, not the kind of bright from sunlight filtering through the window. In fact, the curtains were all drawn.

Why the hell were the curtains drawn?

The overhead light was on.

Had I left it that way when I left earlier?

No.

And I hadn't closed the curtains either.

I blinked again, bringing everything else in the room into focus.

"Blondie. You're late." The familiar sound of his voice made me smile.

"Braeden?" He was standing in the center of the room… my room that looked totally different.

"I've been waiting for an hour."

"I stopped at the library. I thought you were training."

"I lied."

I glanced around again. As inviting as the sight of him standing there shirtless and in nothing but a pair of basketball shorts was, I couldn't get over what he'd done to the room.

* * *

"What is all this?" I asked, wonder in my voice. My eyes couldn't stop staring, couldn't stop moving from one corner to the other.

"I told you I'm no good at talking. So I figured I'd show you how I feel." He motioned with his hands at the transformation.

He turned this room into the beach.

And it was perfect.

There were blow-up palm trees in every corner. There was even a small one on the desk. Paper 3-D pineapples hung throughout the room, tropical paper flowers draped around the ceiling fan, and hanging from the center was a giant red parrot.

The center of my desktop was cleared of all my stuff and set up with a tropical buffet. In the center was a silver bucket of ice and bottles of Corona with several whole limes beside it. There were also real coconuts with their tops cut off. I assumed they were filled with something fruity because of the little umbrellas sticking out of the tops.

Trays of fruit were arranged by color, and there was a round platter of cupcakes, the icing dotted in sprinkles.

Real seashells covered almost every surface, and a big poster of the sun setting over the ocean hung on the back wall.

"I can't believe you did all this."

"Well, I had a little help," he admitted reluctantly. "Rim helped me decorate. And she took Prada for the night."

"It's so beautiful."

"We never really had a beginning. For months, we fought and insulted each other. Then we combusted into bed. We pretended what happened didn't matter, but it did, Blondie. You matter."

"Braeden," I whispered and took a step farther into the room.

He shook his head. "All the shit with Missy, with Zach… hell, even with my father, it got in our way. I let it. This is me swearing I won't let it again. This is me swearing this is our beginning. You're it for me." He took a breath, and I watched his chest rise with it. His dark, chocolate eyes latched onto mine. "Because I still don't like you, Blondie."

I started to roll my eyes.

"I love you."

My heart stopped. Everything stopped. That place deep down inside me burned and tingled.

"I don't like you either." My voice wobbled.

The intensity of his stare drilled right into me, like he was searching desperately for my reply.

"I love you so damn much," I confessed. The words whooshed out of me with momentum, like the weight holding them down had finally been cut free.

"Come here, woman," he growled.

I laughed and rushed the short distance between us. I almost fell when my feet hit something foreign.

"Tell me you noticed," he said, dry. His eyes twinkled with humor.

I looked down and giggled.

I hadn't noticed.

"How am I supposed to notice anything when you're standing there without a shirt?"

"You're forgiven."

Braeden was standing in a blue plastic kiddy pool. It wasn't filled with water. Instead, it was filled with sand.

"Take off your shoes," he whispered.

I kicked them off faster than ever before. I readied to jump in, but he shook his head.

"Hit the lights."

I wrinkled my nose. "But then it will be pitch black in here, and I won't be able to see all your hard work." Our curtains were blackouts so we could sleep in on the weekends.

"Trust me."

The huskiness in his voice was hypnotic. Of course I trusted him. I trusted no one more.

I went back near the door and took one last sweeping glance around. The room plunged into darkness the second I hit the switch.

But it wasn't nearly as dark as it usually was.

The room was filled with stars.

Bright glowing stars.

They filled the ceiling, and part of the walls. Some were even stuck to the curtains, a few outlined one of the blow-up palm trees.

They were in varying sizes, from large to super small. It was exactly what it had been like in Florida when the sun went down and the night lit up.

The sound of ocean waves crashing against the shore filled the room with peaceful rhythm. My breath caught.

He was recreating that night on the beach.

The beach where something between us changed and we spent our first night together.

Our first kiss had been under the stars.

For a man who said he was no good at words, no good at feelings…

He couldn't have done anything any better.

I walked carefully across the room, not worried I would bump into anything because the light from the stars would guide me. Braeden held out his hand and steadied me as I stepped into the pool.

My feet sank in the sand, my toes wiggling with joy. Braeden's arms wound around my waist and pulled me close.

"This is how it should have been that first night down on the sand," he whispered. "This is our beginning Ivy. I want to make it official. I want there to be no doubt, 'cause I'm gonna do stupid shit all the time."

I giggled, and his white teeth flashed.

"I'm gonna leave the toilet seat up. I'm gonna be overprotective, probably bossy, and my temper is always gonna run hot."

"I don't care," I told him, sliding my hands up to rest on his chest.

"Tell me you'll be my girl, and I swear I'll love you with everything I got."

"I'm always gonna be stubborn. I'm not gonna take your shit. My makeup will be all over the bathroom, and I still don't have a major. Oh, and I want to keep Prada. You have to like her, too."

• • •

"I already told Rim to get your adoption paperwork ready for that rat." Then in lower tones, he said, "She's grown on me."

I smiled. He totally loved Prada.

"So what's my answer?" He tightened his arms around my waist.

I pretended to think it over. A girl should never sound too eager—even if she was practically peeing herself with glee.

"Blondie," Braeden growled.

"I'm already yours, B. I have been for a long time."

He kissed me under the stars. A long, fire-filled kiss that not even the ocean waves could put out. It wasn't the first time we'd done this, but it might as well have been.

Braeden made me feel like no one else ever could. All this time, I'd been searching, looking in the face of every man I passed, wondering if he could be the one.

The one my soul would recognize.

He was in front of me all along. He'd just been hiding in the dark. It took the light of a million stars to reveal what a piece of me already knew.

* * *

I never hated Braeden. I loved him, probably from the first day we'd met.

And I'd love him long after the millions of stars faded overhead.

* * *

OMINOUS EPILOGUE

BRAEDEN

I decided not to tell her.

To keep the secret very few knew.

Missy wasn't talking. If it came out she knew a student was assaulted and then used a piece of the evidence to ruin the student's reputation, well, her entire college career would be over. And she could kiss her dreams of theater fame good-bye.

Zach was locked up; with any luck, he'd stay there for a very long time. He wasn't gonna run his mouth because then he might have to exchange his cushy cell for one a lot less comfortable.

That left me.

How could I tear apart the world of the woman I desperately loved? She'd been through so much, it seemed cruel to bring what little bit of footing she was gaining tumbling down.

I wanted to protect her from what was done to her. The way I couldn't ever protect my mother… or even myself.

I didn't know if my decision was wrong.

I hoped I never found out.

All I wanted was for her to be happy. For her to be safe.

And for her to never know.

I had no doubt Ivy could handle this information, but she shouldn't have to.

So everyone was gonna keep their mouths shut… and if they didn't?

There would be hell to pay.

* * *

#TheEnd
... Alpha BuzzFeed

Zach is back.

Hashtag Series #5

Summer 2015

Cambria Hebert

AUTHOR'S NOTE

*This note from me is unedited… Read at your own risk! Ha!

It's a good thing I have a good stylist because otherwise I'd look like a granny with all the extra gray hairs this book surely gave me.

So much went into this book behind the scenes to make it into the finished product that you are reading today. And thank you, for reading it. This book started out pretty easily, I wrote the beach scenes pretty quickly. Then like a car with not enough gas I started to putter out… I was like where do we go now? So I just kept writing, I let Braeden and Ivy pretty much find their way.

And boy did they ever.

Not only did this book give me some grays but it also gave me a few surprises. I really wasn't expecting the book to end the way it did. In my mind I had their story wrapped up with a really pretty bow on it at the end. I didn't intend to leave so much open, to have so much turmoil looming over these characters heads. I also didn't intend to write another novel for them. But I am. Their story just isn't finished yet. ☺

I can honestly say that I love this story though. I love the way Braeden and Ivy have found their way. I feel like we get to learn so much about them, and also watch them grow as people. It's awesome they grew together.

It was very important to me that this book was done right. That #Selfie was done justice. Characters like Braeden don't come along every book and because he is so loved (and not just by me) I so very wanted to do him justice. But not just him anymore, Ivy too. I think it's poor Ivy who really gets beat up the most in this book. She's a lot different than what you expected, isn't she? Deeper, more critical of herself, and more cautious than she appears at first glance.

I really connected to Ivy in this one, in a lot of ways she reminds me of myself, more than I thought she would.

● ● ●

With all of that being said, I will tell you about my granny hair. Ok, my hair is blond. Like I said, I have a good stylist. Ha. A LOT went on behind the scenes of this book. Editing, proofing, worrying, more editing…

There was a time when I thought I might have to push the release date back due to editing issues. Then it was resolved, then I thought about pushing it back again. Basically it's been like a roller coaster ride.

Did I mention I don't like roller coasters?

But through it all I have learned something – okay, I didn't actually learn it. I guess I knew it all along but it was reinforced to me in the past few weeks.

People really care about this series. People genuinely want these books to be their best – and not just me. I don't think I can convey how this makes me feel. Lucky, grateful, humble. But more.

I've said before that writing is a solitary journey, but it takes a team to put out a book. It's so true. An author really learns who her team is when issues arise, personal *and* business, but the work still gets done.

I want to thank Cassie McCown for all that she does. If it wasn't for her my books would look and read

· · ·

a lot worse than they do. I'd like to thank Regina Wamba for always taking my messages, my ideas and my deadlines and working with them all to create one of a kind covers. To Sharon Kay of Amber Leaf Publishing, who always gracefully takes on my formatting jobs even when I tell her it's needed ASAP and we're short on time. I cringe to send the email but the reply it always so sweet.

Another editor who stepped in to also work on this project is Melissa at There For You Editing. Thank you for taking on a job when I know your schedule was full for a client you have never worked with before.

Also, I'd like to acknowledge Melissa Stickney for always having time to devote to beta reading for me, for always thinking of me and if I need something and for running my Fan Club and making it a fun place to be. Amber Garza and Cameo Renae are also my "cheerleaders" and without them I'd probably be more cray cray than I am.

I have more than a few rabid "fans" (more like friends) of this series who make meme's, who cheer me on, who read early copies and who just offer smiles and support. Basically to all the ladies of Cambria's Nerds, thank you.

And so now I am moving on to Hashtag #5. A book I hadn't expected to write. A story I'm still trying to wrap my head around. Even still, I'm excited about it. I hope you are too.

Thank you for reading and if you have a chance please leave a book review. Braeden would appreciate it!

See you next book!

xoxo—CAMBRIA

Cambria Hebert is a bestselling novelist of more than twenty books. She went to college for a bachelor's degree, couldn't pick a major, and ended up with a degree in cosmetology. So rest assured her characters will always have good hair.

Besides writing, Cambria loves a caramel latte, staying up late, sleeping in, and watching movies. She considers math human torture and has an irrational fear of chickens (yes, chickens). You can often find her running on the treadmill (she'd rather be eating a donut), painting her toenails (because she bites her fingernails), or walking her chorkie (the real boss of the house).

Cambria has written within the young adult and new adult genres, penning many paranormal and contemporary titles. Her favorite genre to read and write is romantic suspense. A few of her most recognized titles are: *Text, Torch, Tryst, Masquerade,* and *Recalled.*

Cambria Hebert owns and operates Cambria Hebert Books, LLC.

You can find out more about Cambria and her titles by visiting her website: http://www.cambriahebert.com

* * *